PRETTY
BAD
THINGS

YOLY MARQUEZ

An Original Publication From Yoly Marquez

PRETTY BAD THINGS
http:// yolymarquez.com
Copyright © 2015 by Yoly Marquez.
All rights reserved.

First U.S. Paperback Edition, 2015

Printed in the United States of America

To my mom for her unending love and support. I would be nothing without you. Dad, thank you for always being there for me, bad jokes and all. Los amo con todo mi corazón.

Thank you lots Dennis the Menace. Livvie wouldn't exist without your crazy stories.

Lastly, for all of you guys on Wattpad, who believed in me before I did.

PRETTY
BAD
THINGS

Chapter One
I'm an Introduction Expert

I'm the biggest dork you will ever meet, but I have a secret list that if anyone ever read total humiliation would ensue, because, I, Livvie Jefferson, do not do trouble. Mostly because I can't seem to do trouble *well*. I'm the type of person who nearly dies from asphyxiation at the thought of ditching class or not following an order. I lack lady balls, but at least I'm aware.

How did my list come about? This is the part where I go into flashback and delve into some meaningful detailed exposé. The actual list came to life behind an old receipt I had left over in my purse. In fact, the actual print on the receipt depicted the sorry purchase of maxi pads and ice cream, a lethal combination, maybe even more embarrassing than my actual list. But, since we're talking about the list I might as well get on with it.

#1 Date a guy who rides a motorcycle.

Sure, the idea of potentially having my head knocked off by some misplaced construction beam or simply falling off the side has crossed my mind, but I seriously just want to get on one. The motorcycle, not the boyfriend, although that comes later.

#2 Spit in Mrs. Lasowski's morning coffee.

Okay, the lady has this one coming to her. The day I get to spit a big fat loogie into her drink will be the day I can just die in peace.

#3 Steal a credit card.

I'd probably panic and buy a lot of dumb things with it, like maybe a lifetime supply of toilet paper, but that wouldn't stop me.

#4 Get drunk off my ~~ass~~ butt for the first time.

My mom gave me a sip of her wine cooler that one time, and I thought the world spun right after for a bit. Turns out I just had some bad tuna salad earlier on in the day, but I'd like the feeling back, without the vomiting and diarrhea though.

#5 Lose my V Card.

I know what you're thinking. Your V Card is precious, you can't just punch holes in it and get a free drink, yada, yada... But, do V Cards have expiration dates? They do! It's called menopause and I'm not getting any younger.

Some of those are more cringe worthy than others, but the point is that I'll never get it done. It's just a silly list I made up one day as I realized how boring my life was, and definitely not a list that I'll ever cross things off of. Yeah, sure, I carry it around with me everywhere, even though I *know* I shouldn't because no one should ever read it in my lifetime, or ever. Regardless, I'm perpetually stuck in my boring small-town life, but hey, at least I have my list.

Chapter Two
Getting it Twisted

Like in every friendship, you have your ups and downs.

I'm aware it's nearly every teen girl's dream to have a gay guy best friend—not sure why, since most of the time it's not any different than just having a regular guy as a friend.

Ask me how many times Nick has helped me pick out a piece of clothing. Zero. Maybe if he did I wouldn't dress like I'm still twelve—his words, not mine. Come to think of it, he's pretty good at criticizing my wardrobe choices, but he has the patience of a toddler whenever we try to go shopping together.

I realized I was screwed as I was sitting in English class and felt the terrifying catastrophe in my pants.

Oh, the joys of being a woman.

I slowly swiveled in my desk, as Mrs. Lasowski droned on about Macbeth and his murder-infested conscious, to face my best friend Nick.

"Guys don't have a tendency to carry pads with them, do they?" I whispered so that the entire class didn't become aware of my embarrassing situation.

"Liv, I do everything I can to stay away from girl parts, remember? Besides, even if I wasn't gay, gross." Nick scrunched his pretty face into a scowl.

I tried to weigh the risks of standing up and going on the hunt for a pad against staying planted in my seat. Hoping that it didn't look like I had murdered someone in my pants, my wobbly hand shot up into the air in the middle of Mrs. Lasowski's sentence. The old lady narrowed her eyes at me for interrupting, but hey, it wasn't my fault that she obviously wasn't sympathetic to my plight. I doubted she even remembered what a period was. She was really old, like sixty. I wondered briefly why she hadn't retired already. Wasn't it illegal for her to still be on the job?

The entire senior class pivoted in their seats to look at me for distraction. I awkwardly asked for permission to go to the bathroom and shuffled my way out once she granted it.

The halls were quiet and empty as I practically jogged towards the girls' bathroom. I stopped midway and cursed myself for being so stupid. I didn't even have any spare change to buy a pad.

My options were limited, so I decided to make a small stop at the nurse's office.

Pushing the door open into the brightly lit room, I made eye contact with a girl who lay on one of the mattresses with her hand on her stomach. Her face immediately become pained when the nurse's eyes went to her. It was a pretty weak performance in my opinion. You had to keep your guard up at all times when you were faking it with the nurse, since she practically had a mechanical neck that switched directions at the blink of an eye.

"Hello, Livvie." The nurse sighed as she saw my face. I hadn't acquired my talents in deception without some practice. I gave her a goofy smile in hopes of winning her over. My face must have been off, because she only shook her head before rolling her eyes as I came closer.

"What will it be today? Headache? Stomachache?" She was already pulling out her notepad to write me my slip. So maybe I wasn't so smooth when I came in with a fake illness to get out of gym. I could never actually ditch class, but if I had an excuse, especially when it came to any physical activity, I'd definitely take it.

"You know, Livvie, PE class is not all that bad. If you just gave it a chance you wouldn't have to come here every other day just for—"

I cut the nurse off with a clearing of my throat, partly because I was embarrassed that she knew and partly because the situation was quickly going downhill.

"Uh, not today. I was actually here to see if you were willing to do an act of charity?" My voice went all high at the end, as if I wasn't sure what I was there for myself.

"Charity?" the nurse inquired, clearly suspicious.

"Yeah, well, Aunt Flow made a visit..." It didn't matter that I was a senior in high school, I could never talk about my period. God, I was such a loser.

"Who's Aunt Flow?"

"Well, like, you know, she comes once a month."

"And why do you need me? Do you need to speak to a counselor?"

Things were clearly not going as planned. So, I resorted to being straightforward without being straightforward. I could hear the girl behind me trying to stifle her laughter. Whatever, sick people usually didn't have it in them to chortle the way she was doing, so it would kick her in the butt later.

"I was wondering if I could have a pad?" I asked, in a new tone of voice so that she knew to drop the Aunt Flow subject.

The nurse's mouth grew into a big O when she realized what I had been talking about. Glad we were getting things straightened out.

"Oh!" She laughed. "Why didn't you just say so? Pads are fifty cents."

I did say so, technically. That's when I smiled and started to wring my hands.

"I don't have any change with me." My voice was weak and barely a whisper.

"That's a problem. Livvie, I can't just give you a pad. Just last month Principal River had to talk to me about budget cuts and low funds." It didn't sound like a problem for her. And where was the female compassion? She was a fellow woman out on the field, going through one period after another like the rest of us.

"If I gave every girl here a free sanitary pad, I'd be out by the end of the week. Plus, you all have the tendency to sync up and I can't keep up with that kind of demand..." She trailed off. Was this illegal? There should have been at least one law in place about her refusing to help me out.

I could feel my face morphing into that of an awkward seal, but I couldn't just give up. Time was ticking and the zone below my hips was feeling more and more hazardous.

"What if I promise not to come visit you for a week?" Might as well admit the truth that we both knew. I was giving away my free pass out of gym class for the entire week, all for the sake of keeping my dignity.

That's when the nurse's face glowed with a satisfied smile and I realized that I had been played. Duped, because she would have given me the pad if I had just held out for a little longer. She'd known how bad I needed it.

I was finally handed the coveted package. Thinking that my luck was going to turn around, I started to make my way towards the nurse's private bathroom. Until the girl I'd seen earlier got there first and walked in. The chick even winked at me before she closed the door. A few curse words that I would never say out loud ran through my mind at the sight of her.

Nice. Now I could parade around the whole school on my way to the bathroom. If I was lucky some guy like Harvey Lockwell and his friends would end up bumping into me and miraculously become aware of my existence for the first time. They'd notice me and the giant blood stain on my butt.

I walked out of the nurse's office, pad in hand during the first few steps, until I realized how embarrassing that would be. I cursed for real when I realized my sweatpants didn't have any pockets. I had no choice but to stick the package into my tank top.

My flat chest wasn't helping at all. It was official, after staring at my reflection in a classroom window: I had a third boob in the shape of a square. I should have asked for two pads to at least even things out.

I was so close! I could see the bathroom stick people at the exact moment that a shrill and perky voice called my name. My head snapped up to see one of the office ladies flap her hand in the air and come my way. My body turned to give her a frontal view. God forbid she notice a stain and call me out on it.

My stomach clenched up when none other than Harvey Lockwell came strolling right behind her. A hysterical laugh bubbled up but I squelched it in time. He had a little smirk on his face as if he knew some big joke that no one was in on. Was I standing in front of a reflective surface? Was he smiling at the bloody mess on my butt? No, he'd probably be grossed out by that. Unless he had some weird fetish...

I couldn't shake the feeling that the joke was on me as he walked closer. Did I have something on my face?

I remembered my square boob and crossed my arms quickly. Great, the last thing I'd wanted was coming true.

Well, in reality I had always wanted Harvey Lockwell to come my way and smirk, but not when it was World War III in my pants, complete with the bloody casualties.

Office ladies loved me—heck, all teachers seemed to really like me. Except for Mrs. Lasowski, of course. That woman was an entirely different species, but when I said that teachers and administrators loved me, I wasn't kidding.

That's why the office lady made a huge point of strolling right up to me and beaming. I didn't consider myself a complete nerd, but I did have good grades. I didn't actually put blood and sweat into my work. Good grades were just easy for me to get. That pretty much explained the whole Livvie Fan Club.

If only people my own age found me as appealing.

The woman started talking, but my eyes became transfixed on Harvey Lockwell.

Everyone spoke when Harvey Lockwell was around, not necessarily to him, but about him. He had a huge record of getting into trouble and breaking rules he shouldn't.

It wasn't just his reputation, which everyone in our small town knew about. His older brother, who'd graduated right when I entered high school, had apparently done some time in jail for beating this other guy to a pulp, amongst other things. Things like that don't just fly past people. I did belong to the category of girls who found him insanely attractive. The category was composed of pretty much all girls, and Nick.

Harvey had a perfect jaw that did the ticking thing whenever he concentrated on something. The light freckles on his face should have softened him up, but paired with the piercing gaze they just created a warm sinking feeling in your stomach. His brown hair stuck out from under his cap, while his lip ring caught my attention as always. Yeah, I'd done quite a bit of gazing when it came to his face, mostly from afar.

Harvey Lockwell could come to school wearing a garbage bag and holding a piñata with one hand and still look like he owned the place. The boy had the darkest eyes, almost black. Eyes that were staring right at my chest!

Harvey Lockwell's beautiful eyes were on my chest and his smirk was widening! I was flattered, until I realized maybe I shouldn't be. I mean, what a pervert. He was openly staring at my chest, with no hint of hiding it. Should I have been insulted? If so, why was I getting such an adrenaline rush?

I wore an A cup, but was I getting an A+ in Harvey's boob gradebook? Did I even make the gradebook, or were my boobs so minimal that they didn't even make the cut?

"—and since he's having such a hard time, we figured you could tutor him," the office lady finished, squeezing my shoulder with a smile on her face. I had to break out of my Harvey trance to notice her smiling and waiting for my answer.

When in doubt, just nod your head and hope it was a question, or that a simple reassurance will work.

"Great! You guys can start next week!" The office lady gave me a sweet smile before turning around and leaving me alone in a hallway with Harvey Lockwell.

The silence ticked on as I tried to figure out a plan to leave without looking like a moron. I couldn't just turn around even though the bathroom was right behind me. Walking backwards was out of the question. Harvey was still looking at my chest, until his eyes finally came back up to my face. I could feel my right eye start to twitch under the scrutiny.

It was time to keep my cool. I could keep my cool for two seconds in Harvey's presence. I had to.

I didn't notice when he started to come closer until I found myself looking up and seeing his face mere inches from mine. I could see his freckles up close like I never had before and it was literally the best view of my life. I was stuck with my back against the brick wall. Harvey came even closer.

"What are you doing?" My voice wobbled. I felt the brick texture under my palms. I had never spoken to Harvey in my life, so it was a little weird to do so at that moment.

He smiled and finally leaned in to whisper in my ear. I was mortified at the little shiver that came over me.

"While you were checking me out, you pushed something out of your bra. You might want to try a push-up bra next time." I could feel the smile on his face, and just like that he was gone. He had pulled away and had already started walking in the opposite direction.

I looked down the find the stupid pad halfway up my neck, its horrible mint-green packaging calling out for attention from above my tank.

I couldn't even breathe from the embarrassment. I tried to look up to see if Harvey was witnessing my mental breakdown, but the hallway was empty.

Harvey Lockwell, the badass, the legend, thought I stuffed my bra with pads.

Chapter Three
My Street Cred is Dead

The best thing about tutoring Harvey?

I had no clue when, or where, I would be doing it, so I didn't really have an answer. Not that I thought there were any good things about having to tutor him.

I waited an entire week dreading having to ask Harvey about it. I mean, what girl in her right mind would walk up to him and start a conversation? I wasn't a complete idiot. It was probably an invitation to get gangbanged.

I wasn't really sure what getting gangbanged meant, since I had only heard Nick make a joke about it once. I had made a note to Google it, soon. In the meantime it sounded horrid enough for the occasion.

I wasn't ready to get my face beat in either, though. I needed my face if I was planning to use it in college to at least get one boyfriend. That's the thing, adults respect you for not having a relationship until you're older, but once you start nearing adulthood they start feeling bad for you. Which is horrible because you already feel pretty bad for yourself and don't need everyone else thinking there's something wrong with you.

So, I spent most of Tuesday night pacing like an idiot in my room, with Nick watching me eat candy bars.

I had this horrible habit of eating when I was stressed or worried about something. I could stuff anything in my mouth when I was having a bad day. That night was no different, and I think Nick finally realized that if he didn't stop me soon I would have exploded.

"You've been walking around for, like, an hour. Do you finally want to tell me what's wrong?" Nick asked. He was casually stretched out on my comforter, chewing on a candy bar himself. Nick had been my best friend since I could remember. In fact, at one point I'd even had a massive crush on him. It was, thankfully, short-lived and when he'd finally come out our freshman year of high school I hadn't even batted an eyelash. It was kind of difficult to ignore your best friend checking out the same guys you were, so I had already known he was gay, maybe even before he did.

"Are you sure you really want to know?" I asked him dramatically.

Nick knew I had a tendency of overdramatizing things, so he just rolled his eyes and kept staring at me.

"Livvie, just say it!" he finally ordered, after I'd held out for longer than usual.

"I have to tutor Harvey Lockwell," I said as quickly as I could, then closed my eyes, waiting for Nick to freak out.

Instead, the silence went on for the longest time, so I had to open my eyes again after it became unbearable. Nick was looking at me with his mouth open, making his pretty eyes widen in the process. Nick was too pretty, prettier than me. No wonder I'd had that short-lived crush, I thought as I watched him process what I had just said.

"You. Lucky. Bitch," he finally said, draping a hand over his heart. The action made me giggle, so I swatted him in the arm.

"Not even! I kind of, sort of, maybe forgot to find out when and where, so now I have to ask Harvey," I informed him, wringing my hands close to my chest.

"Oh," was all Nick said in response. I could tell his mind was racing, thinking of ways to help me solve my problem. That was the best part about Nick—he always tried to help me out of my embarrassing situations. I had a *lot* of embarrassing situations happen to me. I was an embarrassment magnet.

"Now I have to ask him, but—"

"Oh," Nick said again, cutting in. I hadn't needed to finish my thought; even Nick knew that Harvey was trouble.

"Well, you're going to have to. What if you don't ask and you stand him up?" Nick said.

I hadn't thought of the possibility of standing Harvey Lockwell up. No one stood him up.

Now, *that* was an invitation to get gangbanged.

"Fine, but I don't even know where to find him! He's never in class!" I half yelled, plopping myself on the bed beside Nick.

I internally chuckled at the irony of my situation. I needed to find him to tutor him, but I couldn't because he was never in class—which was probably the reason he needed the tutoring! It could have been because for all his good looks Harvey just didn't understand certain subjects in school, but I could still remember the time in fourth grade when we went head to head in the school spelling bee. I doubted he even recalled, but I could still picture him beating me. *Ambidextrous.* He'd beaten me with *ambidextrous* because he knew there was an *o* when I didn't. Fourth-grade Harvey had been smarter than me.

"Livvie, my sweet Livvie," Nick snickered, looking down at me like a parent. "If you want to talk to Harvey you're going to have to visit The Cave," he told me in a low tone which made the little hairs on my arms stand up. I didn't have a clue as to what the heck he was talking about, but even the name sounded intimidating.

"What's that?" I asked, bringing a candy into my mouth in the heat of the moment.

"It's an alley behind the gym and the cafeteria. Harvey and his friends are there most of the time." Nick shrugged. Did everyone know this except me?

"I didn't know they hung out there," I finally said, chewing on my candy bar some more.

"If you ever went to gym you'd probably smell them from the track." Nick shrugged again before stealing the last piece of my candy and popping it into his mouth.

I ignored his comment, deciding not to press more. I immediately thought of all the ways things could go wrong if indeed I did decide to go looking for Harvey.

"Could you—" I was about to ask Nick to come with me when I did go looking for Harvey, but Nick started to shake his head violently.

"That wouldn't be such a good idea for me, Livvie," Nick said quietly while looking down at his hands.

I wanted to ask why, until it hit me. Nick would probably get beat up by Harvey and his friends, just because of who he was. I was momentarily mad, but I didn't want Nick to notice. It really wasn't fair that Nick was judged so much at school. We lived in a pretty small town where there weren't many other people who were gay. Last time I checked, Gunnison had a population of 5,854 people and not too many of them played for the other team.

It made it extremely difficult for Nick to make more friends or even go out. I always wanted to tell people off when they gave him weird looks and whispered under their breaths at school, but I was too scared. At least Nick was comfortable enough with himself to accept who he was.

"You're right. Plus, what could possibly go wrong?" I said like a total dork, trying to make Nick feel better.

It sort of worked, because Nick gave me a small smile. Small and partially sad, but a smile.

We finally stopped talking about my Harvey situation and put on a movie to watch. My mom was almost never home, so Nick tended to sleep over a lot. Not that she would really care, since I was pretty sure I had mentioned he was gay in the past. Before we started the movie, I took the time to make my way into Brian's room. It wasn't very late, so I found him sitting Indian style on the floor, playing with his Ninja Turtles action figures. Even though my little brother could make me want to rip all of my hair out, I still loved him to no end. Because my mom wasn't ever around, I usually took care of him every day after school.

I was practically his real mom if you really thought about it.

"How's it going?" I asked him, closing the door softly behind me. My brother looked a lot like me. He had the same wavy brown hair and green eyes. He had just recently turned twelve and was more obsessed with his action figures and his video games than what should be considered normal for a kid his age. The kid was weird, but it was no wonder we were related. If anyone were to ask me, I would say that my little brother was the smartest kid on the planet, but I would probably be biased.

"Wanna play Ninja Turtles with me? I'll let you be Donatello," Brian asked me excitedly. Sometimes I felt guilty about all the time he spent by himself. Our mom never took him to hang out at a friend's house or even to play at the park. I couldn't, because I didn't have a car and the only person who ever took me places was Nick. We were both too busy with school. I couldn't even remember a time when Brian had brought a friend home from school. Heck, I wasn't even sure he had friends. Sometimes the frustration of having such a distant mother really drove me insane.

Why couldn't she do what she was supposed to?

I hadn't gotten pregnant. Why did I have to take care of my little brother?

I knew that last part sounded selfish, but sometimes I felt that the reason I had so few friends was because I never had time to actually go out and live like a normal teen.

Brushing my frustrations aside, I focused my attention on ordering Brian to get ready for bed. I promised to play Ninja Turtles with him the next day; in exchange, he would fall asleep.

I spent the next fifteen minutes asking him about school and what he had done that day. When the only thing I could see from under the covers was the top of his head, I gave him a kiss on the forehead and made my way out. My brother wasn't like regular kids. I waited outside his bedroom door for a few minutes, smiling softly when I saw the soft glow emanate from under his door. I left my brother in his room, playing video games in the dark, believing that I wasn't aware of his gaming habits. He could stay up as long as he wanted; he deserved it.

The rest of the night consisted of watching movies with Nick until we fell asleep. I tried not to think of my impending visit to The Cave and talking to Harvey again.

I really had a knack for putting things off until they came up behind me and bit me in the butt.

Let me explain more thoroughly.

The next day at school I practically kept away from the gym and cafeteria as if they were the sole source of the modern plague. I didn't want to seek Harvey out to talk to him. In fact, if a zombie apocalypse were to have broken out that day I would have welcomed it warmly.

When lunchtime finally rolled around I realized that I had no other choice. It was then or never. Taking in a shaky breath, I made my way to where Nick had described. I hadn't even known that there was a secret place where Harvey hung out, so it took me a while to find it.

I felt like such a dork when I realized that I had my sack lunch in my hand. I usually hated the food they gave out in the cafeteria, ever since an incident in eighth grade. One minute I'd been happily biting into a cheeseburger, when all of a sudden I'd felt the unnerving presence of, literally, a hairball in my mouth. Having to pull out a big wad of hair that had been smack in the middle of my burger had really traumatized me.

I had been bringing my own lunch ever since.

Now there I was, approaching The Cave with my lunch bag in one hand and my backpack straps on my shoulders. I scanned my eyes until I spotted a small opening in between the cafeteria building and the gym. There was a large dumpster covering half of the entrance, leaving just enough space for a person to fit in.

My toes curled inside my Converse when the thought of having to actually go in there crossed my mind. I swiftly pulled my shoulders back and slid my way through the opening. All was well, except my humongous backpack got caught in the tight opening and I was temporarily lodged in between the wall and the dumpster. I had to grunt and pull myself forward with all my strength until my backpack finally decided to follow me inside. The entire alley was sort of dark and musky, making walking difficult for someone who was already challenged.

The alley looked to be pretty long, once I squinted my eyes, and it seemed to curve to the right. Things were freaking scary at that point. I had practically walked halfway inside, but I was ready to bolt from that place quick.

Without thinking twice, I turned around and started to run towards the dumpster opening.

That was until I felt someone or something grab my wrist and pull me back.

I yelled like a little girl at that point.

Chapter Four
Be the Butt of Every Joke

Holy mother of God. That was it, I was dead. I was probably going to get punched in the face, or kidnapped, or...gangbanged.

My entire life flashed before my eyes as I felt the sensation of fingers curling around my wrist. Then I realized how lame I really—my life was the epitome of boring. Even I was bored by the montage of my life. There was absolutely nothing even minimally exciting about me when I thought I was going to die. In fact, the only thing I felt proud about doing was learning how to knit when I was ten, and only then because it had made my Nana proud to teach me.

Having a near-death experience and realizing that your life is a snooze fest can be a little depressing.

I started to yell like a crazy cat woman on crack when I felt the pressure on my wrist exert itself. I finally got myself to calm down long enough to realize that they weren't even holding on that tight. I was simply immobilized by my irrational fear.

I braced myself before I did a full turn to look at my abductor. I was being dramatic since he wasn't even tugging, but still.

I had never seen the guy before. Which was odd because there were less than three hundred students at our school and everyone knew everyone. I could see the faint outline of his skinny, lanky body, but the most interesting thing was his head. With the small amount of light it looked huge, like a pumpkin on a stick. When I got a little closer I realized that it was because he had a full head of dreads.

His facial expression was the exact opposite of mine, a huge grin.

"Daaaaaaamn, do you smell that?" he asked me in a slow but cheery voice. Something told me that he was either mentally challenged or just a really abnormally happy person. He wasn't even bothering with introductions. Instead, he was talking to me as if we were longtime friends.

"S-s-smell what?" I asked him cautiously, trying to untangle my wrist from inside his big calloused hand.

He took that moment to take a big whiff of the air around us and smile widely into the open space. I was leaning toward mentally challenged at that point.

"I don't know but it smells fucking amaaaazing!" he said. I noticed that the guy had a tendency of saying things almost as if they were a song, making all of his words flow and blend together.

I took in a big breath, trying to figure out what smell he was talking about. The only thing I could smell was my lunch bag, which had a chicken sandwich inside. I wondered if that was what he was talking about.

"Do you mean the food?" I asked him in a confused manner.

At the mention of food his entire face lit up even more, which I hadn't thought possible, and he nodded his head enthusiastically, making his dreads fling and dance wildly in the air. He was incredibly skinny, but I was getting the idea that he really liked to eat. Another idea popped into my head. I leaned in with a smile of my own and looked Dreads in the eye.

"What would you say if I made you an offer you couldn't refuse?" I said, making my voice low and persuasive. That's what I got for watching *The Godfather* with Nick the night before. I ended up making business deals in dark alleys.

Dreads nodded his head back and forth, looking at me excitedly.

"If you help me find Harvey Lockwell, I'll give you my chicken sandwich," I singsonged brightly. I decided that if I was already in a scary alley in the presence of a crazy guy I might as well use him to my advantage.

Dreads looked overjoyed at the prospect of chicken and so once again he nodded his head at me like a little boy.

"I can take you to my homeboy, Harvey!" he practically yelled. My fear of Dreads was quickly subsiding the more time I spent with him. I let him lead me further into the alley, all the way to where it curved.

Everything was fine and dandy until I caught a whiff of something in the air myself. The breeze carried a thick and grassy smell that made me scrunch my nose in disgust. It didn't exactly smell bad. It was just unexpected and different. I wasn't sure if I liked it or not, but I was definitely leaning towards not.

Just when I thought that the alley would never end, we finally made it to a secluded spot. The place had a bit more light than the rest of the alley coming from the sunlight above, but not much. I wanted to crawl into a hole and die the minute I saw the large group of people. Alright, they weren't that many people, only five, but they sure weren't kicking it solo like me. I was sticking out with my childish Converse and lunch bag, I could feel it.

The group didn't notice my presence, until Dreads made a big deal of motioning towards me.

"Don't just stand over there! We're here!" He waved me closer, as if we'd just made it to Disney World and I was holding up the line.

I awkwardly slipped my right hand over my face when the entire group of people turned in my direction. I stood there like an idiot, using my measly hand as a barricade from the stares. Four of them, including Harvey, were sitting on some crates that probably used to contain food. They were all guys, except for one girl. She was straddling some guy and practically sucking his face off. When the happy couple turned to look at me, they didn't bother to stop kissing. Their mingling mouths almost made me put my other hand in front of myself, but instead I brought my hand down and hoped that the moment would pass as quickly as possible.

Harvey had been busy talking to another guy before he turned to look at me. He didn't even look very surprised to see me, only smirked my way. As if he had planned for me to be there, which was ridiculous. I tried to keep my cheeks from feeling warm and turning red, but I couldn't shake the fact that I knew Harvey thought I stuffed my bra with pads. I quickly started wondering if he'd told his group of friends. They'd all probably shared a good laugh at my expense.

"Hey, look, Dreads brought in a new friend!" the buff guy who Harvey had been talking to said towards me. I didn't like his tone or the way he was looking at me. He looked like the type of person who would eat me as a weird source of protein.

So, his name *was* Dreads! I half laughed at getting his name right, but not with much humor. Plus, I got weird looks from everyone when I started to giggle.

I needed to get a grip on myself.

I laughed awkwardly once again and tried to find a way to get things over with. Now that I was right next to the group of people the smell was stronger than ever. I could feel Dreads standing right beside me, rocking back and forth on his heels.

Oh, right, Dreads' sandwich!

I ripped open the Velcro that secured my lunch bag with a shaky hand and took out the chicken sandwich I'd spent that very morning preparing. I handed the small package to Dreads, who took it graciously and with a look of wonder. It didn't take long for him to start devouring the thing, grinning and purring with every bite.

"Nice lunch bag," Harvey finally addressed me, looking at the bag in my hand. A few of the people around us snickered, even the couple who were doing the tongue tango. How they managed to laugh at me and put their tongues down each other's throats I would never understand.

"Thanks," I said with as much confidence as I could.

"Yo, guys, this be my homie—" Dreads said enthusiastically, before pausing to look at me with confusion. "What's your name?" Dreads asked, in a serious tone that didn't fit his personality at all.

"Livvie," I managed to squeak out, before Dreads wrapped an arm over my shoulder and finished his sentence.

"Livvie! She makes some dope chicken sandwiches!" Dreads finished, taking in a big bite and focusing on his food. Too bad his arm was still wrapped around my neck between his sandwich-laden hand and mouth. I don't think he remembered, so when he leaned in to take a bite my face was squished into his neck.

He didn't stink, but he was definitely a fan of the horrible body sprays certain boys liked to douse themselves in.

"Dreads," I said in a muffled voice, with my nose getting further squished into his neck.

"Yeah?" he asked, his mouth still full of food, because the sound wasn't very clear either.

"My face," I mentioned, trying to pull away.

"Oh, right! My bad!" he said, finally letting me loose. By then my face was a flaming tomato. The entire group was looking at me with huge grins on their faces. Even Harvey was laughing at me with his eyes.

I took that moment to distract them from my own embarrassment by asking a question that had been on my mind for the longest time.

"What's that smell?" I wondered, looking around for its source. The girl laughed at me, but was quickly shushed by the guy who had been kissing her. All of a sudden the alley turned deadly quiet as they all looked at me suspiciously.

Harvey had stopped smiling and even Dreads had stopped eating.

What had I said?

"Ay, man, I think it's time for your girl to go," said a new guy who hadn't spoken yet. He didn't resume kissing the girl on his lap, only stared at me. He was the least scary, aside from Dreads.

Dreads was already turning to me, but I was panicking. I hadn't gotten what I needed, the information from Harvey!

"Naw, she's cool, man." I got the notion that Dreads was defending me because he thought we were friends.

"We don't know. What if she's a snitch?" The scariest of them all spoke, standing up from his crate. I could see his muscles clench under his tank, right before he started to get closer. You could tell he liked to wear those low-cut tank tops that bodybuilders favored. Frankly I was plenty turned off by his man boobs.

I knew that all three of them had been smoking, but it wasn't as if they would get in big trouble. I was pretty sure that most of them were already eighteen. I wasn't since it was August, but my birthday was in less than a week so I had that going for me. It didn't make sense that I would tell on them, unless they weren't allowed to hang inside the alley, but I doubted it.

Then I finally understood why it smelled so grassy.

My eyes widened when I recognized the signs, which only made the big scary guy come looming closer.

Harvey, bless his heart, took the opportunity to stand up before beefy dude.

"I got it," he said. Even though the beefed-up guy was shorter, he had a lot more muscle. It didn't matter, because it became obvious that Harvey would be listened to. Beefy slowly backed down and nodded his head.

I didn't get to say goodbye to Dreads before Harvey started to walk ahead of me and pushed me along. I decided it was for the best, and so I let him bully me away without a qualm.

Going out was a lot shorter than going in, or maybe it was because Harvey was walking in long strides and I was trying to keep up. I was sort of panting and grunting behind him at one point. All of those skipped PE classes were catching up with me. I couldn't catch up to anything because I was so out of shape. It was true that just because you were thin it didn't necessarily mean you were fit.

When we finally made it to the dumpster opening, Harvey stepped aside and gestured towards the exit.

"Wait! I had to ask you something!" I said quickly, not wanting to leave yet and realizing that we were alone in an alley. He could dismiss me all he wanted, but I needed my answer first. Harvey didn't look so serious now that we had walked away, but he still had a moody look on his face.

I started to take a few steps back when he turned to me with a piercing gaze. He really was too attractive for his own good, and I was in over my head way too much for *my* own good.

My foot got caught in some sort of hump on the ground and decided to give out.

This is the part where I'm supposed to say that Harvey leaned in just in time to catch me and gracefully swept me off my feet in a gust of chivalry. We looked into each other's eyes and shared a special moment where everything clicked and by some miracle Harvey professed that I was the girl he was fascinated by.

Instead, I landed flat on my butt and let out a whine in the process.

"Darnflabbit!" I yelled, rubbing a sore spot while trying to stand up. My balance was crap and I was practically drunk based on all of the wobbly steps I tried to take. Harvey made no move to help me up or even ask if I was alright. His arms were comfortably crossed over his broad chest and he looked at me with a mixture of humor and distance.

"Wow," he deadpanned with one of his eyebrows raised, as if he couldn't believe such a socially awkward creature really existed.

I tried to play it off by finally hoisting myself up and looking him in the eye.

"Thanks for the help." I smiled with mock grace.

Harvey didn't bother to reply, only let his eyes land on my hand, which was still on my butt. I instantly felt self-conscious, so I took it off, not letting the sting continue to bother me. I had probably landed on a rock or something, because it was hurting.

"So, to what do I owe your special visit?" Harvey asked sarcastically, eyes still on my butt.

I tried to get him to look me in the eye again.

"I just wanted to ask you when we were going to start the tutoring."

Hervey finally did bring his eyes up to my face and smirked.

"I can't believe perfect little Livvie wasn't paying attention when someone from administration was talking to her." He did the whole disappointed superior act. I clenched my fists in response.

"Could it have been because she was too busy checking me out?" he continued to taunt.

Usually I would have melted into a puddle at the sight of Harvey Lockwell, much more when he was speaking to me, but I was starting to want to defend myself in these situations where he started to play around with me.

"You wish," I told him seriously, bringing a hand up to my hip in a spur of confidence. Harvey started to laugh loudly at my response, which only caused me to deflate like a popped balloon. Clearly, he didn't wish, only I did.

"Whatever, are you going to let me know or not?" I told him, finally showing my agitation.

Harvey finally stopped laughing enough to answer.

"We start next Monday, after school, in Mrs. Lasowski's classroom."

"After school?" I asked, thinking of Brian.

"Yeah."

"We can't do it before school or—"

Harvey didn't let me finish. He cut in instead.

"I can't do it any other time," he claimed, not looking like he was about to budge. I was such a wimp that I only nodded my head. I needed to figure out what to do about Brian.

"Well, I'll just be going now," I said, my thoughts somewhere else, particularly, my little brother. Harvey didn't bother to say goodbye, but I hadn't been expecting him to.

You know what else I wasn't expecting?

The brush of his hand on my lower back, almost on my butt.

His face looked as innocent as ever when I turned around. I wasn't buying it for a second, but at the same time I couldn't believe that Harvey Lockwell would make a move on me.

"Did you—?"

"Did I what?"

There was a long silence in which I thought of all the ways Harvey could embarrass me by telling me he wasn't the least interested in handling my butt, or near-butt.

"Never mind."

I turned again, almost expecting to feel his hand again. I didn't, thank God. But I did hear a throaty chuckle from deep inside the alley.

Chapter Five
Up in Smoke

"What are we doing again?" Nick wondered, taking a seat right next to me.

"We're interviewing for a babysitter," I told him in my serious business voice.

Nick gave me a crazy look and shook his head. Even though he thought I was being ridiculous by interviewing people to take care of Brian, he was still sitting right beside me. Brian had his own chair not too far from us. That just went to show how used to my weird antics both of them were.

I knew I could just hire some random person from the ads online, but it was my little brother I was entrusting into someone's hands and there was no way I was going to let some stranger take care of him. I needed to get to know the stranger first, thoroughly.

The three of us sat in front of a folded table I'd set up in the middle of the garage. The garage door was open and I had already received calls from people who wanted the job. Now all we needed to do was find someone suitable enough to take care of my little brother. Brian viewed the whole thing with less enthusiasm, too busy flipping through a comic book to pay attention, but no big deal.

The first three people that showed up were definitely not hired. The first girl didn't even get interviewed, since Brian went mute the minute he saw her and scooted closer to Nick. We figured the headgear on her face might have freaked him out.

The next guy looked to be about fifty years old, which instantly gave me the creeps. Finally, some pimply-faced guy from our school showed up, but ended up acting like a total buttface when he saw Nick. It only made me angry to see someone judging my best friend, so I didn't even bother interviewing him and sent him home instead.

Just when we were thinking that all hope was lost, an old Volvo pulled up the drive and a short guy stepped out from the driver's side. He looked around our age, maybe just a bit younger, and at least Brian didn't zip up the minute he saw him. If anything, he became even more engrossed in his comic book, reading it out loud.

Nick and I awkwardly stared him down as he made his way to our table. I had my hands folded over the tabletop and a cheesy smile on my face, while Nick kicked Brian under the table to stop with the narrating. I made a mental note to thank him later.

The guy smiled and waved. He had a cool nerdy look about him, as if he spent his time playing some

weird instrument like a banjo but also discussed
books with intellectuals at coffee shops. Aka, very
hipster.

Nick and I waved, right before we got down to
business.

It only took us five minutes to interview him,
since it seemed like Nick had hired him on the spot.
Brian eventually left to go inside and get another
comic book but never came back out, while we
continued to shoot the guy questions.

We had already discussed wages and hours,
until I remembered to ask something important.

"What did you say your name was again?" I
asked him, smiling awkwardly. Duh, here I was trying
to screen a potential babysitter and I hadn't even
gotten his name.

"Arnold," he told me, smiling. I wrote down all
of his information and let him know he was hired. He
left after some goodbyes.

"I think he's gay," Nick said as we watched the
SUV make a U-turn and drive away.

"Please don't hit on my little brother's
babysitter," I pleaded.

"As long as he doesn't hit on me, I'm still yours,
darling," Nick replied with a wink, making me laugh.

We finally folded up our makeshift station and
put Brian to bed, since the entire hiring process had
taken all day. It wasn't until Nick and I were sprawled
over my bed, stuffing our face with popcorn, that I
remembered about having to tutor Harvey.

A kernel got lodged in my windpipe at the mere thought of the subject.

I couldn't stop remembering the embarrassment of having been caught with a freaking pad inside my bra. The one thing I *was* trying to forget was when he made a move. Was the slight butt grope considered a move? I needed a lot more experience in these matters, I really did. Could Harvey actually be interested in my behind because of some unknown magical force? Was my butt my way in?

I decided to ask the one guy in my life. Sure, Nick had never had a boyfriend either, but he got hit on by girls who didn't know about him all the time. The boy had game, just not in the right court.

I shifted atop my bed. The room was dark, the only light coming from the TV, which was showing some cheesy reality show. I took a big breath before letting it all out on Nick.

"Um, Nick? Would a guy like Harvey, Idon'tknow, do some butt grabbing in an alley? Could that butt belong to me?"

I cringed at how awkward that sounded and waited for Nick to joke about it or maybe even give me an honest opinion. The minutes ticked by, until I realized I wasn't getting a response. I looked over to the big body beside mine, only to come face to face with a sleeping Nick. I rolled my eyes and leaned in to lick his cheek.

That woke him up. He even choked on some saliva before spazzing out and coming back to reality.

"Nick!" I whined.

"What?" he said, his sleepy, droopy eyes looking my way. He would have been really adorable, if he wasn't being so annoying.

"Nothing, you're taking up all of the space," I finally conceded, shifting to let him get more comfortable.

I tried to get my mind off of having to tutor Harvey the next day, but all the thinking only made me restless. It was like one of those moments when you know something big is going to happen the next day and you just can't go to sleep.

It finally happened, though; my eyes got heavy enough to let me rest.

You know how usually when you go to school the hours drag on and five minutes feels like fifty as you sit in class with that dead glaze in your eyes?

None of that happened on the first day I had to tutor Harvey, in case you were wondering. In fact, it seemed like the day was in an unending hurry. Lunch passed faster than ever before. One second I was sitting with Nick, discussing the difference between a weave and extensions, and the next second the last bell rang, letting me know that the school day was done.

I hadn't seen Harvey all day, but I usually never did. He was probably in The Cave with Dreads and the other scary guys he hung out with. My palms started sweating as I neared Mrs. Lasowski's classroom. I guess things got too slippery, because the moment I made it into the room all of my binders and folders fell to the ground in one swift motion.

Lucky for me, Mrs. Lasowski was still in her classroom, putting her things away. I got to have both her and Harvey, who I later saw sitting in his desk, leaning it back, watch me while I scrambled to pick all of my stuff off the floor.

Right as I stood back up, Mrs. Lasowski made her way past me towards the exit, but not without a parting comment.

"Take care of my classroom. One scratch and I'll have both of you on a platter. Am I making myself clear, Mr. Lockwell?"

Harvey stayed silent, but I guess that was answer enough for her. She didn't address me, but she did snort when she passed by. Out of every teacher I had ever had in my academic life, none had ever disliked me like Mrs. Lasowski.

I looked up to see Harvey bang his Vans on top of the desk he was occupying. He even folded his hands behind his back and smiled my way. I didn't understand why he was looking at me so pleasantly, but it caused a nice feeling.

I stood there like an idiot, staring at him. I was so enveloped in his gaze that I didn't notice when he brought the cigarette out and lit it.

"What are you doing?" I asked dumbly.

"Smoking a cig. Want one?" Harvey offered, just as pleasant as his expression.

"Tell me you're not smoking inside of Mrs. Lasowski's classroom," I said with dread. I couldn't believe that he had just literally lit a cigarette in school, and inside a classroom.

He didn't answer me, only took another deep breath from the cigarette and blew it out with a smirk. People who smoked had never been attractive to me, but holy did I want to be that cigarette. I immediately thought of all of the repercussions that we would face if someone found me in a classroom with Harvey smoking. Administration could walk down the hall and immediately see everything from the window on the door.

"What's the matter, Livvie? Scared you'll get in trouble and ruin your track record?" Harvey taunted, bringing the cigarette up to his lips. I made sure to scrunch my nose at the disgusting smell and look at him with narrowed eyes.

"You can't smoke in here," I said as calmly as possible. I used the same voice when I wanted Brian to eat his carrots.

"Why?"

"Because it's against the rules, so put it away!" I yelled with exasperation. My patience didn't last very long. I wasn't going down just because Harvey had a smoking habit.

"Make me." He smiled.

That did it. He was twice as annoying as when Brian would misbehave and my patience wasn't half as accommodating when it came to Harvey..

In one swift movement I had set my stuff down on one of the desks and made my way towards his seat. I tried to grab the stupid thing from his hand, but he had really long arms. He quickly grabbed the cigarette with two fingers and held it as far behind him as he could, at the same time as he pulled his legs down and under the desk. I wasn't thinking when I leaned in to get it, practically crawling on his lap. I suddenly realized that my boobs were in his face when he did. I could see his big satisfied smile on my chest the moment I peered down at him.

"You got any pads in here today, or are these real?" Harvey smiled, pushing the cigarette even more out of my reach. I wasn't going to give him an answer. I reached higher to get the dreaded thing. I don't know when I finally did crawl on his lap and straddle him, but I did.

Things were really getting out of hand, and the smell of the cigarette was making me dizzy. I turned my head towards the window at the door, only to see one of the worst things imaginable.

Principle River's bald head started bobbing up and down the hall. It was only a matter of seconds before he passed by the classroom and saw everything. I didn't think twice, I slid my way down Harvey's legs, all the way until my head was under the wooden desk. I got a clear view of Harvey's neck, chin, and the underside of his face. Not to mention his crotch, but I was trying to ignore that.

My head was right under the wooden table, and I cringed at all of the pieces of chewed up gum that had probably been stuck under the surface. I probably had a nice big glob of Juicy Fruit in my bun.

"Is he gone?" I whispered through clenched teeth. Harvey took his time to look towards the classroom window. His face lit up into a big cheeky smile and with the hand not holding the cigarette, he waved.

I guess Principal River did too, and I could hear the sound of his footsteps get further away when I focused.

"Fudge nuggets," I whispered, trying to crawl out from under the table. I ended up crawling out and sitting Indian style the second I was back out. Harvey was having the best time chuckling at me when I came out.

I reached my hand up to my head, only to feel various sticky substances in my hair.

"Fudge nuggets!" I said more forcibly, picking out what felt like a huge glop on my head. My hair was stuck together in certain parts from the gum.

Hearing my dorky curse, Harvey started to laugh even more. I sent him a bitter glance before standing halfway up to plant myself in a desk chair. He had a deep laugh, and even though he was laughing at me, it almost had the power to make me laugh with him. I was pathetic, trying to please him when I was just some big joke.

At least he had put the cigarette out. I realized when I saw it dead on the floor.

"Stop laughing!" I said like a little kid, cringing at the pitch of my voice.

Harvey's laughter died down quickly, until he was just smirking at me.

"Come here," he told me, his tone doing a 360-degree turn from playful to serious. Even though everything that had just happened would have made me really distrustful, his tone left no room for disobedience.

I awkwardly walked closer, waiting for him to stand. Was it weird that the smell of smoke didn't bother me anymore? It was almost a natural smell, laced with whatever the heck Harvey smelled like. It was all woodsy and smoky, and not necessarily bad just then.

I started to freak out when Harvey's fingers came up to my head and started to run through my hair, even though it was up in a bun. It wasn't for long, because he pulled the elastic band out quickly and let my hair tumble down.

"There's nothing in your hair," he claimed, even though his fingers were still running through it. It wasn't even special, he was brushing through the locks with quick efficiency, but I stood there with my eyes open, just feeling the chills that went down my spine. It was really weird how he was completely interested in my hair. I knew I shouldn't have let him, but there was some weird stuff happening to me, particularly in my chest, right where my heart was supposed to be. It was beating so fast I could almost imagine him feeling the thumping through my skull. I didn't want to ruin it by pulling away or saying something stupid.

Harvey gave a half smirk before he pulled his hands away. He had probably messed my hair up, but I didn't think it was that big of a deal during those moments. Harvey coughed, although it seemed forced. I was still kind of shocked about what had just happened, so I didn't stop him when he reached behind me and pulled something out.

"What's this?" he asked, his playful attitude coming back out. I looked down to see the last thing I ever wanted in Harvey's hands. A receipt for maxi pads and ice cream.

My secret list was suddenly right in front of me, after Harvey pulled it out of the messy folders that had been carelessly set on the desk behind me.

"Number one...date a guy who drives a motorcycle..." Harvey read, his grin widening.

I swear, a part of me died as I started to hear him read it.

Chapter Six
Do the Creep? Better Not.

You know when your brain goes into panic mode and you try to function correctly, but you can't?

I would like to think this a good explanation as to why I decided to jump on top of Harvey the moment he started reading my note. My lunch threatened to make a new appearance when I realized that The Harvey Lockwell had my stupid list in his hands and was freaking reading it.

I flung myself at him like a cold fish to get the dreaded piece of paper back, but Harvey's reflexes were obviously much better than mine. I took those few moments after I missed Harvey and ended up on the floor to chide myself for never going to that stupid PE class. Why couldn't I be fit and athletic enough to save myself from the embarrassment?

I was nothing but determined, though. Harvey was trying to scan the piece of paper while I practically picked myself up by climbing his leg. I would have time to rethink my strategy later.

"Give that back!" I yelled, reaching my hand forward to rip the paper away.

Harvey finally focused his attention on me. I was too caught up in making eye contact with him to notice when he hid the paper. I swear, one minute I was bent on reclaiming my dignity and the next I was too busy looking at Harvey grin at me.

I was weak. Weak, I tell you!

"I'm freaking serious Harvey. Give me my...English homework back!"

"English homework? I hardly think Mrs. Lasowski would assign you to spit in her coffee."

I stood there with my mouth open for a full minute in realization that Harvey was a much faster reader than I had given him credit for. Granted, it was the second item on the list but couldn't he have stumbled over the vocabulary a bit?

"Which by the way, is weak. Everyone pretty much did that freshman year," Harvey told me in all seriousness.

"You've spat in Mrs. Lasowski's coffee?" I asked with a little pang of jealousy. Had everyone gotten the chance to spit in her coffee but me? I wanted to slap myself for practically admitting that it wasn't my English homework. The excuse had seemed so golden in my mind for a millisecond.

"Like I said, the shit on your list is weak. Although some of them aren't that bad..." Harvey spoke with a hint of appreciation. I was going to agree until I realized that I'd written down losing my virginity as something that needed to be done.

"Well, now that you had a good laugh, you should give me my paper back," I said with a fake smile, before sticking my hand out in front of me. I hated the conflicting emotions that surged through me when Harvey smirked at me before shaking his head slowly. Part of me thought that he shouldn't have been looking so attractive doing something so evil.

"I think I'm going to keep it for a while," Harvey said, making his way around me. I stood there dumbfounded for the longest time, swirling on my heels to face him again. What was wrong with me? It was like my brain was malfunctioning or something.

"Where are you going?" I asked.

"Time's up, Little Livvie. Thanks for all the help. I really feel like I learned something today." I could practically hear the cocky smile in his tone.

With that parting statement I watched Harvey's broad shoulders disappear through the classroom door. He left as if nothing had happened and I guess nothing had for him. My eyes darted to the clock resting on the wall over the chalkboard and I realized that our time was up.

A part of me had been expecting a bigger meltdown or maybe having Harvey taunt me so bad I would have wanted to move to Alaska, but none of that had happened. Yet, why was my heart still beating frantically? Something told me that Harvey's response to my list hadn't been normal. He was holding something back, or worse, he was planning something.

Plus, he hadn't given me my list back.

I quickly gathered all of my things back into my backpack and scrambled my way out.

I had to take the city bus to get home, which was the icing on my already perfect day. Nick hadn't answered his phone and it was way too late to take the school bus. The bus was practically empty when I got on. There was one stop before mine where a creepy homeless man decided to get on and sit right beside me. Never mind that the entire bus was empty, he had to take the seat right beside mine.

I kept trying to figure out what Harvey was planning, except the smell of urine made it hard to focus.

By the time I got home I was beyond stressed out. I expected to find Brian's babysitter when I entered the doorway, but was greeted by something else, my mother's wrath.

"A babysitter?" My mom stood directly in front of me with a hand on her hip and the biggest frown on the planet. My eyes quickly noted her tan suit and perfectly styled hair.

"Why would you hire a babysitter without my consent?"

My mom kept going, choosing not to wait for a response. That's how it was between us. She would talk until the sky turned pink and I would never get a word in. This time was no different.

"I spend hours every day working my ass off trying to provide for you two and the only thing you have to do is help me with Brian!"

I gulped.

"You think I like coming home to a stranger in my house?"

For a second I panicked, thinking that perhaps my mom had fired the babysitter, but I knew my mother would never do that. My mom was extremely nice to everyone who wasn't me. I usually didn't mind her intolerant attitude, as long as she wasn't the same way with Brian.

I tried to apologize. "I'm sorry, it's just that I have to tutor someone after school now and I didn't—"

"So you would rather help some stranger than your family," she stated without batting an eyelash. I watched her walk around me towards the mail that had been dropped through the slot on the door, as if she hadn't just made me feel guilty. A part of me felt hurt, but a bigger part felt angry. Brian wasn't my son! I wanted to scream at my mom for being so judgmental, but I would never do that.

Just when I thought she would chew me out some more, her attention was gripped by something else.

I turned just in time to see her rip an envelope in half without bothering to even open it. Apparently she was done with me, because she walked off into the kitchen without a second glance. I wanted to call Nick, since he knew about my mom and always found a way to cheer me up, but I didn't want the subject of Harvey and my list to slip. No one knew about my list. It was so embarrassing that I hadn't even had the guts to show it to my best friend.

The list sounded nothing like me because I didn't want to be me anymore. Being me sucked.

I focused on the letter my mom had ripped in half. I was almost ninety percent sure who it was from. I wondered if maybe I could find a chance to read it, so huffing, I followed her into the kitchen. I tried not to be too thrown off by the various pots and pans on the stove.

Something was off, way off. My mom was almost never home to cook. In fact, we always went out for Thanksgiving because my mom hated cooking. I could count the times I'd watched my mom cook on one hand.

"Are you making dinner?" I asked, dumbfounded. My tone even had a little hint of hope in it, which was murdered by my mother's response.

"Jim's coming over."

Just like that, my day got ten times suckier. Jim coming over still didn't suck as much as knowing that my secret list was probably in Harvey's hands at the moment, but it was pretty close.

I didn't even want to get started on Jim. He was the creep who was half of the reason why my mom was never home. I guess you could say they had been 'dating' for a while, but a part of me never wanted to accept that. She canoodled with the enemy on a regular basis, but I was going to be ignorant of it as long as I could.

He was tall, skinny, middle-aged, balding, and creepy as all heck. The few times he had come over to pick up my mom, I had made sure that Brian was in bed and far away from him. My mom had never invited him over, despite them being whatever they were for more than a year, so it was a total surprise that she wanted him coming into the house. That was just like my mom, making plans as if Brian and I didn't exist.

I gulped, trying to think of an excuse to miss dinner, but I was too slow.

"Tell Brian to take a bath before he gets here. I want you two to look nice," my mom ordered, straining some sort of spaghetti near the sink. I internally rolled my eyes, knowing it was an order. I would have to get the letter later from wherever my mom had thrown it away.

It took me forever to get Brian looking presentable. I didn't want my mom to chew me out later about not doing a good job, so I even made him wear one of his cute little button-down shirts he hated so bad. Brian was being really fussy, almost as if he knew how sucky our situation was. He kept complaining about some villain in his comic, which was his way of complaining about Jim.

When it was my turn to get ready, I opted for some skinny jeans and a dressy shirt. I knew my mom was expecting me to wear one of my dresses, but I wouldn't for Jim. Plus, there was only one dress I would ever wear and my mom would have flipped out if I did that.

She didn't want anything reminding her of my dad. The last time I had seen him he had bought me the most beautiful white dress. It was the last thing I remembered him by. The dress still fit and it was locked away at the very back of my closet. It sounded weird, but I checked for it almost every day to see if it was still there, fearing my mom would throw it out.

My stomach did a weird flip when the doorbell rang. I was already seated, with Brian in the chair beside mine. He kept jiggling one of the table legs and the whole shebang was going to fall apart if he decided to wiggle the table a little more. I was too busy trying to get Brian to stop to cringe at my mom's flirty greeting.

"Jim! You made it," my mom gushed. No duh, he made it. Was she expecting him not to? Was there some dragon he had to slay to get here and that's why she was surprised? That's when I heard the awkward slapping sound of lips. I lied to myself and decided it was the sound of their hands shaking, no more.

"I wouldn't miss seeing you, Virginia." Ack! I flinched at Jim's voice.

My mom led him in way too fast, so I had no time to wipe the constipated look off my face. I got a dirty look from my mom, though, so I fixed it quick. That's when Jim's beady eyes made contact with mine, making it harder for me not to look like I smelled a fart.

"Livvie, you look so grown up," Jim said appreciatively after a few tense moments. Who the heck said that? I'd seen him like three months ago. I doubted being three months older had made me grow up. I was silent until my mom made a small huffing sound, meaning I should cooperate.

"Jim." There, I acknowledged his presence. Someone should have given me at least a cookie then. I never really had the guts not to do exactly what my mom wanted, but Jim was on a whole other level. I didn't like him.

"And here's Brian!" my mom exclaimed, taking the attention off of me. My brother became instantly cooler when he refused make eye contact. In fact, he started playing with the tablecloth and continued to jiggle the table with his foot.

Thus proceeded the most awkward dinner of my life. Once everyone was seated my mom tried to act as if we were a family. I noticed it right off when she asked Jim to sit at the head of our dining table, in my dad's seat, which she seemed not to remember right then. I started attacking my spaghetti in anger. No one sat in his chair. It was like an unwritten rule that the head of the table was my father's, not slimy Jim's. He didn't deserve the same butt space.

Things got even worse when she sat to his right and ordered me to move seats so I could sit on his left. As if sitting next to him and smelling his creep musk was going to make us a family. I dragged my plate over grudgingly, watching Jim's bland smile.

Just when I thought the dinner, also known as Livvie's torture hour, was about to be over, my mom decided to go get the dessert. That's when things got bad.

I wasn't expecting the bony hand. I felt movement going on under the table until the warmth enveloped one of my knees. I was practically dying in my seat when my mom came out with the pie.

I wanted to yell at my mom that her boyfriend's hand was on my leg under the table. She had no freaking clue that his hand was just there, all nice and comfortable over my knee cap. In fact, scratch that, I didn't want to tell anyone. It was so embarrassing that the only thing I wanted was to rip his hand off.

Oh my God.

I don't know why I thought it, but for a moment I wanted Harvey to be in the room. It was so weird, thinking of someone like Harvey inside my dining room with my mom and her boyfriend, but I wished so bad that he were there to protect me and make sure Jim's slimy hand left. I slapped myself mentally. Who was I kidding? As if Harvey would ever care about me enough to do something like that. I was just being wishful and stupid, I hardly knew the guy. But something told me a badass like Harvey would probably punch Jim in the face just because he could.

"Virginia, if I could have your attention for a second," Jim spoke up, hand still on my leg, completely casual as if he rented the very spot under his name and everything. I tried looking at my mom with wide eyes and a pleading stare, but she was too busy giving her attention at Jim's request.

I felt like I could breathe again when his hand disappeared, until I wished something I would have never thought. I actually wished Jim would have kept

* * *

62

his hand on my knee if it meant him not doing what he did.

"Virginia," Jim said, reaching the knee-grabbing hand into his suit pocket and pulling out a small black box.

Oh no, oh no, oh no—

"Will you marry me?" he asked.

I watched in horror as my mom's face lit up. She had known this was her proposal dinner. The stupid spaghetti and everything was for this moment.

We all knew her response, but she didn't have the chance to say it, because just then the entire dining table came down with a bang. Wine and leftover breadsticks flew in the air, while a big slice of pie landed right on my foot. I swiveled over to Brian to see if he was okay. His much-too-innocent eyes told me he wasn't entirely, but he was pretty pleased with himself.

If my mom hadn't just gotten engaged she would have thrown the biggest fit on the planet. Instead, Jim made some joke about how even the dining room table was excited about their marriage, which was so lame only my mom acknowledged it with a giggle. I had to spend the rest of the evening cleaning the mess up while the happy couple left to celebrate their engagement. Brian was partly guilty about the mess so he helped me clean up a bit.

When the hour was late and Brian was finally asleep, I snuck into the kitchen and pulled the torn envelope from behind a cookie jar. I'd taken it out of the trash before I started throwing all of the other food away. I had to take both parts of the paper out and then, after hunting for some clear tape, put them back together.

My dad never called, it just wasn't his thing. He either showed up unannounced out of the blue or he sent a letter. Usually I got my hands on his letters before my mom did, but this time she'd beaten me to it, so I had to put it together like a pirate trying to fix his treasure map.

He had doctor's writing, meaning you could only decipher half of his messy script and guess the rest. I'd gotten some practice throughout the years, but I still got stuck on certain parts. The letter was short, addressed to Brian and me, and only held a few abrupt sentences. He asked about our wellbeing, even my mom's, and then mentioned that he was somewhere really hot. The letter didn't have a return address and his message didn't betray his location, which wasn't new.

Only the last sentence caught me off guard.
I'll be there soon.
For the first time in the entire day, I smiled.

Chapter Seven
If I Were in Your Shoes

I couldn't stop thinking about my dad the entire day.

I was sitting in Mrs. Lasowski's class, busily battling with a stubborn hangnail and remembering Jim's slimy hand on my knee. I had seen Nick in the morning, but my best friend could obviously tell something was bothering me and so with a sad smile had left me alone for the first part of the day.

I couldn't bring myself to tell Nick about Jim being a pervert or even about the marriage proposal. It couldn't be happening to me, it just couldn't. Plus, my mom and the Creep had decided to head back to our house the night before. It had been so gross and depressing to see my mom close her bedroom door with him inside. The only thing that kept me feeling super depressed was the fact that my dad would be home soon enough and all hell would break loose.

It was the first time he'd spent the night and I had to crawl into bed with Brian because it freaked me out so much. I kept the door locked the entire night, but I still clutched one of Brian's action figures under the pillow to club Jim with.

My dad couldn't come home soon enough when Jim came out of my mom's room the following morning and smiled at me before going into the bathroom. It wasn't even a casual smile. He gave me an intense creeper smirk that sent me practically running down the stairs and into the kitchen. I even bumped my hip on the wall and sent a few picture frames falling on the ground. At least he wasn't standing outside long enough to watch me scramble to put the stupid things back on the wall.

I couldn't stand being in English class, so my hand awkwardly shot up into the air while Mrs. Lasowski was midsentence. If looks could have killed I would have been a bloody mess on the ground. Mrs. Lasowski was definitely not pleased to be cut off.

"Yes, Livvie?" she asked curtly. Like I made a habit of cutting off her speech, which I didn't, on purpose.

"I need to pee!" I said without thinking. I heard a few people snicker behind me and mentally slapped myself. It wasn't even true, but I had needed a quick excuse.

"Well, don't be crude. You may be excused." Mrs. Lasowski turned her nose up in the air before turning back to the whiteboard.

I quickly walked out of the room with my head down towards the ground. It didn't take me long to reach the girls' bathroom. I made my way towards one of the stalls and promptly sat on the toilet. I didn't think of how gross it was, since I could only focus on the letter. Sometimes the letters had money, other times they just contained a funny story, but never had they actually given me a hint of when he would be back.

For a second I wondered if Jim knew the truth about my parents. He wouldn't have proposed if he did, though. Even he wasn't dumb enough to propose to an already married woman.

I closed my eyes so hard they scrunched on my face. I missed my dad so much at that moment. My parents had never gotten divorced, but my mom had told my dad to leave when I was ten. I could still remember them fighting until my mom finally forced him to go. I had begged him to stay. He hadn't wanted to leave either, but told me it was for the best. In the years after, my dad had come and visited Brian and me, but never for long.

He was like a storm that would come into our house and pass. A storm because every time I saw him my mom flipped out, but he always whirled everything around after passing through and the aftermath was always a little better than what we started with. My dad was like no one I knew. In fact, once, when I turned fifteen, my dad had picked me up at midnight, right on my birthday.

We got on a plane that night and I spent the day with him in New York. He took me to the zoo, even though I was turning fifteen and not ten, but I didn't care. After the zoo he hailed a cab took me to an art museum on the Upper West Side filled with artsy people with different hair colors and designer tastes. In one day he'd treated me like his little girl but also allowed me to feel closer to an adult.

Then when the day was about to end, after we'd dined in a luxurious restaurant and done some more sightseeing, we flew back. He left me on our doorstep and kissed my forehead, right before my mom opened the door along with a cop in uniform. By the time the cop started to question me on my doorstep, my dad had already left, as if he'd never even existed.

I never really knew what my dad did for a living, but I always thought it was the reason my mom made him leave. I couldn't bring myself to believe anything too bad, though. He was the most important person in my life aside from Brian. I just couldn't think like that about him. If anything he was probably a secret agent or something just as exciting.

I kept recalling memories with my dad until at one point I started staring at the bathroom walls and reading the writing on them. My heart jumped a little when I saw Harvey's name. All memories of my dad faded while I tried to understand the writing on the wall.

harvey lockwell was the best fuck ever

Apparently some girl thought he was good enough to scribble with sharpie on a bathroom stall? I wasn't sure if that meant he was really talented. I mean, she had written this on school property.

"Wow, Lockwell, you really know how to get it in," I said out loud after reading several other messages that had been written under the original one. Some of them even started describing the things they did together. It was getting kind of graphic and awkward.

"Damn right he does," a new voice replied to me from the other side of the stall. I felt my face getting hot when I realized that someone had heard me. I was going to act like I wasn't there, until I stiffened and set off the automatic toilet flushing system.

"I know you're in there," the unknown female voice called out. I finally popped open the door to face the girl who had been speaking to me. My eyes widened when I realized it was the girl from The Cave. It did take me a while to recognize her, since she wasn't sucking anyone's face off.

"How was your shit?" she asked nonchalantly. In shock, I watched her as she started fixing a bobby pin in place on her head. She had crazily teased hair that was obviously dyed black. The front was in a huge poof that she was trying to bring up even higher.

"I wasn't—"

"Hey, it's cool. We all shit, even though most guys like to believe that since we're girls we only poop out butterflies and rainbows."

"They really think that?" I asked, confused.

❀ ❀ ❀

69

"Yeah, it's like they don't function thinking that our assholes are for anything other than—" The girl paused, probably taking in my horrified expression. "Oh, yeah, I forgot you're a nun," she finally picked up, shrugging her shoulders.

"I'm not a nun!" I defended quickly. I had an alarming habit of falling asleep in church—something in the holy water knocked me out—and I wondered if I should include this little tidbit in my defense.

"Whatever, see you around, Livvie," the girl said, already walking out the door.

My eyes were busy looking at her swaying hips. For a second I wondered if that's how all girls walked. Why didn't I walk like that? Wait, she knew my name! I realized with wonder that the girl knew who I was. My life was getting infinitely weirder by the second.

By the time I got back to class it was close to ending. I feared for a second that Mrs. Lasowski would give me detention or something horrible, but for once she wasn't out to get me. I decided to spend my lunch period in the library, away from Nick. I knew he was probably eating alone, but I was scared he would ask questions I just couldn't bring myself to answer.

My stomach was in knots when it was finally time to tutor Harvey. I really couldn't handle any more stress. By the time I got to Mrs. Lasowski's classroom, the old woman was long gone. Harvey was sitting on one of the seats with his combat boots propped up on top of the table. He had a pair of

earphones in his ears and one of his shoes was kicking
up and down to a beat.

When I got closer I could see his head rocking
back and forth to the same tempo. He noticed me
right away, because his eyes slowly opened when I got
close enough. Instead of being caught embarrassed or
anything like that, a smirk slowly crept onto his face. I
was stuck like a mouse in front of a lion all over again,
but I didn't even care. I was right, though, my heart
really couldn't handle any more stress. With how fast
it was beating I was almost ready to faint.

I watched him slowly take the buds out of his
ears and bring his legs back under the table. Squaring
my shoulders, I got down to business. I brought my
desk right next to his, as if he hadn't just mesmerized
me like an idiot for five seconds. A part of me was too
tired to let myself get carried away. If anything I was
just his tutor who was a complete loser, and I needed
to get things over with.

"Alright, what do you need me to help you
with?" I asked, already looking over my notes to have
him copy from.

"Nothing really," he said casually, bringing his
hands up behind his head. There was a weird feeling
to his tone, as if he was inside some joke, again.

"That's funny, anyway I was thinking I could
help you with some Cal homework to start—"

"Already done."

"What?" I was really confused. What was he
doing?

I watched in a daze as he brought out some papers and handed them to me. I was surprised when I saw that all of the problems had been neatly worked out.

"You paid someone to do this?" I asked, thinking that was the only way. I mean, I remembered him being smart, but there were at least two problems in the homework I still hadn't figured out.

"Ouch, Livvie, be careful—you'll hurt my feelings with questions like that," Harvey said, touching his heart dramatically. He obviously wasn't the least bit hurt. But I liked the sound of my name coming from him, even when he was mocking me.

"If you know how to do all of this, then why did the office lady make me tutor you?"

"Don't know. Something about my less-than-impressive attendance or some shit like that."

I sat there with my mouth wide open for about ten seconds, until I heard Harvey's next words.

"So, virgin, huh?"

I almost choked on my own saliva, which would have been really gross.

"No. Well. Yes. But that's none of your business!" I really didn't know how to say anything at that point.

Harvey had a full-on smile. He was enjoying watching me squirm.

"No one's popped your cherry?"

"I-I..."

"Ready to hand in your V-Card?"

"Oh my God."

He just kept on going. It was like there was no appropriate answer to anything he was asking. It was kind of sad to say the truth, and at the same time I wasn't going to lie. He wouldn't believe me.

I was steeling myself for another round of sexual innuendos, when the door burst open. The door was pushed so hard that it banged against the wall once it opened. My eyes connected with the big scary guy from The Cave. He was sweating as if he had just run a mile. There was a wild energy coming off him that made my heart start beating faster. It was in part because he wasn't someone I felt the least bit comfortable with, even less than Harvey.

I relaxed a little when I caught sight of Dreads. He skidded in right behind Beefy. His dreads were flinging wildly in the air in alarm, which killed my momentary calm.

"Fucking shit! They found us, man!" Beefy yelled towards Harvey.

I turned just in time to watch Harvey's mouth open into a little O shape. He looked confused, then panicked.

"Don't fuck with me, Rex," Harvey said in a soft but serious tone.

Big Scary Guy was clearly named Rex, because he leveled his gaze towards Harvey and spoke in a deadly tone. "I wouldn't fuck around with this. We need to leave, now."

Had he said leave? Where? Before I knew it Harvey had jumped from his seat and hurled himself over his desk before pushing past me. I watched all

three of them run out the door. I don't know what
propelled me to follow them, but it was probably the
fact that there was hardly any excitement in my life.
This was it. There was something inside me screaming
at my legs to run after them. Suddenly I was right
behind them as the school doors burst open.

It was only a little bit after school and so there
were still some students milling around at the front
entrance, but even with the small crowd I caught sight
of the black SUV that was parked beside the fire lane.

"Holy shit, man!" Dreads' voice cracked. He
was staring at the same black vehicle that we all were.

"We need to go now. They won't do shit here,
but we can't stay any longer," Rex said, already getting
ready to run towards the student parking lot.

Harvey finally noticed that I was standing right
beside him. I was so close to him it was a wonder that
he hadn't noticed me before. The look on his face
betrayed just how much he was freaking out.

"Come on, bitch, we need to go!" Rex was
yelling. For a moment I wondered if he was referring
to me, until it dawned on me that the bitch was
Harvey.

Harvey took one last look at me before
following in Rex's footsteps. My heart was practically
banging inside my chest. I had no clue what was
happening, but something about the expensive black
SUV with nearly black tinted windows was making my
legs feel wobbly. It just looked so out of place and it
felt like trouble. I had no clue if the people inside the

SUV could see me, but when I looked in its direction I felt like I was making eye contact.

"Harvey, bro! What are you doing? We can't ditch Livvie!" Dreads yelled. He was the only one who still hadn't left my side.

I watched as Harvey turned around and realization touched his face.

"She doesn't know anything!"

"They saw her with us. They're gonna ask her questions!"

"But she doesn't know anything!" Harvey was practically yelling now. Some of the students around us were starting to pay attention, which was probably what made Harvey roll his eyes at Dreads and start to run towards the school parking lot again.

"Dreads, what's happening?" I finally gained the courage to ask. Dreads tried to smile at me, but it looked weak and forced.

"Looks like you're coming on a little road trip with us, Livvie."

I didn't ask any more questions, because the purr of a motorcycle was right in front of me.

"Get on, dork," Harvey Lockwell ordered from his bike.

The entire senior class was watching me as I debated whether or not it was the best idea. Before I saw it coming, Harvey threw his helmet my way, deciding things for me. I put the stupid thing on and practically hopped onto the back of his motorcycle. I had never touched him on purpose before, so the tingle that shot from my fingers to my chest when I

wrapped my arms around him was unexpected. I had never touched anyone like that, with excitement and fear vibrating inside my body. I watched as Dreads crawled into the passenger seat of an old beat-up Corolla.

Harvey quickly drove us out of the school lot and onto the road. The wind that was hitting my body almost knocked me off the bike, so I made sure to wrap my arms around him tighter. I could feel the Corolla driving behind us, following our lead.

I had no clue where I was going. I didn't know what the heck was happening to me, but I was almost sure I was in a real-life high-speed chase, because when I gained the guts to turn around I could see the black SUV right behind us.

I wondered what my mother would think of me being gone. I was leaving our little town, and I hadn't even decided to. It wasn't like I was being abducted, especially when we started to get far away and the shots started being fired. At first I thought they were fireworks, but then I realized how stupid I was when my ears started ringing. No, I wanted to leave just as much as Harvey and his friends, to go somewhere especially far away from the guns.

What would happen to Brian? What about my mom's impending marriage? What would Jim do in our house? What if my dad arrived and found I wasn't there? Would he be worried?

All of these questions popped into my head, which was kind of crazy to think about since there was literally a car following us and gunning us down.

I practically became one with Harvey when he accelerated and made an unexpected exit from the freeway we had been on. The speed we had been going would have made it impossible to do without crashing into the divider, but it was clear that he'd timed it so that the Corolla even made it, unlike the black SUV, which had no time to turn.

I watched from behind my helmet visor and started to breathe a little better as the truck continued on the road we had been on just moments before. Luckily they were bad shots, because I wasn't dead yet. I was confused, but full of adrenaline. Even though it felt like everything was going so wrong, there was a little voice in my head telling me that this was what I had been waiting for.

It was time for my mom to take responsibility for Brian. She needed to be the parent now. The more I thought about it, the more I started to believe that the reason my mom had been so angry when my dad took me to New York when I was fifteen was because she would have had to take care of Brian. It wasn't that she was worried, not really. Her babysitter would have been gone, that's all. I was tired of feeling like everyone made the decisions for me. I was sick of taking care of someone I loved and resenting it. I was terrified of Jim the Creep and frustrated because my mom was never going to believe or notice how messed up he was. That was it, I had successfully rationalized everything in my head right then.

This was fate.

Chapter Eight
Can't Believe I'm Not Butter

Once the excitement of being in a high-speed chase with the school's most attractive boy wore off a little, reality set in. I was really leaving home. I was really leaving Brian and Nick. My arms tightened around Harvey reflexively and I felt his abs tighten. That was definitely not the appropriate time to realize how close I was to him. I needed to clear my head.

It felt like we had been driving for hours, and I realized that it was true when the sun started to set and nighttime neared. It had been at least three hours. I couldn't believe that they were really going through with this, especially when I noticed that the Corolla was still behind us. At least the black SUV was nowhere to be found, but something in the back of my head told me that they weren't very far. What had Harvey done that people with guns wanted him and his friends badly enough? Was it wrong for me to be more peeved about the fact that Harvey wasn't wearing a helmet than the idea that crazy criminals were on our tails?

I tried to look at our surroundings as we whizzed on by, but the speed of the motorcycle pretty much terrified me. Every time I wanted to look sideways, my arms got a little looser and I would feel like my head was going to be blown off by the air around us. I was beginning to have a love-hate relationship with the bike under me. At least I got a few glimpses of the scenery. At one point the road stopped looking so civilized and the pine trees we were used to grew thicker. I wondered what Harvey would do if I got the chance to tell him about the new problem facing us.

I needed to pee.

I was also hungry. Oh, and I was pretty sure I had just left my little brother in the hands of a perv.

Just when I thought we would continue driving for the entire duration of the night, a gasoline station popped up. It was the only building in sight and my bladder practically rejoiced. Happiness surged through me when Harvey made the turn into the station and the Corolla followed suit.

Harvey started to stand up right as he cut the engine. The bad part was that my legs weren't used to being in the same position for such a long time, and so they'd fallen asleep. I was still straddling the machine when Harvey stood. He obviously forgot I was behind him or something. I was left trying to balance myself on the stupid bike and before I knew it, my entire body was being pushed down towards the opposite side. I was going to face-plant in the cement along with the bike. I would be lucky to find a boyfriend in graduate school if I messed up my face.

"Shit," I heard Harvey curse from the other side, right before one of his hands grabbed the bike's handle and held it in place. My nose was like two inches away from the dirty, gasoline-splattered ground. I felt my body right itself slowly. Even throughout all of that my legs were still wrapped around the sides of the bike.

I watched Harvey run a hand over his face, as if he were infinitely tired, before he gestured for me to get off. Someone was grumpy.

I forced my legs to untangle themselves and stand up. I tried not to look retarded when they wobbled, but it felt like a thousand little needles were piercing every inch of my legs. Yup, definitely asleep.

"I need your phone," Harvey said, extending his hand out to me.

"What for?" I don't even know why I was being difficult. It was clear that Harvey wasn't happy that I had joined the escape and I was just making it harder.

"You're eighteen?" he asked, but he looked like he already knew the answer.

"No," I replied sheepishly anyway.

"You want the cops to track you? We can't take any chances. Hand it over."

Right, I wasn't an adult; I was a runaway. My nose twitched before I finally complied and pulled my Blackberry out. With one last sad look, I watched Harvey take out everything from the inside, pocket it, and take the actual phone towards the Corolla that had parked on the opposite gas pump. I wondered if I was supposed to wait for him to come back, but when I took a look around at the deserted space around me I figured he wouldn't mind me following him again, at least I wouldn't.

I trailed behind Harvey. Rex was the first to exit the car from the driver's side. Dreads and the people in the backseat followed not long after. The girl from the bathroom earlier that day caught sight of me and looked surprised, right before forming a smile.

"Damn, when I said I would see you around, I didn't think it would be so soon!"

I felt my face redden as the people around us looked confused. The girl didn't bother to explain, so neither did I. The guy she had been busily making out with the first time I met her walked up to Harvey and they began to speak in hushed tones.

It wasn't long before Dreads and Rex formed a circle with the other two and joined the discussion. It seemed like us, the girls, weren't going to be included.

"I didn't know you were a part of this—" the girl began, before the guy who I was assuming was her boyfriend broke away from the circle and gave her a look.

"Lexi," he chided, pretty much making her quiet, before turning back to the group.

"Um, I'm not really sure what's going on here." I shrugged. Even though she was someone who I would have never talked to in school, it seemed like the girl wasn't entirely mad about me joining the group. In fact, the girl, whose name was Lexi, seemed a little relieved to have me there.

The circle of guys finally broke up, but not before I heard Dreads say something a little too loudly.

"So, we just have to make it to Jesse's, then?"

Harvey nodded before looking right at me. For a second I almost felt like he was debating something in his head. Whatever it was, I didn't want to be there when he decided it. He wouldn't leave me stranded where we were, right?

I wondered who Jesse was for a brief second. As if I were still in school, I brought my hand up into the air to grab Harvey's attention. Whatever he had been trying to decide in his head was erased by a smirk.

"Yes, Livvie?" he asked in a mocking tone, eerily similar to Mrs. Lasowski's. Heck, he even had a hint of Mrs. Lasowski's facial expression. I tried not to let my cheeks get red when Lexi's boyfriend snickered alongside Rex.

"Can I make a phone call? Since I'm kind of, well, running away, and all." I started to wring my hands in front of me.

"No, we can't risk—"

"But, there's a payphone right there! Plus, I'm calling someone I can trust." I motioned towards the payphone that I had been eyeing since we arrived. I almost thought he was going to say no, but he sighed and nodded his head. I skipped over to it, before realizing that I was being followed by the entire group.

Rex gave me a look that made my skin crawl, which pretty much meant that if I wanted to call someone, he would be right behind me to listen to it all. For a second, I pictured him strangling me with the payphone cord if he thought I was betraying the group. Definitely didn't like Rex.

I wasn't going to be more of a burden than I already was, so I sucked it up and walked to the payphone again. That's when I hit a wall.

Smiling awkwardly, I tried to make my voice as innocent as possible.

"You guys wouldn't happen to have any change on you?"

I watched as the entire group rolled their eyes and started to stick their hands in their pockets. It wasn't my fault that my backpack, along with the rest of my belongings, had been left behind.

"Here," Lexi's boyfriend finally said, handing over some change. There was some lint in there too, which I had to separate to get to the quarters. It didn't take very long for Nick to pick up. I wondered if he had been expecting me.

"Hey—" I tried to greet smoothly.

"Where the hell are you, Livvie? Oh my—I can't even—do you know how freaked out everyone is?" He couldn't pick which sentence to finish, apparently.

"Yeah, see, about that—" I was cut off again, this time by Harvey. He had brought a finger up to his lips.

"You were on the news, Livvie. On the freaking news. On the back of Harvey Lockwell's motorcycle, no less."

"Oh my God, really?" I asked a bit too excitedly. "How did I look?"

"I can't believe—wait, what? You looked fine. Well, aside from the cardigan, but—"

"What's wrong with my cardigan?" I wondered, holding the bottom of it up for inspection. I wasn't paying attention to Harvey's eye roll.

"It's just, well, the color."

I noticed that Harvey had been trying to get my attention. He was telling me to wrap it up. I cleared my throat quickly and got back to business.

"Um, Nick, I think I'm going on a little trip. Would you mind taking care of Brian for me? I know he has his babysitter, but Jim kind of sort of proposed to my mom."

"Jim the Creep?"

"Exactly. It won't be for long, just until my dad gets there." I took the opportunity to see the confused looks I was getting.

"Yeah, sure. You know I would do anything for you, Livvie, but what the hell are you doing with Harvey? Why are you running from the cops with him? Did he make you do anything? Why didn't you tell me?" Nick was throwing way too many questions at me. Some that I couldn't answer. Even though I felt like a butthole, I tried to bypass his questions.

"Nick, I have to go, but please do that for me?" I asked, talking quickly.

I heard him sigh. "Yeah, sure."

"Alright, I love you."

"Love you too, Livvie."

"Nick?"

"Huh?"

"You were right. The cardigan is an ugly color." Someone snorted behind me, who sounded a lot like Lexi.

I tried not to get clumsily emotional when I finally hung up. Before I knew it, I was straddled behind Harvey again and the motorcycle had come to life under me. We were a few miles away from the gasoline station when my bladder came knocking. I mean, how horrible would it have been if I'd just peed behind Harvey? There had been no time to go at the gasoline station, which was the worst part of it all.

I willed my bladder to be made of steel and wondered if we would be stopping again soon. It didn't seem likely, so I rested my head against Harvey's back and tried not to think. I obviously couldn't sleep, even though I was getting tired enough for it, but I wasn't going to risk falling off the back of a moving motorcycle. That was one excitement I was going to have to pass on.

It felt like forever, and now that I didn't even have my phone with me, I didn't know how many hours passed. Probably two more. My heart started beating a little faster when I cracked an eye open the saw a fast food restaurant whiz by. We were back into civilization.

I didn't know how late it was, but it seemed like a lot of the places around us were closed, which was why I was a little weirded out when we finally pulled into a parking lot belonging to a pawn shop. A sign overlooking the building claimed it was open twenty-four hours. Because you never knew when you'd need to pawn a family heirloom.

This time, thankfully, Harvey waited for me to get off the bike first. I watched the others exit the car and come near us. Lexi had her arms wrapped around her body, trying to fight off the cold that her miniskirt wasn't shielding her from. I mentally patted myself on the back for my cardigan. It might have been an ugly color and possibly ruined the chances of having an amazing high-speed-chase recording, but it was doing its job.

"Alright, babe, work your magic," Lexi's boyfriend ordered her, handing her the bulk of everyone's dead phones.

Lexi nodded her head resolutely and had already turned to make her way towards the pawn shop, when Dreads spoke. "Hey, why doesn't Livvie go with her?"

I heard the rest of the guys snort and Rex laugh before getting the hint. What could Lexi do that I couldn't?

Even Lexi looked at me up and down and smiled. It was clear that I wouldn't be helpful, and so Lexi started to make her way inside. I finally understood what I wasn't going to be helpful for when I caught sight of Lexi and a pawn shop employee through one of the windows. You could tell from where we stood that Lexi was using all of her 'womanly' skills. Even her boobs were pressed up against the display glass, right next to the hunting rifles.

I remembered I had to pee, and without thinking started to walk up to the building.

"What are you doing?" Harvey asked from behind me.

"I have to go to the bathroom," I claimed, without bothering to look behind me. I didn't hear or feel any footsteps behind me, so I concluded that they were letting me.

A chime screeched throughout the room when I entered, letting whomever was inside know of my presence. I was only going to look for a bathroom, until I heard a man's voice.

"Sorry, can't help you. How do I know those things aren't stolen?"

"They aren't!" Lexi sounded agitated now. I wouldn't call myself a flirting genius, but even I knew that the flirting boat had long sailed and Lexi was about to lose it.

I didn't think twice before walking up from behind a row of secondhand guitar amps and right up to the employee. The man had a huge beer belly that made it hard for him to stand next to the counter. He sported a long gray beard, which was in weird harmony with his many tattoos. Even with all of those characteristics, I couldn't stop thinking of Santa Claus when I first set eyes on him.

"Hello! What a fine-looking establishment!" I greeted him cheerfully, eyeing the cracked ceiling. Fine, indeed. This was my chance to prove my worth. Lexi sent me a panicked glare.

"I already told your friend here that I'm not interested in the phones." A look at the man's name tag told me his name was George. George Claus, perhaps?

"Oh, but I can assure you that the devices aren't stolen." I don't know if it was my vocabulary, or my tone, or even the cardigan, but George's resolve looked like it was starting to weaken.

"Yes, but—"

I didn't let George finish before my attention was caught by something else. "Is that the entire seven seasons of *Buffy*?" I had a short attention span when it came to good TV.

"Why, yes it is!" George's entire face lit up as his eyes were directed to the DVD boxed set. Something told me he'd made sure they were behind the counter not because of worth, but because of personal value.

"Wow, I've only watched the first two and have been wanting to see the rest, but haven't been able to." It was true. On the weekends that my mom was never home and Brian was asleep, I would spend my time watching *Buffy* reruns. Too bad they only reran the same two seasons.

"Well, I'll tell you what! I'll buy the phones and throw in the boxed set!"

"No!" I exclaimed.

"Yes! Anything for a fellow *Buffy* fan. I've been worried about this baby falling into the wrong hands."

"I completely understand," I said seriously.

By the end of it all George and I were grinning widely at each other. It didn't take long for him to evaluate the phones, fill out the paper work, and hand over the DVD set. I tried not to freak out when Lexi took out her fake ID. What George didn't know wouldn't hurt him.

"Alright, well, thank you so much!" I said, waving my hand in his direction. I had the *Buffy* set already cradled in my other arm.

"No, thank you! Enjoy those! Anything for a fellow Scoobie!" I had never seen a grown man look so excited.

I took a small break, setting the box set in Lexi's arms like a newborn, to go to the bathroom. We left right after. I turned my head to our waiting group, smiling. Lexi took the opportunity to wave the money that George had given us in the air. The rest of the guys looked pretty excited about our new economic standing. Rex was hollering and hooting everywhere.

"Damn, babe, good job!" Lexi's boyfriend cheered. I really needed to know his name.

"Don't thank me. Thank Livvie. She did the deal, not me." I watched Lexi's boyfriend look at me with newfound respect. Even Harvey looked at me, but I couldn't really tell what was going through his mind. I wished I could read him as well as I could Lexi's boyfriend.

Harvey finally spoke up. "Let's keep it moving."

I didn't miss the fact that everyone had no qualms about handing him all of the money. Harvey was definitely in charge, but something told me that he might be the one person that the people chasing us wanted most. It only made sense, in a twisted, ironic way. I couldn't hold my *Buffy* set in my hands for the rest of the motorcycle ride, and so Dreads was kind enough to pop open the trunk and help me put my new treasure away. I seriously thought we were going to continue driving, but even Harvey looked tired. It took us all of five minutes before we pulled into another lot.

This one belonged to a motel. I wasn't sure how this was supposed to work. I mean, things were becoming official right then. I was on the run and I was going to be spending the night with them. Not just them, Harvey. Well, probably not Harvey. Right?

I wasn't going to lie. I knew that even with the money that George had handed us, we really weren't loaded. I didn't have any money on me, but I wasn't so sure about the rest of the guys.

We all walked into a small office. There was a little floral couch and nothing else except a potted plant and the counter. I didn't know that fake plants could look dead, but the one that had been set beside the couch did. I was about to sit down, until I noticed a suspicious-looking stain. Yup, this was definitely going to be some night for me. Lexi and her boyfriend didn't find a problem with the furniture, because they both plopped down on the coach before making out. I wondered if they had been doing the same thing in the car. At this rate they'd probably have their lips fall off soon.

"Bro, can you stop dry humping your girlfriend for a minute? You're making the rest of us horny," Rex said, leaning against one of the peeling-wallpaper-adorned walls. The rest of us? I tried not to cringe when he looked at me right after he said it.

That was my cue to walk next to Harvey, who was talking to a pimply-faced guy working the other side of the counter. What I really wanted to outrun was all of the perverts in my life.

It was clear that the pimply-faced guy really didn't care if Harvey's ID was fake or not, but I had long ago figured that almost everyone in the group aside from me had a fake ID.

"Is that room I mentioned okay?" the guy asked, checking with Harvey that the one room available was up to his standards. I wasn't sure anything in the motel was up to anyone's standards, but whatever. I tried not to freak out when Harvey nodded and was handed a set of keys. They didn't even have key cards, they handed him actual keys. I wondered how easy it was to make a copy of those keys if you were a crazy psycho killer. What were the chances that someone like that had had the room we were being given before and had thought the same thing?

No one asked any questions as we followed Harvey. He knew the room number. I scanned the area around me, realizing how dark and dangerous the location we were in looked. The old metal stairs under our feet groaned with our weight as we made it to the second floor. Our room was the fourth down the hall.

I wondered how we were all going to sleep. At least Lexi was holding her boyfriend's hand. I tried to stick close to Dreads and Harvey, while Rex brought up the tail of the group. That's exactly where he should stay all the time—at the end, far away.

The room smelled like urine, which only made it worse because by that point of the night I was ready to just let it all go and forget about my sanitary standards. I didn't even wait to take a look at the room and have someone check if there was in fact a crazy killer before dashing for the bathroom again. I could hear the rest of the group shifting around the room and a television was turned on. Peeing had never felt so good. I tried not to think about the diseases I could have caught by using the toilet and moved on to wash my hands.

I was in the middle of turning the water off when I finally got a good look at myself. Who would have thought that in the morning my only problem had been Jim the Creep?

A knock sounded on the door.

"I have to shit."

It was Rex. Cringing, I dried off my hands and took a good look at the cigarette burns around the sink.

"All yours," I tried to say smoothly. Rex only grunted in response before slamming the door closed. Lexi and her boyfriend were too busy sprawled on a loveseat making out to notice anything. Dreads was watching the TV screen avidly like a little kid when I glanced at him. For a second he reminded me of Brian when he watched his cartoons. Looking at the TV screen I realized that Dreads was even watching Brian's favorite show, Ninja Turtles. I already missed my brother. What was he doing? Was he safe? Was my mom worried about me, but still taking care of him? Either way, I knew Nick would come through for me. He always did.

I took a seat beside Dreads on the edge of the bed and tried watching the show with him. I noticed that Harvey looked deep in thought standing in front of our only window. Once you got used to it the room didn't smell so bad. Although even the bedspreads felt dusty.

It wasn't until Rex emerged from the bathroom that things took a turn for the worse.

"Holy shit, man!" Lexi's boyfriend exclaimed, ripping his mouth away from Lexi's. I wondered what he was talking about until I got a good whiff. Rex had held nothing back.

"I wouldn't say they're holy." Rex smirked, unabashed by the offensive odor.

"Damn, Rex," Harvey said, bringing his hand up to shield his nose and ripping himself away from his thoughts. I expected Rex to look at least a smidge embarrassed, but the butthole was looking pretty proud. No shame. Dreads must have really liked Ninja Turtles because he hadn't noticed the smell. In fact his mouth was kind of sagging open from the lack of personal attention he was giving himself. Rex eventually closed the door, though.

"Alright, it's time to go to bed." Harvey said, trying to swipe away the stench from the air. He really was like everyone's parent, I was starting to realize. I was used to being the person telling people to go to bed, not the other way around. I watched as Dreads slowly let himself fall onto the floor, claiming it as his improvised bed, without ripping his eyes away from the screen. Lexi and her boyfriend were already getting comfortable on the loveseat, which left Harvey, Rex, and Me.

I almost cringed when Rex took a seat right beside me. The beams holding up the bed made a cracking sound from his weight.

"Looks like it's just us three on the bed, then," Rex said, giving me a half-open smile. I looked over at Harvey with a pleading look on my face, but he ignored me. Everyone had already taken off their shoes, and Harvey started to do the same, so he was too busy doing that.

I tried to slide as far away from Rex as possible, towards the back of the bed. He followed suit, but so did Harvey, who had already taken a seat on the opposite side. It looked like I was going to be in the middle, like some uncomfortable ice cream sandwich.

Dreads eventually turned off the TV and someone else made sure the room was dark. I was officially lying down between Rex and Harvey, except unlike Rex, Harvey had turned his back to me and was miles away. I could feel Rex's hand creeping close, and

I tried to scoot as close to Harvey as I could without actually touching him. There was no way I was going to sleep right next to Rex.

"Babe," Lexi's boyfriend said before grunting in mild pain. "You're squishing my balls."

Dreads and I snorted at the same time, which set me at ease. Maybe I could just sleep on the floor? Even though it sounded a hundred times more disgusting than the bed, anything was better than Rex's hand, which had brushed my chest at least six times. I was almost sure he was doing it subconsciously while asleep by that point. A long while passed before I finally got the guts to decide on the floor. I didn't want to step on Dreads, so I decided to just half jump over Harvey and sleep on that section.

Everything was going smoothly. I was halfway off of the bed. Sure, I could have been straddling Harvey if only I let my weight down, but I was going to be suave. Like a freaking ninja. That's right, people should start calling me Livvie the Ninja, because I was so smooth...

"What are you doing?" Harvey whispered, turning his back onto the mattress and causing us to be face to face. I was poised on top of him with my hair just barely brushing his shoulders.

I was going to explain myself but was interrupted by a scream. I really thought it was Lexi, before the lights were suddenly turned on and Rex was sitting up on the bed swinging his arms in the air. Dreads' big head had popped up from the end of the bed, Lexi was standing next to her boyfriend, who had his fists poised for a fight, and I was frozen on top of Harvey.

"Get it, girl!" Lexi said my way. Everyone except Rex turned their attention to Harvey and me. My mouth dropped open and I started to shake my head, except I had given up on hovering over Harvey and had actually sat on him, which in retrospect was a dumb idea. Actual chairs didn't get turned on when we sat on top of them. I turned my panicked look down towards Harvey, who looked to be in pain.

Even throughout all of that, Rex was still screaming like a little girl and flinging his arms everywhere.

Harvey started to scramble up from under me while I tried to plant my feet on the ground.

"Rex, what the hell?" Lexi's boyfriend finally asked.

"T-t-there was this—this fucking—it touched me in my sleep!" Now that the attention was turned away from Harvey and me, people started to listen to Rex. Lexi was the second to catch sight of it, aside from Rex when it slithered on his pillow.

Lexi screamed along with Rex, while Lexi's boyfriend jumped on top of the armchair. Dreads looked too confused about everything to even process it, and my entire body shivered when Harvey grabbed the sides of my arms and stood behind me. He was just as freaked out as everyone, I realized, when he scrunched behind me as if I were a human shield. Rex was trying to slide himself off the bed without startling the creature on his pillow.

"It's a lizard," I said, looking at the little guy, who seemed to be just as scared as everyone else. I wasn't thinking or even hearing as Rex, the guy with the bulging muscles, practically whimpered, before I made my way towards the dresser. I was pretty calm when I grabbed a complimentary Styrofoam cup that even the crappiest establishment offered for coffee and walked beside the bed. I offered the little lizard entrance to the cup, while everyone calmed down the slightest bit and stared at me.

"Come on, buddy," I coaxed, bringing the cup closer. The little guy scurried into the cup in the blink of an eye, earning a cumulative yell from everyone in the room, including me. I was all business again as I walked towards our only window and pushed it open with one hand. The chilly night air hit me strong, but I ignored it while tilting the cup onto the windowsill. I was almost sure that the lizard would be able to crawl down the side of the wall, and I was right—he scrambled out and started to slither down the stucco-covered side.

"There," I sighed, turning back to the group, who were now watching me in awe. I finally made eye contact with Harvey, who had an incommunicable look on his face, until he half smiled. The same smile that I hadn't seen since before our entire runaway spectacle. The one that reminded me of a little boy who had done something he knew he shouldn't have. So I smiled right back.

* * *

Chapter Nine
Cuddle Buddies Stick Together

I hadn't expected Rex to grumble thanks, throw a pillow on the floor, and leave me alone in the bed with Harvey the night I practically saved his life from a lizard. I mean, I guessed that Rex probably felt indebted to me. I was so relieved that I wasn't going to spend the rest of the night dealing with Rex's groping or sleeping on the grubby floor that I hadn't noticed everyone else's smirks, excluding Harvey, who grimaced when Rex relinquished his spot on the bed. Except, right as I pushed my legs under the covers and lay my head on the pillow I realized that it was just Harvey and me in a bed.

Just us. On one freaking mattress. Holy smokes.

I awkwardly turned so that I wouldn't have to face him. I thought that things would become less awkward, but in my hurry I ended up wrapping the covers in my legs and pulling them completely off Harvey.

"Uh, could you give me some of that?" Harvey mumbled in the darkness after the lights had already been turned off.

"That's right Harv, get some of that!" Lexi's boyfriend encouraged in a perverted tone from somewhere off in the room. I was about to say something, until I heard a slap and Lexi's boyfriend yelling out in pain. I figured Lexi was the attacker.

"Lexi, I didn't know you liked it like that. Kinky," Rex said in response, leaving his previous humiliation behind him and opting for his usual perverted self. Someone snorted.

Lexi shut him down. "Shut up, Rex."

We all kind of shifted in the room and you could hear fabric moving back and forth as we all tried to get comfortable. I tried handing Harvey some of the comforter, but my hand shot out awkwardly and I ended up running it down his arm. Oh God, for a second I wondered if Harvey thought I was coming on to him. First I straddled him and then I ran my hand down his arm. I was practically seducing him without trying!

Alright, maybe I was giving myself too many props. If anything he probably thought I was more of a dork than usual.

"Thanks," he mumbled again, before the mattress rocked as he turned completely away from me. That definitely settled that. I scooted all the way to the opposite side of the bed and tried to curl myself

PRETTY BAD THINGS

into a ball. I mean, how awkward would it be if I drooled or started talking in my sleep? I had never realized how weird it was to sleep next to someone. You had to worry about being socially acceptable in your inactivity. It was all demanding way too much of my social skills.

I thought I would never fall asleep when I started to think about Brian and how he was doing, but I mildly surprised myself when I drifted off after remembering that Nick was there. Nick would take care of everything. He always did.

The next morning I woke up because my butt hurt. I knew it was way too early and that I was probably the first one awake, but the throbbing in my butt was the first thing that greeted me. I learned two things when I opened my eyes that morning.

One, motorcycles were horrible on a girl's behind, and two, Harvey Lockwell was a cuddler. One of his arms was draped over my middle and his head was dangerously close to my chest. His other hand was hovering over my butt and I couldn't ignore the adorable innocent look he had on his face. Even his parted lips killed my ovaries. I tried to relax before I passed out, but the excitement of having his arms around me was kind of killing me.

This was pathetic of me. I was having the most intimate moment of my life, and he wasn't even conscious.

I snorted when I realized the irony of the situation. Harvey had been the one to turn completely away from me the night before and now he was the one who had traveled all the way to my side by the morning. My snort made him stir, until his blue eyes opened slowly and peered right up at me. I watched in half wonder as the realization washed over him that he was the one who was all over me. That's right, he was on *my* side of the bed.

I almost went into full cardiac arrest when Harvey shook his head, blushed and quickly lifted his arm off from atop me. Harvey freaking Lockwell blushed. It was all too much. That was it. I was dead.

"Sorry," he mumbled sleepily before quickly turning away, back to his previous position from the night before. All I could do was nod and try to stop myself from begging him not to leave from my side.

Everyone else awoke a bit after Harvey did. It was like they were all just waiting for him to wake and get ready. The last one to wake was Dreads, who seemed to have enjoyed his spot on the ground way too much. I giggled when I watched his giant head pop up from under the bed. His dreads were all tangled and he gave me a lopsided smile when he saw me.

It didn't really take us long to get ready. We were all still wearing the same rumpled clothes from the day before and the only thing that delayed us was a few bathroom breaks from everyone who needed to pee.

By the end of it all, we walked back to the main office of the motel to hand in the set of keys. I had absolutely no clue where we were going, not even when I was already behind Harvey on the motorcycle again. This time, without the high-speed chase, it was even more daunting. Plus, my butt felt super sore from the day before.

I didn't know what town we were in, until we rode for a bit and I realized we were in Colorado Springs. We drove by lots of tourists, who seemed unperturbed by the lack of snow, the main attraction when you went almost anywhere in Colorado. In fact, I could have sworn it was almost ninety degrees now that it was daytime. Eventually we stopped at a diner. I didn't realize how hungry I was until I saw a giant rotating piece of pie that looked worse for wear over the sign belonging to the diner. I could see huge chunks of the sculpture's paint chipping from where I stood below it. The sign read Betty's Pies.

We entered as a group into the large establishment. There was a kitchen and a bar right in front, where a biker-looking guy sat eating a piece of, you guessed it, pie. There were other people scattered around the room. There was even a family of eight who had all crammed into the same booth. The booths were candy apple red and we were finally led to one by an older waitress whose name tag read Betty. I had a hunch that the pies being served were hers—you know, just a hunch.

The woman had short and very curly white hair. She eyed the group warily as she led us to our table and her eyes lingered on me. Just meeting her gaze I could get the message she was sending me.

What's a girl like you doing with these kids?

I gave her a shy smile and a small shrug, kind of answering her unspoken question. I wasn't really sure either.

"Your waitress will be with you kids shortly," the older woman said, never tearing her eyes off me. After she left and the guys started to have a conversation, I took the time to really look at them. I tried to see what Betty had seen when we walked in the door. I noticed Lexi's overly teased hair, which didn't have its usual volume from the day before. Her eyeliner was really smudged, but still looked good on her. She was one of those girls who didn't even have to try to be sexy.

It just poured out of everything she did. She was playing with a packet of sugar while I watched her, and I could tell that her boyfriend was having a hard time talking to the rest of the guys. Clearly, I wasn't blessed with such an appeal, because no one turned my way while I analyzed them.

I moved on to her boyfriend, whose name I still hadn't discovered, and noticed the beanie on his head and the chain of tattoos that curled around his arms. They didn't look like the type of tattoos that everyone got. They looked thoughtful, artistic, like they meant something. Rex didn't seem to have any visible tattoos, and neither did Harvey. I moved on to Dreads, who was already a character of his own. Sure, he wasn't as scary as the rest of the guys, mostly because he looked like Bob Marley's godchild, but still, he was different, on a different level.

PRETTY BAD THINGS

Finally, my eyes landed on Harvey. He seemed to be explaining something to the guys as he played idly with a saltshaker. He made the plain black T-shirt he wore look attractive. I could see the muscles on his back move back and forth while he talked, his shoulder blades straining under the fabric. His eyebrows were drawn and his lip ring moved every time he spoke.

The fact was, every single one of them looked exciting. It was as if none of them were scared of anything. More importantly, they looked like trouble. And then there was me. I was so busy thinking all of this that I didn't notice when our waitress arrived. By the time I finally looked up I was met by a perky girl who looked to be in her early twenties. Her hair was bleached blond, almost white, and she was wearing the brightest shade of pink lipstick known to man.

I was sitting between the wall and Harvey. He hadn't really spoken to me since the morning incident. Not that he would have spoken to me anyways, but now it was like he didn't even notice I existed. Lexi was sitting in front of me, already looking through the menu. I mean in any other situation, it would have made perfect sense for the waitress to ignore me. Harvey was doing a banging job. Except the moment her eyes landed on Harvey it was like no one else was sitting in the booth. We all watched as she ran her fingers through her hair and poised her glitter pen over a notepad, ready to take our order, but more specifically Harvey's.

"My name's Candy and I'll be your waitress. What can I get you?" she practically purred at him. Candy? Did her mother name her that? Why not take it one step forward and just name her Milk Dud? Harvey looked up from his menu at her with a smirk, which kind of made my stomach drop weirdly. Geez, one awkward morning cuddle and I was already feeling jealous.

"You can get me anything you want," Rex purred back from the end of the seat opposite us. I looked over at Lexi, who rolled her eyes, and couldn't stop from snickering. I wasn't sure if Rex hadn't noticed her obvious interest in Harvey, or maybe he was just choosing to ignore it. Rex's interest in her didn't seem to register, because the girl only looked at Harvey. Dreads was too busy coloring in the kids' menu to notice anything, and I wished I could be as oblivious.

Lexi took the opportunity to order for her, her boyfriend, and Dreads since he was still engrossed in his coloring page. Rex then made a big show of ordering. He made a cup of oatmeal sound sexual, which even I had to give him credit for. I think we were all waiting for Harvey to speak and when he only ordered a coffee and handed her the menu without looking back at her, it was almost a letdown. You could tell that Candy, the waitress, was disappointed as well.

I watched her turn and slump away as my chance to order breakfast left. I didn't know if I should have called her back or just sat there. I had been completely forgotten. It wasn't until I faced forward that Lexi gave me a perplexed look.

"You didn't order," she reminded the table and me.

I felt my face growing hot, since I realized I was stuck in one those uncomfortable situations where you're ignored and then other people notice.

"Nah, I wasn't really—" I couldn't finish, because Lexi cut in.

"Harvey, call her back, Livvie didn't order."

I watched as Harvey looked beside him as if he hadn't a clue that I was pretty much being crushed by him and the wall beside me for the last thirty minutes. He rolled his eyes before calling Candy over. Our waitress was quick to come back. You could practically see the excitement on her face. Right when she arrived back at our table and ate Harvey with her eyes like he was her breakfast, everyone else turned to me. They were all waiting for me to say something.

"Yes?" Candy, the waitress, said perkily. Her eyes were begging Harvey to ask for something, anything.

I was frozen in my seat. It was all levels of awkward around the table. I couldn't get the guts to divert Candy's attention to me and I couldn't really order with everyone watching me.

I heard Harvey sigh before saying curtly, "You missed her. She'll have the scrambled eggs, bacon, and double stack of pancakes."

He had officially ordered for me, as if I were a little kid, and a fat one at that. Oh God, things could have not gotten any more awkward. Once again defeated, Candy walked away from the table with a pout.

I tried not to make eye contact with anyone else while our food was being prepared. It wasn't very hard because Dreads was still engrossed with his coloring, Lexi and her boyfriend were busy making out, to the disdain of the family of eight in the table next to us, and Harvey was back to ignoring me, talking to Rex.

I had to give our waitress props for being determined. Even when she brought out food for the last time she made a show of batting her eyelashes. At one point it looked like she had a nervous twitch, but what did I know. Guys probably found it appealing. Rex obviously did, because he started throwing her sexual looks from the moment she started to set the plates down.

It was obvious that Harvey ordered way too much for me. I was sure I wasn't going to eat it all, but I wasn't going to risk another uncomfortable moment, so I would endure.

By the time I was through the eggs and one pancake I was ready to explode. I never ate this much. Even when I was nervous, which I was, I didn't believe I could finish everything. I finished the last strip of bacon, losing my ability to move, which was why when Lexi turned to look at me with a glint in her eye and Dreads started to jump up and down in his seat, I started to panic.

"Ready, guys?" Lexi spoke in a hushed tone, looking at all of us with an excited smile on her face. I looked over to see Harvey back to his old self, smirking while nodding. Something was happening and I had no clue what.

"What's happening?" I whispered to her after Harvey paid the bill and Rex started stretching. Rex took everything as a serious workout.

Lexi leaned close to me to whisper back, "It's dinner tradition. You'll see right now when Harvey gets up."

In the blink of an eye Harvey had propped his Vans on the red leather booth so that his feet were under him and not on the floor. Everyone followed suit so that they looked like they were about to lay an egg on the vinyl. I wasn't sure if I was supposed to do it too, so I just sat there, frozen.

"Don't get caught like last time," Harvey warned, right before springing up on his feet and planting them on the table we had been eating on before. Just like that, I watched as he started to literally walk on every table and booth towards the exit, completely ignoring the floor. The rest of the guys followed, while people started freaking out that a bunch of teenagers were walking over their tables. No one stepped on their food, which I guess was because of the obstacle course theme they were going for. It was the craziest thing I had ever seen, which was saying something considering that I had been on a high-speed chase.

Lexi was last to follow and stretched her hand out to me when I wasn't keeping up.

"Liv, come on, we can't get caught!"

Without thinking, I let her pull me up and started to run on top of every booth and table that led towards the exit. I tried my best not to step on anyone's plates as we winded over people's outraged heads and giggling kids. It wasn't long before Lexi and I were laughing at the rush. At this point Betty from earlier had come out of the kitchen and started yelling at us to come down. The cook seemed to be behind her, waving a spatula in the air, when I looked back.

"Young lady, you better stop right there!" Betty said, looking right at me.

I shook my head and smiled dazedly at her. Not happening.

Lexi and I both jumped down to the ground after the final booth, following the guys who were already opening the door to leave. I could feel Betty and the cook both trailing behind us, so I didn't dare look back again.

Harvey was already straddling the bike, so Lexi pulled me into the Corolla. Before I knew what was happening, we had sped out of the lot and were following Harvey's lead again. I was in the backseat with Lexi and her boyfriend as we made our way away from the restaurant. Rex was driving, but not very smoothly. Rex had a need for speed. I took those few moments to take in the car. It smelled like old cigarettes and coffee. The seats were dusty, but the car looked to be more put together on the inside than the outside.

I was seriously grateful that our trip back would consist of me being inside the car. I didn't think my butt could take another motorcycle ride. A part of me would have been fine with the motorcycle so that I could be close to Harvey, but it was getting clear that he still didn't want me with him.

Harvey led us into the parking lot of some sort of shopping complex. The buildings were almost completely next to each other, if it weren't for the small spaces in between each store separating them. We eventually parked in front of the furthest building towards the end. It didn't look like any store I had ever seen before. Every wall of the building had been purposely covered with graffiti.

"Woo! I was wondering when we were going shopping!" Lexi exclaimed excitedly from beside me. She was right, it was getting kind of gross being in the same clothes from the day before, especially given the fact that none of us had showered.

We all eventually made our way into the store. The lights were dim, music blasted heavily from a few speakers around us, and the overall atmosphere was musky. It was the weirdest place I had ever been in. A bald guy with several piercings on his face sat behind the counter, taking a phone call. He smiled at us and waved in greeting when we walked in.

I watched the guys head in the opposite direction, right before Lexi pulled me towards a rack of clothes.

"You know what this means, right?" she said.

"We won't wear the same clothes forever?" I guessed, confused.

"No!" Lexi replied, her face lighting up. "It's makeover time! Girl, I've been wanting to burn the cardigan you're wearing since forever."

"It's not that bad. I mean, my friend did comment on the ugly color..." Again, I was defending the cardigan.

"Trust me, it's bad. Don't get me wrong, it's cute...if you were five," she said, her face kind of scrunching up.

I looked down at what I was wearing. Maybe Lexi was right and I needed a makeover. I would have never admitted it, but hadn't I always wanted to be different? Now was my chance.

"So, are we doing this?" she asked hopefully, bouncing on the balls of her feet. Something told me that it was really hard to say no to Lexi anyway, so I smiled and nodded.

"Hell yeah!" she exclaimed, grabbing ahold of me and pulling me towards the studs and sequins.

Lexi really liked to shop. She had almost every single garment imaginable in her hands and in mine by the time we finally made it to the fitting rooms. I'd shaved the day before, thank God. Everything was going fine. Lexi and I were running all over the place, picking up pieces of clothing and letting each other see what we were wearing. At one point we both got matching leather skirts that surprisingly looked good on both of us.

I seriously had never had so much fun in my life. Some of the things Lexi picked out for me I would have never even dared touch, but I tried them on that day. But, like in everything that happens in my life, there was a speed bump. It was the last dress I was trying on and possibly the tightest that acted as the little bump in the road. I just knew that if it hadn't been for Harvey's megabreakfast I would have made it fit.

I was stubborn, until I had half the dress on. I knew for sure I was stuck when I couldn't bring my hands back down to my sides and the dress was wrapped in a big ball around my shoulders. I tried taking it off the same way I had put it on, but it wouldn't budge. I was in my bra and underwear with a dress stuck on my shoulders. No matter how hard I tried the fabric wouldn't stretch. That was it. I was going to die in the dress. They were going to have to bury me in it. It would be an open casket because my mom loved to go against my wishes and everyone would see me in a dress cocoon because not even the paramedics could rip it off.

Dead at seventeen from skanky dress suffocation

"Lexi?" I whispered urgently. I really didn't want to call any attention to myself, especially when I could hear the boys playing around outside the dressing room. They had finished a while ago and were just waiting on us.

"Yeah?" I heard her muffled voice from the other dressing room.

"Could you, uh, come help me with something?"

"Sure thing," she responded, her voice getting closer. I watched as she opened up the curtain and slid in. I also watched the open-mouthed look she gave me when she caught sight of me.

"Holy shit!" she cursed, immediately running over to my side and tugging the dress up. I noticed that she had only put her strapless dress on, but hadn't bothered with the zipper. We were both struggling to free me from the dress's clutches. I tried turning my head and lifting my arms higher. Lexi was leaning over me trying to pull it off without ripping it. At one point I was crouching on the floor and she stood over me. Her dress had slid from her shoulders and her lacy bra was out in the open. Mine was just blue and clearly outshined by hers. That was the last thing I thought before losing my footing and face-planting on the carpet. Lexi's hands were still wrapped in the dress, and so I brought her down with me. It was just us two yelling and grunting, before she fell over me and we started rolling.

The curtain was no use in holding us from tumbling out into the open. In the middle of us rolling out Lexi was able to pull the dress off, leaving me completely without clothes when we appeared in front of the guys. Lexi stood up triumphantly and swung the dress in the air when she realized that she'd gotten it off. That caused her dress to slide from her hips and onto the ground. We were both in our bras and underwear, while all four of the guys got an eyeful. Things were silent while they stared. I could practically hear my dignity breaking.

Finally, Rex broke the silence. "I don't know about you guys, but that was hot!" he said before fist pumping the air.

"Remind me to tag along next time you guys go shopping," Lexi's boyfriend said, grinning at Rex and doing a bro handshake like they were the wittiest human beings ever.

I scrambled to stand up and made the mistake of making eye contact with Harvey. His eyes were right on me and for a second, I froze. My head snapped towards Lexi when she flipped Rex and her boyfriend off and walked casually back into her dressing room. Like she didn't actually care if they caught a good look at her butt.

I whipped around and did the same, still remembering Harvey's look. Even Dreads had looked happily excited when we tumbled out, but the look on Harvey's face showed that he wasn't even a little amused—he was bored, peeved even. It made no sense. I hadn't done anything to him. It wasn't my fault that he was still mad about the morning. I wasn't even sure why. I almost wanted to cry as I put my normal clothes back on. It didn't matter if I got a makeover, I was still the same lame Livvie.

By the time I walked out of the dressing room I wasn't surprised when Harvey was nowhere in sight. Lexi had everything that we were buying already in the guys' hands, so much that you couldn't even see their heads. I knew I should have followed them towards the cash register, but something was pulling me back.

Maybe it was the confidence the new clothes had brought me, but I had never been this confrontational. In fact, I hated confrontations. That was the reason why I couldn't confront the waitress earlier that day. Just the thought of seeking something out and facing something head on freaked me out. But I was confronting Harvey then.

I found him leaning against one of the brick walls, taking a cigarette out of its slot. He stopped when he heard me coming towards him. I saw him exhale loudly before leaning his head up towards the sky. Just seeing me exasperated him. The guy needed Jesus to deal with me.

"Did I do something wrong?" I asked without even thinking. I wasn't sure where this gutsy Livvie was coming from, but I kind of liked her. Harvey clearly didn't, because he leveled his eyes at mine without any expression.

He didn't reply, so my nervous tendency to fill in the silence with rambling kicked in.

"Look, I don't really know why you're mad at me. I mean, it's not like we're close friends or anything. I'm just the girl you're stuck with for this trip and I'm sorry."

He still hadn't said anything, so I carried on.

"I shouldn't have followed you. I really can't think of any other reason for you to be so mad. If it's about this morning—"

I finally got a reaction when he shifted uncomfortably and started to look around, his mouth in a hard line.

"Well, I'm sorry that I'm so lame and clearly not someone you want to be close to. I can't help it if I'm not good enough or—"

Something clicked in Harvey's expression when he heard those last few sentences. I watched him shake his head and come towards me. He was so fast that I hadn't even stopped talking when his lips came over mine. My heart started beating wildly when he brought a hand up to cup my cheek, pinning my mouth in place.

Kissing him wasn't what I expected. After hearing countless stories about Harvey Lockwell and his intoxicating kisses, I had always imagined something stronger and more rash. I had only been kissed one other time in my life. It had been in eighth grade, close to the time when Nick was realizing he was gay. We both just sort of brought our mouths together while watching a movie. Nothing had happened for either of us, and when he came out I wondered if it was my fault, like I'd scarred him for life, until I remembered that I had always known he was gay.

This time something happened. Everything felt hot, like the temperature had spiked up several degrees and every place where Harvey made contact with me felt super sensitive. It wasn't how I'd imagined it at all. It was slow and sweet and it took my breath away. I didn't even notice when he spun us around and had me caged in between the brick wall and him. I officially understood what every girl had been talking about. His thumb made slow circles on my cheek while his mouth explored mine. I never wanted it to end, but Harvey was the first one to pull away. We were both breathing a little erratically. Our gazes locked and I was sure he could see how I felt. The problem was that I could see how he felt too.

He looked like he was feeling a lot of regret right around then.

"Fuck." He breathed out, looking down towards the ground. His body was still pressing into mine and the cool brick wall behind me was the only thing holding me up.

The haze was broken when we both heard the clatter of the door opening and the rest of the group chatting. As if I'd burned him, Harvey took several steps back and walked towards the entrance, turning the corner. I stood on the other side of the building before sprinting back behind him. I was sure we looked suspicious, but the way Harvey was acting really made it hard for anyone to guess. I walked alongside the group as if I hadn't just received the most mind-blowing kiss, but it was the hardest thing to do.

I unconsciously started to walk behind Harvey towards the bike, before he turned back to me.

"You should go with them," he ordered, turning around again and not giving me a second glance.

"What was that all about?" Lexi asked, giving Harvey the stink eye and already pulling me towards the Corolla.

I didn't have the guts to say what had happened. Plus, it still hurt, because even if he had kissed me, his reaction meant that everything I had said was right. I wasn't good enough for him. No one would believe that he'd kissed me anyway.

Chapter Ten
Panic! At the Party

Harvey's lips had made contact with mine.

That was pretty much all I could think about as we pulled out of the lot and back onto the road. It was practically the middle of the day when we headed out of the town we had stayed in. I tried to act like Harvey's rejection didn't hurt, but he should have just punched me in the face and it would have been better. Or at least made more sense.

The more I thought about it, the more I started to panic. What if it wasn't because I was lame? What if I had done it wrong? What if I was a bad kisser? What if I was lame and a bad kisser?

That was it. I was a bad kisser. I probably did everything wrong. Was I supposed to do something more? Where were my hands even supposed to go? I couldn't remember where I put them when he kissed me. Did I just let them dangle there? God, I was so stupid. I should have done something with them! I looked over to Lexi, who was practically lying in her boyfriend's lap and kissing him to death. At least someone wanted to kiss her.

I noticed her hands were braced against his chest. Her boyfriend's hand was over her butt, but that wasn't my focus. I needed to know where my hands would go. Plus, Harvey hadn't touched my butt when he kissed me. Sad how that kind of disappointed me. Then again, he hadn't even wanted to kiss me in the first place.

I felt someone's eyes on me and looked up towards the rearview mirror. Rex was using it to watch me watch Lexi and her boyfriend kiss. I felt my face get flaming hot when he started nodding his head and smiling devilishly. I felt like such a perv, I even started to shake my head to make him realize it wasn't what it looked like. I mean, it was, but Rex didn't need to know that I was trying to learn how to kiss by watching other people.

I turned towards the window beside me and made a show of being incredibly interested in the scenery. Once again we were on the road and nothing but trees whizzed past us. I could see Harvey leading us when I looked forward, as well as Dreads, who was fiddling with the old radio dials, trying to get a station going.

I thought of sleeping, but I really wasn't tired. Sadly, I was still on a Harvey high, which was hard to shake. We drove for hours and eventually Lexi and her boyfriend stopped kissing and cuddled. Which was even worse to my forever-alone soul. We finally pulled into a fast-food restaurant and got some food to go. I noticed Harvey waited idly while we went through the drive-through.

It was nightfall when we pulled into another city. The Welcome to Denver sign greeted us upon entering. Everything was a lot more populated and even though it was ten o'clock, from what the dashboard told me when I glanced at it, there were tons of cars and lights still going. Even the radio started playing clearly. Our little town practically shut down after eight.

"We're gonna crash with Garrard, right?" I heard Dreads mutter to Rex, who nodded in response. It was clear that they had been in the city and knew someone there.

The curiosity got the best of me as we started to drive away from all of the buildings and closer to a forest. Pretty soon we were driving on a dirt road and I wondered who this Garrard person was if we had to drive all the way into the middle of the woods and away from the city to get to him. I was getting kind of creeped out when it got dark enough that I could only see the small dot of Harvey's taillight in front of us.

"Who's Garrard?" I whispered to Lexi in the darkness. I wasn't sure if she was facing me, but her response came quickly.

"He's a friend of Rex's. Girl, honestly, just stay with us when we get there. The first time I met him it was scary as hell."

My eyes widened at Lexi's tone.
"Why?"

"Well, he's kind of a big deal here and well, you know, the guys buy from him now and then. None of us owe him money so we're technically fine, but that doesn't mean you let your guard down."

By then I was freaking out. We were going to a drug dealer's home. His casa would be our casa. After the few days I had spent with the group I wasn't nearly as scared of them as before, but I still remembered how much trouble Harvey was supposed to be. To think that they were hesitant around this Garrard guy was even worse.

I was shocked when the trees cleared and right in front of us on a large section of land stood a huge modern house. Most of it was made of glass, and it could have been considered a mansion if it were only a bit bigger. There was music blasting loudly from inside it and all of the lights were on. From the window you could see tons of people dancing and moving around.

The front section of the land had rows of cars and motorcycles scattered throughout. Some of the cars were shabby; others were luxury. It was a weird combination.

People were either walking to their cars or getting out of them. We finally found a small spot to park the car and started to exit. I knew I was going to stick out in my cardigan and Chucks the minute I looked back to the house. Everyone looked like they belonged except me. I was terrified when a group of guys stopped walking for a second to look at me questioningly, laugh, and continue their way to the house.

The music sounded a lot louder now that we were outside, and all I could hear was a rapper yelling about his bitches and chains. The Beethoven of our time. Everyone started to walk towards the house, until Harvey stepped in front of Lexi and brought her walking to a halt.

"She can't walk in like that," he told her, not bothering to look at me. It was like I was someone he didn't want to know.

"You're right," she finally said, turning and grabbing my hand. The rest of the guys were a little further ahead, waiting for Harvey to join them. I watched him turn and walk away before Lexi started to speak.

"Looks like it's time to put that leather skirt to work, Liv. You can't stick out."

"What would they do to me?" I asked, half in wonder.

"You never know with them, but it wouldn't be good for Garrard to pick you out or something." Lexi said all of this while she pulled some bags from the trunk and rummaged through them.

"Ah, yeah, definitely the crop top for this one." I watched as Lexi pulled out half a shirt and my leather skirt from one of the bags, along with a pair of super-high wedges I wasn't sure I could walk in.

"But that's your, uh, shirt," I mentioned, not wanting to be rude and tell her that it was practically a bra with studs.

"Yeah, but it goes way better with the leather skirt, so no complaining!"

"But—" I was more than hesitant.

"Livvie, you're like super skinny. You have nothing to worry about."

Both of us crawled into the car and quickly undressed in the darkness. I panicked when I heard a few guys laughing as they walked by, but thankfully none of them noticed how shirtless I was inside. I hurried to get the bra over my real one and lastly put on the skirt. Lexi was ready way before me and had hovered over me, trying to put my hair up. It had been in a ponytail all day and so I couldn't put it down. I felt her hands make my hair into a bun and then start to pull a bunch of it out.

"What's the point of doing the bun if you're going to mess it all up?" I wondered, not understanding.

"Because messy buns are cute. Oh my God, Livvie, you have so much to learn," Lexi huffed, still putting the finishing touches on my hair.

I finally put the last wedge on my foot and followed Lexi out of the backseat. My feet wobbled when I set them on the dirt and I worked hard to keep my balance. I looked over to Lexi, who was wearing a dark purple minidress with a faux fur vest. Her heels were just as high as mine, but even though they were wedges too, they had studs all over the sides and backs.

"Alright, I'm gonna have to do your makeup in the house because I can't see for shit." Lexi grabbed hold of my arm and pulled me towards where the music was blasting. I wasn't gonna lie, my heart was beating a little frantically from excitement and fear. A guy with about twenty piercings pushed past us towards the house and I freaked out from all of the metal on his face.

The volume of the music and the number of people increased as we pushed on. I turned to see a guy take a breath from some sort of cigarette and then promptly pass out on the hood of a nearby car.

"Shouldn't someone check to see if he's alright?" I asked nervously. Lexi glanced at him, shrugged and continued on. We walked up the porch steps, past a guy who had been peeing on some of the bushes. He waved at me, but it messed up his aim so he refocused. I was steering away from any guy with his boy part out as a resolution for the night.

Inside, the house was super big, but dirty. Bottles were everywhere, along with cups and trash that littered the floor. The furniture looked to be really expensive but no one cared if they stood on it, or in one guy's case, passed out on it. The volume of the music had officially given me a headache and we had only been inside the house for a couple of minutes.

A really meaty-looking guy pushed Lexi, and me, out of the way without bothering to glance at us. He had been carrying a giant keg of beer, which seemed to be his priority. There was a large living room to our right, a bar towards the back, and I figured the only wall visible covered the kitchen. Other than that one wall, the entire place was open space. There was a large set of grand stairs to our left that Lexi veered us off to.

"They don't care if we go upstairs?" I yelled through the bass.

"If we get caught we act stupid!" Lexi yelled back, pulling me with her. I looked down at the craziness under us and was secretly glad to be away from it.

We walked into the first room we saw. There was a large king bed in the middle, a dresser, and nothing more. Even the walls were bare. As if the person who lived here hadn't really settled in.

Lexi didn't waste time in taking out her bag and attacking me with products. I had never worn any of the stuff she put on my face and I had no idea how to put it on myself. We were there for a while as she applied eyeliner and mascara. There's something nice about someone putting makeup on you. You start feeling worth the effort. She was a shade darker than me, but told me I didn't need the concealer anyway, so we skipped that.

I thought we were done, until Lexi cursed. "Shit, too much eyeliner."

I looked over to a window that was on the wall beside me, where I could barely see my reflection. Despite that, I looked nothing like me. My eyes popped and I looked way older. Instead of looking like a twelve-year-old, I actually looked older than my age.

"I'll be back. I'm gonna go look for some water to take some off."

I wanted to call her back, but before I knew it she was gone. I sat there, waiting for her to return. I knew only a minute passed, but panic shot through me. I should have just gone with her.

My body blasted up from the bed and I started for the door, except right as I was going to pull it open, someone else entered.

It was a guy. A really tall, good-looking guy. He had short blond hair and both of his arms were covered with tattoos. There was even a tattoo on his neck, which looked painful just glancing at it. He looked confused to see me, then angry, then kind of pleased. It was like a million emotions flashed through his face and none of them seemed like the one he was really feeling.

"You want to tell me what you're doing in one of my rooms?"

I felt my mouth drop and I started to fidget.

"Your room? As in...your house?" I asked with a nervous smile. I was wringing my hands by then, which he found amusing, since he was sending me a Harvey-like smirk.

"Yeah, my house. I want to know what a hot girl is doing in one of my rooms all alone," he said in response, coming closer to me. I backed up until I felt the bed hit the back of my legs.

"Oh, Lexi? She just walked out," I responded, not understanding.

"There's another hot girl?" he said, grinning.

"Oh, the first one was me?" I asked, my voice rising at the end from the surprise. Well, Lexi had told me to act stupid. At least it was coming to me naturally.

He laughed, a loud, strong sound, like he didn't care if you heard him, he was going to be as loud as he wanted, before coming right up to me and grabbing my hand.

"Come on, let's go back downstairs and you can tell me all about your hot friend."

I let him pull me out in a daze. I seriously thought I would feel some sort of shock from having him touch me, but his grip was too strong. A super-attractive guy had called me hot and held my hand, but I wanted to get away from him. What was wrong with me?

A super-hot guy named Garrard, who was a drug dealer. Right.

Lexi was still nowhere to be found as we descended the stairs. I realized she was coming up when she caught sight of us and started to walk off the stairs backwards. The rest of the guys were also standing by the entrance and looked up the moment Garrard put his arm on my bare skin. Darn my half-shirt.

It wasn't just the guys who had their eyes on us, it was practically everyone at the party. Some of the guys started to look at me in a way that they never had. I guessed that the makeup had done the trick, along with my half-there clothes. Mostly, I think it was the fact that Garrard was claiming me in front of everyone that made the girls give me angry looks and the guys look at me with desire but holding back because they didn't want to get on Gerrard's bad side.

It was the second most exhilarating feeling, besides Harvey's kiss. Lexi was looking at me with shock and I looked back at her in fear. I didn't want to be on his arm. I really didn't. I watched Lexi's boyfriend slap Harvey in the stomach because he was the second to see us after Lexi. Harvey's look was unreadable. At least Dreads gave me a wounded puppy look, like he felt kind of bad for me. Rex was the only one smirking, but I had no idea why. He looked like he'd just had a really good protein shake. I realized he felt pretty good about himself when he walked up to us and spoke.

"I see you've met our girl, Livvie." It almost sounded like he was taking the credit for giving birth to me.

"Yeah, she was all alone upstairs. I told her she could be my company tonight."

He had? Did I bang my head somewhere and forget the last five minutes?

"Harvey." Garrard only said his name as a greeting. Harvey looked up to him and they did one of those boy handshakes where they lock hands and half hug but not really because they can't even brush shoulders.

"'Sup, man," Harvey said in a bored tone. He gave me the harshest look before ignoring me completely. It was him being mad at me times a thousand. I almost wanted to cry.

Garrard didn't bother with the rest of the guys and moved his attention back to Rex. "Mike has your shit ready."

"But, we weren't going—" Lexi's boyfriend started to say before Rex shut him up.

"Alright, cool, man," Rex said. Something about his tone made him look nervous, like he agreed with Lexi's boyfriend but didn't want to admit it. Some sort of plans had changed. His shit? Like drugs? He was talking about drugs. I was witnessing a drug deal.

Garrard nodded before pulling me away, and I lost sight of the group as he took me to the center of the room. A bunch of guys started to huddle around us. Garrard sat down on a stool before pulling me onto his lap. I felt like I was about to give him my Christmas list, to be honest.

The guys and two girls around us started to talk about random things I had no clue about. After a while no one was talking to me, so I began to scan the room. I officially knew what it was like to have a guy be interested in your boobs and butt, but not your personality when I met Garrard. It was almost as bad as not having a guy be interested in either.

He hadn't even asked for my name, now that I started to think about it. He only knew because Rex blurted it out. I thought things couldn't get any worse until I saw a red dress and a pair of boobs sliding up against my Harvey.

My Harvey?

I was as territorial as Garrard, it seemed.

Harvey was grinding up against a blonde girl with huge boobs in the middle of the living room, where other couples were also dancing. Where had she even come from? Her dress was just as short as mine, except she had lots of curves, which made it racier. She and Harvey were pressed up against each other. She had an arm over one of his shoulders and was using it to hold herself up as she pressed herself all over him. It was the most sexual thing I had ever seen and probably wouldn't even be considered dancing. Granted there were other people dancing the same way, but that was Harvey. My Harvey. I mean, not mine, but...kind of mine. I knew him first. She probably only knew him five minutes, and they'd gotten twice as far as Harvey and I had.

At first, my heart plummeted. That was it. He didn't care about me. I'd been dumb enough to think that maybe because he'd kissed me he did care, even a little bit, but I was wrong. Something came over me. Something made me stand up quickly and make the people talking around me pause.

"We should dance!" I exclaimed, pouting like I never had before.

I guess it had the effect I was going for because Garrard shrugged and let me pull him up towards where everyone was dancing. I was planning on dancing with him the same exact way as the busty blonde was dancing with Harvey, but a minute after getting to the dance floor I realized there was no slutty dancing in me.

I tried pressing my back against him and shimmying down his front but I stopped midway, feeling completely ridiculous. I was like a retarded worm and the words 'Abort Mission' flashed in my mind. I tried one more time, never tearing my eyes away from the blonde. At this point Harvey had stopped being completely entranced by her and had caught sight of me. His face hardened, but then turned to confusion as I tried to half hump Garrard. It was a weak attempt, even if he did try to hold on to my hips. At least he was into it. I just felt awkward, like I wasn't doing it right. How did girls do this?

In my frustration and increasing embarrassment I started to panic dance. My arms took on a life of their own when they started to wiggle up in the air and I started to shake my body side to side as if I were doing a tribal ritual. I just needed to start howling to complete it. Garrard started to get turned off, I could tell, but that wasn't the point. Harvey and the blonde were dancing with less vigor and that was all of the encouragement I needed. Some cheesy rap song with a repetitive beat was playing, and I held my arms bent in front of me and pulled them into me, doing a hip thrust to every beat.

I was officially turning into the Napoleon Dynamite of the party. The air hump slowly turned into a robotic chicken dance. People had stopped dancing around me but I didn't notice in my dance haze, until I looked around me. People were watching me now. Should I stop? Stopping felt more embarrassing, but to keep going was just as embarrassing. I started to do the Sprinkler as I pondered the possibilities. Garrard was standing off to the side with a look of confusion and embarrassment on his face.

I thought I had really messed things up until I peered over to Harvey and watched him smile at me. He had stopped dancing and now stood several feet away from the girl. He started to laugh softly and looked around, just as embarrassed for me, but the good kind, like I was a cute puppy he found.

He didn't look angry now, only entertained by my horrible dance moves. I eventually had to stop when someone unexpectedly shut the music off. My dancing came to a slow, painful halt, while people just stared.

I coughed and stood there in equal silence.

"I'm...gonna...go...now." I spoke slowly and robotically, pushing past a group of people in haste. I had officially done the dumbest thing of my life. I had danced the chicken dance to a Lil Wayne song for God's sake!

I sprinted out the back door of the house, where there were less people. Eventually, the further I walked out, the more alone I became. I heard the music turn back on in the distance while I walked deeper into the trees before they closed around me. The last thing I needed was to get lost in the woods, although it was starting to sound like a prime idea.

I was startled when I heard the ground crunching beneath someone's feet. I couldn't lie, seeing Harvey when I turned surprised me.

"You are the worst dancer I have ever seen," he commented, coming up right in front of me.

"Thanks," I said half sarcastically, but mostly embarrassed.

"I was expecting you to do the moonwalk." I saw him smile in the darkness.

I snickered and responded, "Actually, that was my next move if they hadn't shut the music off."

"Damn, would have killed to see that."

I couldn't help smiling back at him. I existed again, weirdly. We stood there smiling at each other for a few moments until he tore his gaze away and his mouth hardened. Oh, no. I felt him going back into Anti-Livvie mode, until his eyes met mine again and softened, just a little.

"You've never gotten drunk, right?" he asked me, unexpectedly changing the subject.

"Um, nope," I answered.

Minutes passed by while I waited for him to look at me and respond.

"I think your first time should be with me," he finally said quietly. Something about the way he worded it made my heart race. Context. It was all about context. My first time with him.

"Okay," I was quick to say, looking up to him and giving him a wide-eyed stare.

Oh, Harvey Lockwell, you were such a contradiction.

Chapter Eleven
Cheers to That

I watched Harvey's silhouette coming from where the illuminated house stood. Clearly I had been forgotten by Garrard, which was pretty darn great by me. The music had been brought back to its initial volume.

That was it. I was going to get drunk for the first time. A part of me was kind of excited and another part was terrified. What if I went completely berserk? Oh God, what if I was an emotional drunk like my mom? I could count the times I'd seen my mother drunk on one hand, only because I could count the times I saw her at all on both hands. Yet, the few times she had been drunk she had been completely emotional.

My mom was really cold and detached normally, so it was always surprising to see her stumble around the place in tears when she got tipsy enough. Most of the time she cursed my dad and then

she cried for him. It was the one time I didn't want
Brian to be near her and usually set him to bed early.
There were other problems with me getting drunk, but
Harvey already had my list so there wasn't much to
lose.

I already danced like an idiot sober.

"Do you think my dancing will get better or
worse if I try it while tipsy?" I asked suddenly when he
reached me. I could see several bottles cradled in his
hands. I wondered if I should have started with beer
or something light, because it looked like Harvey was
ready to go all out.

"There's really nowhere to go but up with
that..." He trailed off, smiling faintly at the memory.

I watched him slowly sit down with his legs up
on the dirty gravel and followed suit. I couldn't sit
with my legs up because of the leather miniskirt, so I
had to keep my legs out in front of me. We were facing
the trees while the party carried on behind us.

"Ready?" he asked, opening the first bottle and
glancing at me. I could feel my wide-eyed stare
meeting his, but I nodded with resolution.

The liquor he had with him didn't look like the
cheap kind, which made sense because everything
inside the house looked expensive.

"What is it?" I asked, leaning in to get a closer
look. Harvey stopped pouring when I leaned in but
then continued as if he hadn't paused. He wasn't
filling the solo cup even to the middle, which I found
weird. It looked like a really small amount.

"Grey Goose," he answered. I had no idea and so I stayed silent. I guess he figured, because he said something else shortly after.

"It's vodka. The first time, you wanna get completely hammered, but you also wanna drink the good shit. That way you won't get such a bad headache the next day. I would have you try other kinds, but I don't know if you have a light stomach and getting sick on your first time sucks."

I nodded my head in the darkness, making sense of everything. I didn't realize my unconscious effort to sit closer to him, but before I knew it we were shoulder to shoulder. Was it me that moved right next to him?

Probably.

Harvey was about to set the cup in my hand, but he paused midmotion. I quirked a brow and looked at him in confusion.

"Let's make this interesting." He smirked. Confused, I couldn't help smiling at his new tone while I took the cup slowly from his hand. I watched him put a hand into his jeans pocket and pull something out in the darkness. The light from the house illuminated us just enough so that I could see exactly what he took out.

"Cards? You carry around a deck of cards with you?" I asked, noting the strangeness of it.

"You don't?" he answered incredulously.

I took him seriously until I grasped he was just being sarcastic. He started laughing when I realized and so I slapped his arm, kind of how I'd seen Lexi do to her boyfriend. I watched him in wonder as he shuffled the deck expertly. The cards almost floated over the gravel as he shuffled them back and forth. I had no clue how to shuffle cards, but something about the way Harvey was doing it felt like déjà vu.

"Cut the deck," he ordered, bringing the cards up to me. I don't know why I felt like I had done it before when I cut it right in the middle and watched him bring to top section towards the bottom. Suppressing an emerging memory, I tried to focus on the present.

I listened avidly while Harvey explained everything. At first it was hard to keep up with all of the rules, but I made myself remember once he really started to explain what was at stake.

"Alright, you got all of that?" Harvey asked me once he had described what every card meant. I nodded my head like a good student and smiled goofily at him. He probably thought I was drunk already. My heart did a little flutter when he shook his head and smiled faintly. I watched him set the deck in between us, even though there really wasn't much space. He waited for me to go first, and with a nervous hand, I picked up the first card on the deck.

My eyes scanned the Two of Hearts before I showed Harvey. He nodded and waited for me to do what I was supposed to, which was take two sips. I brought the cup to my mouth and with anticipation I let the drink go down my throat. The liquid burned my throat, bad. I was about to spit it out. It was gross and tasted like rubbing alcohol. I knew Harvey was watching me though, so I took the second sip like a champ with a puckered face.

It didn't taste so bad once you got used to it. I don't know why I thought I was going to feel any different, but I was shocked that I wasn't feeling crazy or anything.

Harvey picked a Ten of Spades next, which meant that we both drank. My next card was a Jack, so Harvey had to drink. Back and forth we started to pick cards up and do what they asked us to do. By the middle of the game, I was already feeling kind of light-headed and I honestly hadn't had so much fun before. The thing was, it wasn't like normal fun, where I felt self-conscious. Suddenly, almost like a punch, I became someone who didn't care. I could feel my heart beating fast from the last card I had picked, which made me chug my cup till the end with Harvey.

He refilled our cups before he picked his next card. When he drew the Six of Hearts, that was when we both of kind of calmed down from our highs and looked at each other. We both knew what it meant. I tried really hard to hide my enthusiasm but I had no clue if it was showing all over my face. That was the thing about being drunk, you didn't know what you were really doing. Also, everything was tingly, even my lips.

I was getting ready to clap and do a jig when Harvey sat up and pulled his shirt off. Six of Hearts was definitely one of my favorite cards. Oh heck, who was I kidding? Six of Hearts was my favorite card of all time.

I tried to keep it cool when he sat back down, shirtless. I kept telling myself to control the urge to look, but I was weak. I glanced over to see his back being illuminated by the lights coming from the house. I'd had no idea there was a tattoo there, but I could see the outline of a scripture-looking design. I felt my chest constrict when I saw the muscles on his back go back and forth. I wished I could see his tattoo better. The urge to run my hands over it almost overwhelmed me. I didn't know what came over me. I wasn't usually that sexual, but when I glanced over to see his chest I was thinking some really racy things.

Then I realized.

Drinking made me sexual.

Mother of Jesus.

I mean, I usually fantasized about Harvey when I was sober, but this was a whole new level. Some of the things I started to think when I saw his abs and the scripture tattoo he had from one shoulder to the other were way out of my league of imagination. I really needed to control myself.

"Your turn," Harvey said with a smirk after I gawked at him for a full minute. I felt myself blushing as I picked up another one of the cards quickly.

I got the Six of Spades and looked up at Harvey just in time to see him gulp. I mean, I was already wearing half a top. It was practically a bra already, right?

With shaky fingers, I gripped my tube top and pulled it over my head, left in only my plain black bra. It was a relief when Harvey didn't immediately look at my boobs and only gave me a half smirk, then it was a bit of a downer. I mean, I had my boobs almost out in plain view and he wasn't even looking. I knew there wasn't much to show, but still. I looked at his freaking back for an hour!

We continued playing, flipping every card faster the more we drank. At one point, I was a giggling fool. One card made him give me a word and I had to reply in words that rhymed for a full minute. I was so drunk that I tried rhyming the word blue with cantaloupe, which made us both laugh uncontrollably and I had to drink the rest of my cup for being a loser.

I always freaked out when either of us pulled any card with a Six, because it meant that another item of clothing was coming off. The height of my night came when Harvey unbuckled his belt and stepped out of his jeans. He was a boxer briefs guy. Harvey was a boxer-briefs guy and God was real. I tried not staring at him after that and even less when it was my turn to take off my mini skirt. I was so hammered at that point that my wedge got stuck in the tight fabric of the leather skirt and I tumbled onto the ground. Before I knew it I fell right over Harvey in a fit of laughter, not even caring when his arms came around me to catch me. I don't know if either of us really realized that I was lying on top of him, but we continued to play like that, with me looming over him, skin to skin.

I didn't even care that I was practically naked on top of a boy, who just so happened to be Harvey. I had other, racier thoughts running through my head. Vodka was my new best friend.

Half of the cards were almost gone when I pulled up the Five of Hearts. I was supposed to say something I had never done, and I said the first thing that came into my mind.

"I've never..." I paused to drunkenly giggle at him because he was staring at me. He gave me one of his boyish smiles and I recovered.

"...fallen in love."

I waited for him to take a drink, letting me know that he had, but he never did. I tried to store it in my permanent memories, because I didn't want to forget his answer, but my head wasn't really doing what it was supposed to.

The next card Harvey pulled was a Four, which meant that we had to fire questions at each other before one of us cracked. He brushed away a stray hair that had fallen out of my bun before beginning. I tried to put that into the list of things I was going to remember the next day, too.

"Why do birds fly?" he started.

"Is there a life after this?" I counter-asked. Back and forth we both continued.

"Why does life suck?"

"Is Mrs. Lasowski's hair real?" That one almost made him crack, I could tell, but he carried on.

"Why is the sky blue?" he said.

"Why is the grass green?" I said.

"Why are you so pretty?" I was about to ask him another question, but his last one made me pause. I was almost sure I imagined it, but no. Harvey was still smiling up at me, thinking he had me.

"What do your tattoos mean?"

"How come time exists?"

"Am I a bad kisser?" That last question came up from the dark depths of my conscious memory. There wasn't much left on my mind, but that was one of the things from before I was so drunk I still remembered.

"No," he answered immediately. He flinched for a second, realizing he lost, but then continued.

"You're not bad, just...inexperienced."

"Well, that's because you're mean and won't kiss me again!" I whined. Wow, drunk me was desperate. The real me was pretty thirsty but not this much. He didn't even think twice before leaning up and kissing me. I was already on top of him anyway.

His mouth tasted like vodka but better, just like earlier that day. This kiss wasn't like the first one. We were both clawing at each other and he kept running his hands up and down my back, sending an army of shivers all over me. Drunk me didn't think twice before running her hands over the muscles on his chest and kissing him back. I had no clue what sex was like, but it felt like that was exactly how it started. It still wasn't how I expected a Harvey kiss to be. It wasn't as slow as the first one, but even though it was urgent this time, it was still sweet, which was completely unexpected. I could hear us both panting from when we would break off the kiss and then continue.

Harvey stopped kissing me and started to make a trail of kisses down the side of my throat. Then, the craziest thing happened.

I moaned.

Hearing yourself moan for the first time has got to be the weirdest thing. I mean, at that moment you don't care, but since it was definitely one of the things I remembered from that night, it was weird. Then something even crazier happened.

Harvey moaned back. His moan was way better, by the way. More throaty, less strangled-cat-like, than mine.

Sexual Livvie was pleased. I was so caught up in the moment that I didn't hear it at first, but Harvey did. I was about to whine dramatically, when he ripped his mouth away and focused his attention on something else. Something in the distance.

"Cops! Cops! Cops!" someone kept yelling from the house. I could see the red, white, and blue glow coming from far off into the distance when I finally looked up.

"Shit!" Harvey yelled, standing up and picking me up with him.

"What are we doing?" I asked, letting him pull me into the woods and away from the cop lights. The music was cut off for the second time that night and people started yelling. I turned just in time to see people swarming out of the house like ants. One guy in the distance was trying to hold two six-packs of beer in between his arms and he ended up tripping over something. The drinks flew all over as a woman cop ran right over and belly flopped onto him. Talk about dedicated. The guy had already been down.

I let Harvey lead me into the woods then, not wanting to get tackled the same way. I wasn't going to come this far only to be caught by the cops. It hardly seemed fair. Harvey and I were running through the trees and I got a slight chill from the air, which reminded me that I was in my underwear and bra.

Harvey made some random turns and pulled me along. We were both running especially hard when we saw the glow of a flashlight illuminate one of the tree trunks.

I wasn't sure how long we were running through the woods, but somehow it seemed far enough. We both stopped to catch our breath. As I tried to stop breathing like an asthmatic, I started to look around me. God, I really should have stuck with those PE classes.

A bigger worry gripped me when I tried looking around me and only saw darkness. I stuck my hand out and felt someone.

"Harvey?" I whispered.

"Yeah?"

"You know how to get out, right?" I asked, my voice rising close to hysteria. The adrenaline rush had cleared my mind a little, even though I still felt like I slurred my question.

I heard him sigh for a long period of time with no answer.

It was enough for me to figure that we were lost. I was lost in the woods with Harvey in my underwear. It sounded bad, but not as bad as being lost in the woods with Harvey in my underwear and hearing a wolf howl, which was exactly what happened after Harvey sighed.

I was definitely going to remember that the next day.

Chapter Twelve
The Girl Who Cried Wolf

"You heard that, right?" I exclaimed, grabbing hold of Harvey's arm and squeezing tight in my terror.

"Uh, yeah. It's probably really far away..." Harvey sounded like he was trying to convince himself that the wolf's howl wasn't a threat. He sounded distant, kind of like his mind was far away. The sound of his tone made me nervous so I held on to his arm tighter. I was probably squeezing off his circulation.

"What do we do now?" I asked, still a little tipsy. Maybe it was the vodka that was making us sound weird. A breeze ran through the trees and hit my bare stomach. I was in my freaking underwear. So was Harvey though, and having him be in the same situation without his clothes was kind of nice, like we both got ourselves into it. For the first time, I wasn't the only one stuck in the awkward situation.

"I guess we wait until the sun comes back out. It can't be that long. It was four in the morning when I went into the house."

I counted in my head the probable hours that had passed. He was right, it wouldn't be too long for the sun to come out. We were going to walk out unscathed. Going around trying to get out in the darkness would be useless if neither of us knew how.

Everything kind of calmed down once I knew we had a plan, until my bladder decided to make an appearance. I swore I would hold it in the moment I got the urge. I didn't know how many minutes passed while Harvey and I just stood in the darkness waiting for the sun to come up. All the while I was getting ready for my bladder to explode. I couldn't just pee in the woods in front of Harvey. The idea of actually peeing in his presence made me sick.

I had to hold it.

Neither of us had said anything for a while, so the chatter inside me bubbled up. I realized I couldn't deal with silence when I was with him. It was too hard to know what he was thinking, especially in the dark.

"So, this is...interesting," I mumbled, still grabbing on to his arm. I was scared of letting go and losing him in the darkness. Although with the urge to pee I was grabbing on tight. I knew it, but he wasn't complaining, so I kept my grip.

Harvey snorted before answering, "Yeah, it's something."

The minutes ticked by while I looked around my head for something else to say. I was feeling

* * *

pressured to say something, which led to me making the next embarrassing statement.

"Uh, you're a boxer briefs guy?"

Why did I say that? I wanted to slap myself. It was just that I would have been okay with boxers. Nick wore boxers and he usually slept in them when he stayed over. It was no big deal. But these were boxer briefs. They outlined everything without looking dumb like regular briefs. I couldn't deal with his underwear choice. Maybe it was still the remnants of super drunk and sexual Livvie.

"Yeah, you're a boyshorts girl?" I could finally hear something in his tone, like laughter.

My cheeks reddened in the darkness.

"They're comfortable, okay?" I sounded like a defensive little kid. There really wasn't anything wrong with my underwear choice, it wasn't a thong or anything.

"These hold my junk pretty well."

"Harvey!" I yelled a few seconds after I heard what he said. I could tell he was teasing me when he began to laugh in the darkness.

"Thank you, for bringing your junk into the conversation," I said half sarcastically.

"Welcome?" I could practically see his grin even though the sunlight still hadn't made an appearance. I don't know why I chose that moment to register the texture of his arm in my hand.

"You know, you really need to moisturize," I said offhandedly.

"What?"

I was going to say something else but the leaves rustled at that very moment and Harvey hadn't moved beside me. In fact, Harvey hadn't moved at all during our entire conversation. The leaves rustled and I could feel something coming closer. I couldn't see it, but I could feel its presence. My heart beat crazily in a quiet way. Kind of like when you panic but don't make a sound. I was sure I was gonna pee myself right then, and I didn't even have the urge to before.

Harvey wasn't moving beside me, yet there was a crunching sound coming from the dead leaves on the ground. I was still as a tree. Come to think of it, that's how Harvey had been during our entire talk, still as a tree.

Something growled.

"H-H-Harvey?" I stuttered out. I hadn't even noticed the sun coming out. You can't notice those kinds of things anyway. One minute it's dark and then the light comes and envelops everything without you noticing.

The next place I set my eyes was on the wolf. He was huge and growling right at me. His eyes were black and his fur was an opaque gray color mixed with white. If I hadn't stopped myself right at the last second, I really would have peed myself.

My mind went into panic mode. I knew I shouldn't run away from it since I was obviously the center of attention, but I wasn't thinking with my fear.

"Harvey! Let's go!" I yelled, pulling at his arm, which was still in my hand, and trying to run. But Harvey wouldn't budge. I kept trying to pull him. I was like a pickup truck stuck in the mud. Every time I pulled, trying to get away from the wolf, Harvey wouldn't move beside me.

"Livvie, what the hell are you doing?" I heard Harvey whisper to me, like he didn't want to disturb anything, which was what I should have been doing instead of panicking like an idiot and trying to pull the guy beside me. That's when I realized that Harvey hadn't sounded distant earlier because his mind was somewhere else. He himself had been somewhere else. My head whipped around to the side just in time for me to realize that I had been holding on to a tree and was now trying to pull it with me in a run.

I was an idiot.

I finally gave up long enough to see Harvey at the other side of our small clearing and the gray wolf in between us. I swear, even the wolf was looking at me like I was retarded.

No wonder I'd told him to moisturize, I had been holding on to a freaking tree trunk. The bark was pretty ashy now that I really thought about it.

"Livvie, you need to stop moving," Harvey said a little bit louder. It was an order, and so I followed it because there was nothing I could do. What if I played dead? Wasn't that what you did with wolves? Or was that with bears? Could they tell the difference? I was a terrible actress, though. I was sure not even the wolf in front of me would buy it.

The wolf crept over slowly, growling as it got closer. It wanted me. Why me? I mean, Harvey was the attractive one. The wolf obviously had bad taste in people.

I looked up to see Harvey whistle. The wolf turned just in time towards the sound and I watched Harvey leap and sprint right to my side. He could have easily run and fed me, literally, to the wolves, but there he was beside me in an instant.

I don't know why, but it was the single most romantic thing ever. I said so, since I was almost sure we were both going to die then. My last words to him wouldn't matter.

"Aw, you just jumped in front of a wolf for me?" I crooned, half-shocked he would do something so sweet on my behalf.

I thought he would say something sweet for our last moments alive. We hadn't been a couple and the most he had done was kiss me, but he jumped in front of a deadly animal for me so it had to mean something.

"I think I'm still drunk," he said, kind of in shock himself.

"Well, I like the drunk Harvey, then," I said back, considering he was risking his life for me.

"I like drunk Livvie too. You're not sloppy like most girls."

"But I am slutty—" I was cut off when the wolf growled loudly this time, annoyed about the exchange and lack of attention towards him. Maybe it was me accepting I was going to die and not caring anymore. Maybe it was still the vodka, but I let myself get weird. There were very few options left, so if we didn't come out alive from what I was about to do, then we were going to die anyway.

I decided to talk to him.

"I know you want to eat us," I said, as if I were talking to a little boy. This was Brian in wolf form, no big deal.

"Holy shit, Livvie, don't speak to it!" Harvey exclaimed, trying to pull me back.

"Harvey, you're hurting his feelings."

"What the hell? He's not a real person, Livvie!"

I ignored him and started to walk forward. I wanted the wolf to know that I wasn't scared to the point of almost peeing myself, even though it was a lie.

"See, although I'm sure eating us wouldn't be that bad for you, it would kind of suck for us. My name's Livvie and that's Harvey." I pointed at each of us. This was normal. I was just chatting with a wolf that wanted to eat me.

The foam forming around his mouth wasn't a big deal, right? Having rabies was in these days.

The wolf's attention shifted to Harvey when I pointed at him, and his wolf eyes narrowed. He was still several feet away from us but had been slowly creeping closer.

"What's your name?" I asked.

"I take it back. I think you're fucking crazy when you're drunk," Harvey amended from behind me.

I ignored Harvey and continued to speak. "You look like a Bob."

Slowly the wolf closed his mouth and stared at me. I was confusing him, but maybe for the better. With his mouth closed and his expression less menacing he was almost cute.

"So, what do you say, Bob? Bobby? Bobbert?" I was trying to butter him up. I tried to keep the ghostly expression off my face when the wolf crept right up and peered up at me. He didn't look deadly anymore, just kind of neutral. Actually, the more I looked at him the less he looked like a wolf.

His giant head brushed my hand that was resting at my side. I went with my gut and touched one of his ears. The wolf leaned more into my hand and closed his eyes. My fingers slowly started moving over his thick, coarse fur and around the top of his head. He looked like he was liking it, so I started to get comfortable.

Pretty soon, I was giving him a head massage.

"I want my own nature show. Something like Livvie the Wolf Whisperer," I mused, still trying to keep Bob happy. When I was sure I had done it long enough, and Harvey had been quiet for the longest time, I stopped.

Harvey finally spoke from where he stood. "Livvie, I didn't say anything because he can still kill our asses, but...that's a dog." I looked at him and then back at Bob, repeating that a few times with a dumbfounded expression, until it hit me.

"Seriously?" I asked, glaring at a tail-wagging Bob.

"He's wearing a collar."

Indeed he was. I was petting a dog, not a wolf. A freakishly big dog, but definitely not a wolf. I needed glasses.

"Alright, well I gotta head out. It was really nice to meet you— " I leaned down to his name tag. "Tiny. Nice to meet you, Tiny."

Harvey stifled his laughter behind me. I walked towards him and grabbed his hand. I waved at Tiny before pulling the real Harvey and not a tree in a random direction. I just wanted to get away from the freakishly big husky dog and his ironic real name.

"You thought he was a wolf too!" I accused, one of my fingers stabbing into his chest.

"Yeah, for like ten minutes." He laughed.

We were silent for a few minutes.

"Do you want me to address you as Ms. Wolf Whisperer now, or...?"

I whacked him over the head before he could laugh at me again. "What was he even doing in the woods?" I wondered aloud, completely offended by Tiny now that it was all his fault.

"He probably ran away. There's a ton of houses scattered throughout the woods and up the mountains."

We walked through the woods in silence after that. I wondered if we would get lost again, but didn't say anything. Frankly, I was still kind of mad at myself. I was worse than my nana, and she put her shirts on backwards all the time.

Finally, after we'd walked barefoot in the woods for a solid hour the trees started to become sparse and we met with a lonely road. I looked over at Harvey and then at myself, realizing that we looked like a pair of modern Indians. I knew I had leaves in my hair and so did Harvey. We were both dirty from tumbling around on the ground during our makeout session, along with the coat of dirt we'd acquired from simply walking around the woods. I had stepped on some berries earlier and tried to wipe my feet off with my hand, then forgotten, and wiped my face, so I had purple stains on my cheeks. I had freaked out and wondered if they were poisonous, and perhaps I almost killed myself, but then Harvey put my worries to rest.

He had been in Boy Scouts when he was little, so he knew they were fine. Harvey, the bad ass, in freaking Boy Scouts, tying knots and everything. It was the most adorable thing.

We stood beside the deserted road in silence. I decided to break it with an important question.

"So, if we had stayed lost in the woods you would have been able to start a fire and stuff?" I couldn't keep the enthusiasm out of my voice. Harvey rolled his eyes and shook his shoulders. He didn't want to plainly admit it, but I knew he would have.

"What are we going to do now?" It seemed like that was the question I always asked him. I realized I was just like the rest of the group, waiting for him to make the first move. I don't know when it happened, but it felt nice to let someone else come up with all of the answers.

"We wait to hitch a ride from someone," he said plainly.

"In our underwear?" I wondered.

He turned to me and gave me a once-over for the first time. He nodded, then brought his eyes forward again. I was so red I was sure even my arms changed color.

We stood there, waiting and looking into the distance to see if something was coming. It was luck when a car and someone on a motorcycle started driving toward us in the distance. We couldn't see who it was, but for a moment I was sure it was the rest of the group.

Harvey met my eyes and we both smiled, understanding the same thing. As the group got closer we both stuck out our thumbs and smiled wider. It was completely crazy, the night we had spent. Our thumbs stood out in the breeze as we jokingly asked for a ride.

I realized Rex was the one driving the motorcycle when he got close enough. The Corolla wasn't very far behind and Lexi stepped out the minute the car stopped in front of us.

"Holy motherfucking shit sticks, you guys!" Lexi came over and hugged both of us. No one could string curse words together like Lexi.

"I told you they were fine," Lexi's boyfriend said, coming out of the driver's seat of the Corolla and standing by the door. Dreads came out from the back and quickly ran up to Harvey and held him in a huge dramatic hug.

"Damn, we thought the cops got you!" Dreads sounded off, like way more mellow than normal, even though he was saying something really intense. He almost squeezed the pee out of me when he wobbled over and put his arms around me. I took a big whiff of Dreads and remembered the smell from the last time we were all in The Cave. Dreads was high as a kite.

Harvey just smirked, while Rex took the helmet off and walked over with the keys to hand them to him.

Lexi was back at my side, asking us what had happened the night before.

"What do you think happened?" Lexi's boyfriend joked, wiggling his eyebrows at me.

That's when I remembered I was in my bra and underwear. I looked over at Harvey, who was only smirking wider, and just rolled my eyes. He walked over to the trunk of the car to get some clothes, and I followed, ignoring Lexi's question. She looked a little bit thrown off, but I just nodded my head at her, promising to tell her later with my pointed stare. There would be girl talk soon, just how it was with Nick, only this time I actually had something to talk about.

I stopped short when Harvey opened the trunk and a hard look crossed his face. Something stopped me from coming over to his side and seeing what he saw inside the car's trunk.

"Rex."

I looked over to see Rex look down at the ground while he made his way over past me, to Harvey.

"Yeah?" Rex said, kind of sheepishly. I looked over at Dreads, who was chasing a nearby butterfly with his eyes, like he didn't even notice what was going down. He was loopier than usual.

"You bought from him? That wasn't what we agreed to do, shithead!" Harvey looked pissed. His mouth was set in a hard line and you could see an angry red glow under some of the dirt caked on his face.

"Dude, I couldn't say no! Blame it on her for blowing him off at the party!" Rex pointed an accusing finger at me.

"Blame me for what?" I asked, kind of insulted. I stalked over to the trunk to see what he was accusing me of, only to have my mouth drop.

There were several squares of it in the car, all scattered throughout the compartment.

"Is that what I think it is?" I asked, freaking out more and more by the second. I had never seen it in my entire life, and there it was, in bulk, right in front of me. I felt like part of a Mexican drug cartel.

Harvey ignored me. "You bought all of that weed from him just because Livvie didn't fuck him?" He was getting ready to throw punches, if his clenched fists meant anything. I flinched from his crude attitude and knew I looked like a lost animal when I met Lexi's eyes.

"You guys need to just shut up and deal with it later. You're scaring Livvie," Lexi said, obviously used to them fighting, unlike me. I let her grab my hand, use her other hand to get my clothes from under the drugs, and push me towards the backseat. I didn't even want to wear them now that I knew they had been in the same trunk, but I put them on anyway when she handed the clothes over.

"Why did he buy that stuff?" I asked.

"Don't listen to him, it wasn't because of you. Rex is a pushover when it comes to Garrard. He was too much of a little bitch to tell him no and so he blew all of our money on it. We were going to buy from him anyway, but just not so much—that was the only way we could have stayed at his house."

I tried to make sense of everything Lexi had said. That obviously explained why he owned a freaking mansion in the middle of the woods—the guy was selling in bulk.

"At least Dreads is happy about it," I said, looking out of the window and watching him try to catch the butterfly that was long gone.

Lexi laughed. "Yeah, he's high as shit."

I finally asked what I'd been wanting to for the longest time.

"Is that why those people are chasing you guys?" I was a part of it too, but not really.

"No." Lexi's eyes turned a little dark, like she really didn't want to delve in the specifics.

Regardless, I waited for her to say something, anything, but Rex decided to climb into the driver's seat and start the car with a grunt. I hadn't seen what happened while I was in the car, but now Rex looked just as angry. I realized his nose was bleeding when he used the back of his hand to wipe some blood off. Lexi's boyfriend took the passenger seat, wearing a neutral expression. Dreads was last to stumble into the car and sit beside me. He quickly fell asleep on my shoulder. His dreads tickled my nose, so I moved some of them aside.

I saw Harvey's newly clothed back in the distance. He looked like he was trying to get as far away from us as possible. I knew he wasn't mad at me, but at Rex for not following his orders, but it still didn't feel good.

"Isn't he going a little fast?" I asked, my eyes glued to him as he got further and further away from us even though we were going pretty fast ourselves.

"Nah, it's not like he's trying to ditch us." Lexi said, but it sounded more like she was convincing herself.

I sat back and closed my eyes, not wanting to see when he would inevitably take an exit at the last minute and lose us. I didn't want to see him drive fast enough to leave us behind.

Instead, I thought about Nick, Brian, and even my mom.

I ignored the fact that we were officially broke and had an abundance of weed but nowhere to go.

I didn't know who was chasing us or why, but I knew they had guns.

Plus, Harvey was gone.

I ignored all of it.

The most amazing night of my life had morphed into that very moment and it sucked. I wished I could have climbed onto the back of the bike with him, just so that he couldn't have deserted me.

I sighed, officially giving up and letting Dreads' hair tickle my nose.

Chapter Thirteen
Kiss Me? I'm Different.

"Wasn't gonna ditch us, my ass," Lexi's boyfriend grumbled from the passenger seat. Lexi made a point of flashing her middle finger next to his face and sitting back in her seat after she was satisfied with her work.

The car was silent for a few moments before I spoke up.

"I think Dreads' hair is giving me allergies," I said, trying my best to breathe. "How often does he clean this thing?" I pointed with my free hand to his giant head.

"The last time Harvey ditched us," Lexi's boyfriend responded drily. I tried not to cringe. I was going to move away but Dreads looked so comfortable, just how Brian looked when he would sleep next to me. My big sister instinct took over and I let him rest his head on the same spot for the time being.

At one point someone started sniffling louder than me. It started slowly but picked up speed eventually. I looked up in confusion, only to find Lexi's boyfriend leaning towards the driver's side and speaking sternly.

"Keep it together, man!" This was directed at a tearful and emotional Rex.

"I can't. I fucked up, Rowan!"

Finally learning his name was Rowan and not Lexi's boyfriend made me giggle. My giggling died down when I realized big and mighty Rex was literally in tears. I wondered for a moment if his watery eyes were going to affect his driving. Lexi looked at me with a question in her eyes, and I felt kind of embarrassed when I leaned over to whisper something over Dreads' head.

"It's just that I finally learned your boyfriend's name."

It took Lexi a few moments, but she replied after Rex let out another wail.

"You just now caught his name? You could have asked!" she said, laughing silently.

While the mood towards the front seat was melancholic, at least the backseat portion of the car could laugh.

"That reminds me." Lexi leaned in even more, ignoring Rex, who was practically breaking down, and her boyfriend, who was acting as if they were both in some emotional drama. Rowan kept telling Rex to keep it together in an intense coaching voice.

"What happened between you and Harvey? You guys disappeared and then when we found you at the side of the road you were both pretty much naked. Did something happen between you two?" Lexi had a huge smile on her face, as if she couldn't wait to hear the juicy details. We were both whispering, and the guys in the front seat were too busy with their emotional moment, but I still leaned in closer so as to not be heard.

"Nothing, really," I finally relented. "Well, kind of, but I'm not really sure..."

I knew I wasn't making any sense and Lexi's confused stare was proof enough. I tried to elaborate.

"He...kissed me, that's it."

The moment became more awkward with Rex's sobbing, but Lexi only looked at me with a blank stare in her eyes. I tried wringing my hands to give myself something to do, but the silence was getting to me.

"I told you it wasn't anything—" I tried to amend, but Lexi cut me off when her mouth dropped open. She was still giving me the same blank stare, but at least she had movement.

"He...kissed you? On the mouth?" Apparently, location was very important here.

"Yeah, where else?"

"He kissed you last night when he was drunk?" Lexi looked at me like my answer was crucial to our very existence, so I nodded my head.

"Oh, alright. I mean, it's still pretty crazy to hear, but maybe he was really drunk—"

"Well, that was the second time..." I felt the need to add more info. You know, to get our facts straight.

"He kissed you when he wasn't drunk?" Lexi looked about ready to pop a blood vessel.

"Yeah, he just sort of...kissed me." I was hesitant, waiting for Lexi's response.

"Livvie, Harvey doesn't kiss girls."

"Huh?"

"What I'm saying is that Harvey doesn't kiss girls, he fucks them. Ask any girl who's ever been with him, he's never kissed any of them." Lexi was dispensing critical, albeit confusing, information.

"But, isn't that a little weird?" I interjected, wondering why all of those girls ever let him get so far with them, but he never even kissed them.

"It's common knowledge that Harvey doesn't kiss any of the girls he's with. He's pretty good at everything else, or so I've heard." Lexi nodded her head to make her point.

I tried to understand what made me so different and if being different was a good or bad thing with Harvey. It didn't make sense that he wouldn't kiss any of the girls he was with and I could tell Lexi knew I was wondering these things.

"But, why?" I finally asked, since I couldn't come up with an answer on my own.

"I guess because kissing is personal. Fucking isn't, and Harvey has never been serious with anyone. To be honest, I think the poor dude has commitment issues."

Great, yet another reason for me to believe that I wasn't good enough for him. Just another thing drunk kinky Livvie was confused about.

"Are you sure?" I asked, one more time before my hopes were completely crushed.

"Yeah, she's sure," a new voice said from out of nowhere. I jumped a little when Dreads spoke up and looked at me with a huge grin on his face.

So much for girl talk.

I wondered how much Dreads had heard, but my question was quickly answered with Lexi's next words.

"Do you know what this means?" she finally said, a small smile on her face mirroring the one Dreads had given me.

I shook my shoulders, having no clue.

Dreads answered Lexi's question. "It means you're different." He had straightened up but was still grinning at me. Rowan and Rex, thankfully, were past the tearful moment, but were still too distracted with their own problems to notice what was happening in the backseat.

I didn't know what to make of that, but Rowan took the opportunity to turn around and talk to Lexi. With the attention diverted from me I looked out the window and thought about what Lexi had told me.

Was it a good or a bad thing that Harvey would kiss me? Honestly, it was only confusing. I had no clue what to think of things.

After a few hours, most of our stomachs were grumbling. We still had no clue where Harvey was or if he was coming back to us. Eventually, we stopped at a large gas station. It was in the middle of nowhere, but there were a lot of truck drivers milling around with their large cargo trucks parked throughout the entire lot.

The gas station was divided into two and one side held a sandwich shop. Since we didn't appear to have enough money for gas *and* food, we looked towards the restaurant wistfully from our seats, while a composed Rex went outside.

Dreads had fallen asleep once again, and Lexi was busy straddling her boyfriend on the front seat of the car. They'd been apart for most of the ride, the longest I'd seen them, but they were back to sucking face. Things were getting a little too sexual for me to feel comfortable, so I stumbled out of the car and offered to go inside and pay.

Rex seemed distracted when he gave me a few crumbled bills and started to pull the nozzle out.

The air was kind of chilly, but I didn't have anything to wrap around myself. We'd been on the road for about four days and I had no clue as to where we were since I hadn't thought to ask. A few of the truck drivers looked me up and down as I walked past them and I regretted asking to go towards the building alone. Their stares reminded me of Jim the Creep, which caused the hairs on the back of my arms to stand up from apprehension.

I walked quickly past the glass doors and into the main building. The lights were dim and there were more truck drivers, some waiting in line to pay for their gas and others scattered around the aisles. I steered away from a particularly large bearded guy and made my way towards the cashier in a hurry.

I was walking through the candy aisle when I felt a pair of hands grab hold of my hips. My heart pumped faster until it felt as if it were lodged in my throat. I clutched the thing nearest to me before turning around.

With a warlike cry, I hit the person behind me with the object I'd grabbed. I ended up slapping Harvey in the face with a stick of beef jerky before realizing it was him. Harvey closed his eyes briefly once the jerky made contact with his face, and cringed like he smelled something bad. His hands remained on my hips, since he seemed frozen for a moment.

"Sorry," I mumbled, kind of shocked at seeing him.

"Did you really think beef jerky was a good weapon choice?" Harvey asked me, hands still resting on my hips, as if he had already expected me to pick something ridiculous.

Was he going to move his hands soon? I sure hoped not. My heart quickened its pace when I noticed the faint outline of stubble going on. The rest of the guys had it too, but on Harvey it just made my knees weak.

"Have you smelled this stuff? It could drive anyone away." I tried to sound casual, as if not seeing him for the entire day and then running into him at a gasoline station was perfectly normal.

"Yeah, that's true," he agreed before scrunching his face up.

I wanted to both hug and strangle him, both at the same time if that made sense.

Instead, I wrapped my arms around him in a hug that almost made him topple over. It was unexpected for the both of us. He didn't push me away, but didn't exactly return the hug either.

I pulled away a little and spoke without thinking.

"Sorry, people always leave and it sucks, even when you think you're used to it," I said, the words rushed and a little jumbled, then capped it off with a weak laugh. I could feel his arms start to come around me, but the last thing I wanted was a pity hug, so I slipped under them instead.

I wanted to undo the last few minutes, but I didn't have the right words to make it less awkward. I'd practically invited him to my pity party and then done the limbo out of his pity hug.

I finally looked up towards Harvey's tense expression, but I couldn't decipher everything going on.

"About what happened—" Harvey started. I stayed quiet, waiting for his next words. He seemed to pause out of feeling awkward.

"We were both kind of drunk. You know that it didn't...mean anything, right?"

I was dead. This was what it felt like to be so mortified that you couldn't even form a coherent response. I shouldn't have been standing there, in that

• • •

gasoline station, getting rejected by a boy. I should have been at home, stuffing my face with junk food and watching movies with Nick like always, not there getting my hopes stomped on. Running away had been the biggest mistake, because getting rejected majorly sucked.

"Oh, look, chips!" I mentioned randomly, turning towards the aisle beside us and frantically making my way towards it. The aisle I chose supplied dish soap and condoms, not chips, but my movements were too scattered and shaky for that to be the real issue. Harvey followed behind me, but since I hadn't turned to see his expression I was able to take a few deep breaths and wipe the humiliated look from my face.

"We should get going," I said, still randomly walking with him behind me. I had forgotten to ask him if he was back or still apart from the group, but that didn't really matter to me at the moment.

Harvey sighed, grabbed hold of my hand, and led me towards the cashier. It was the worst time for him to hold my hand, ever, but the feeling of his hand enveloping mine was still amazing and that just made me hate everything even more.

There was a woman ahead of us in line who had her small son with her. I peered outside to see a man putting gas into a large RV. I figured it was her husband. The woman was fumbling with the little boy beside her. The kid was whining and pulling at her shirt because he wanted to get his hands on an ice cream from the cooler beside us.

She had already taken out her credit card, seeing as she was the next person in line. Once the last trucker paid his bill and walked away, our line moved forward. I felt Harvey lean over and whisper towards me.

"Number three." He didn't say anything else before straightening.

I was about to ask him what he was talking about, but I focused on the woman, who was busy trying to control her wailing child. Number three suddenly made sense.

Number Three: Steal a Credit Card.

I looked over at Harvey and locked eyes with him. He smirked before gently kicking over a tub filled with discounted candy. The little boy at the woman's leg went insane.

The lady wrestled with him, while simultaneously trying to get the items she purchased from the cashier. Her card lay forgotten on the counter and before I knew what I was doing, I walked over to a display with sunglasses and put a pair on. The cashier was so caught up in the mess happening on the opposite side of the counter that he didn't even look at me.

I slipped the card into the palm of my hand and, acting like the glasses weren't exactly what I was looking for, I set them back down.

I walked back to Harvey, and we both watched the woman pick up her son and her things, then walk away. It had been way too easy. That's when the guilt hit me.

Oh my God, I had never felt so guilty.

The card burned my palm the minute I realized it was still there. I quickly looked towards the woman and then the cashier. With shaky legs I walked up to the cashier, practically yelled my pump number and slid the card into the machine. He didn't even ask for any identification. I ripped the receipt from the man's hand when the transaction was over. Before I knew it I had turned towards Harvey.

"We need to give it back!"

I ran out of the building towards the RV. To my despair the vehicle was already thundering towards the exit. I pushed my legs harder until I was running alongside the moving vehicle. I waved my arms around like a crazy person, but it was no use. It reminded me of when I was in fifth grade and had missed the bus.

All of my classmates had watched me follow the bus for a full block while the bus driver acted as if he didn't see me. Eventually the bus driver relented and stopped the bus, but not before I fell into a puddle of rainwater from the day before. No wonder my dorky reputation followed me into high school.

I knew the rest of the guys were looking at me from one of the pumps, and I was almost sure Harvey had followed me out, but I didn't care. I needed to get that dreaded card back to its rightful owner, or I would have broken down from the guilt.

I could practically see the RV nearing the exit. While I ran, I couldn't help but admire how well kept the RV was. Did people wax an RV? With the sun just setting there was a crazy reflection coming off from the shiny exterior. I had my eyes on the prize, regardless of the glare.

Which is why I didn't see the giant pole right in front of me.

But I felt it when I smacked forehead first into it.

I felt my entire body vibrate like a tuning fork from the impact. I heard a roar of laughter belonging to several nearby truck drivers and felt my face heat up. Both my hands were on my forehead as I tried to press on it to make the pain go away. I was walking around like a drunken lunatic now, trying to find the direction of the RV. My legs were tripping over each other, but eventually the man who had been driving the RV ran towards me.

"Miss, are you alright?"

"Your wife—" I stuttered out. The woman ran up not too far behind him. They were so nice, getting out of their RV to see if the girl who stole their credit card was okay. I felt twice as guilty then.

I pulled the card out from my pocket and waved it up in the air, one hand still gripping my throbbing forehead.

"You—" I breathed in from the exertion of running and from having the air knocked out of me.

"—forgot—" Another asthmatic breath followed.

"—your card!" I finally puffed out.

"Thank you so much!" The woman walked up to me and took the card from my wild hand.

"No problem," I mumbled.

"Have a nice day!" I yelled with a dumb smile on my face. I turned back towards the station with my dignity far, far, behind me. I heard the rumble of the RV starting up, and kind of smiled. I was guilt-free at least.

I looked up just in time to see Harvey giving me a small smile. I saw his eyes shoot up to my banged-up forehead not long after.

"The fact that you ran into a pole sucks. That wasn't how I pictured you giving it back, but I should have known." Harvey was smiling down at me when we reached each other. I knew the rest of the group was surprised to see him, but they stayed away. I knew they didn't want to do anything that would drive him away again.

"You knew I was gonna give it back?" I practically screeched in surprise.

Harvey smirked at me before grabbing my free hand and leading me towards the group. I was under the impression that there was nothing between us, so what was up with all the hand-holding?

"Same direction," Harvey said towards the group.

I let him lead me away from them and towards the other side of the building. I looked behind me, only to see Rex nod like a trained soldier and Lexi still straddling Rowan's lap but no longer kissing him. They nodded as well. Only a sleeping Dreads had no response.

Harvey's bike was parked on the opposite side of the lot. He handed me his helmet, but first made me pull my hand away from my forehead.

I heard him suck in a breath through his teeth as he eyed whatever was happening on my forehead.

"Is it that bad?" I asked in horror.

"I'm not sure you can get the helmet over that bump." I believed him for five seconds before I saw him grin a little. "Don't worry, it's a little bruise. No big deal." He set me at ease before pushing the helmet over my face.

He took that moment to straddle the bike and start the engine, drowning out any more sounds. I sighed before putting a leg over the motorcycle and wrapping my arms around him.

I rested my head on his back as he pulled out from where he was parked and towards the exit. I closed my eyes for just a second, letting the wind whip past me.

It didn't mean anything, it didn't mean anything, it didn't mean... I chanted until it hit me. I'd already done two out of five things on my list.

Three more to go.

Chapter Fourteen
Breaking the Ice are the Windows to the Souls

My arms wrapped themselves tighter around Harvey. I was beginning to miss the warmth that the Corolla provided. Plus, I didn't know how long we had to drive until we stopped again.

Thank God it wasn't long. I looked over Harvey's shoulder in time to see another motel sign coming nearer. The motorcycle parked first and the car followed shortly. I remembered we didn't have any money and wondered what we were going to do.

I was growing better at getting off of the bike, but my foot still got stuck when I tried to unhitch it. I thought no one saw, until Harvey walked past me with a grin on his face. At least I kept impressing the guy.

I followed close behind him as our group came to a halt at the entrance. We didn't need to pay until we checked out, thankfully. Harvey grabbed our room key from the old woman behind the desk and it wasn't long before we were climbing a new set of stairs towards our room. I wanted to ask how we were going to pay for it, but that would have been awkward so I kept my mouth shut.

I hadn't thought it possible, but the room was worse than the last. The wallpaper was peeling from the wooden walls and the carpet had several unknown stains that grossed me out immediately.

"Alright, Rex gets the shower last cus' he's a little bitch, everyone else gets to fight for it." Everyone stood in the middle of the room and agreed silently. Dreads and Rowan had brought in our "luggage," which really just meant all of the clothes we had bought from the store that were still in the plastic bags, along with my *Buffy* DVDs.

Rex nodded his head solemnly, as if he truly believed he deserved to get the shower last. He was pretty gallant about the entire thing. I had no clue how we were supposed to fight for dibs on the shower, but I soon found out after Harvey did a countdown.

I was the last to figure out what to do because I had never done it before, but I sprinted towards the bathroom behind everyone. Dreads ended up fiercely holding on to Rowan's leg until he brought him down with him into some sort of wrestling move. They were a mess on the floor, both of them tackling and fighting like boys usually did. I was behind Harvey when he sprinted and leaped over them, but it was clear that Lexi was in the lead. She made it to the door handle and quickly pulled it open.

"I win, bitches!" she yelled happily, doing a little shimmy.

Seeing her win, Harvey cursed. The boys at my feet stopped fighting. Both of them needed the shower more now that they'd rolled around on the floor.

"Damn, she always wins!" Dreads hollered. I glanced over at Rex, who was bouncing on the balls of his feet and nodding along to Dreads' statement. The rest of the guys groaned and nodded their heads as well. Looking pleased with herself, Lexi was about to close the door, until her boyfriend sprang up from the floor.

"Damn right, my girl always wins!" He said this in a smooth voice while he made his way towards her. We all watched as he grabbed her hips and started to push her into the bathroom. Lexi rolled her eyes, but laughed nonetheless.

"Got room for one more?" Rex asked behind me. I turned around in time to see him wiggle his eyebrows towards the bathroom.

"No," both Rowan and Lexi said in unison, shutting the door. Everyone laughed at Rex's crushed expression.

Dreads didn't take long to turn on the old TV. The problem with that was that there was literally nothing except for mangled noises and bad reception coming from the thing. I walked over beside him, catching his dismayed expression. I checked to see if there was at least a DVD player before going over to my *Buffy* set and picking out the first season disc. The guys watched me put the disc into the slot and press play.

I figured if Lexi and her boyfriend had the bathroom first then it would be a while until it was my turn, and I was right. After an hour and a half, Rex, Dreads, and I were all too engrossed in the TV show to think too hard about what they were probably doing.

Harvey tried to act like he was too cool to watch *Buffy*, but eventually he cracked. I realized it when I felt the bed dip from his weight. Buffy and her friends were suddenly a hundred times less interesting with him beside me. I tried focusing on the show but I couldn't stop noticing how nice it was to have him there.

He was just sitting next to me and already all I could think about was him. Was it hot, or was it just me? Or maybe it was Harvey...

I internally shrugged off my less-than-normal thoughts. It wasn't like Harvey was interested in me. He'd made that pretty clear earlier on in the day.

Lexi and her boyfriend eventually fumbled out of the foggy bathroom and I tried not to cringe when the boys allowed me to be next. They made it seem like they were being nice, but I knew none of them wanted to really take a shower after Lexi and her boyfriend.

I tried not to think too hard about what had probably gone down in the shower just minutes before. I made it a quick one and put on the clothes that Lexi had put out for me when I was done. I'd bought some sweats to sleep in, but Lexi said we were going out somewhere and so I was forced to wear what she picked out.

At least it wasn't like my party outfit. I slipped on the black skinny jeans before pulling the sheer lilac top over my head. You could see my bra under the shirt if you really focused, but I doubted anyone would take the time to. The sleeves of the shirt had little studs, which I would never have worn before but could deal with.

Lexi wore a hot pink wrap skirt and a half-there tube top, making my outfit appear modest in comparison.

It didn't take long for the rest of the guys to get showered and ready. I had no clue where we were going, even when I found myself on the back of the motorcycle again and holding on to Harvey. I felt his abdomen flex under my fingers once when we stopped at a red light and almost lost it.

I wasn't just thirsty for the guy, I was practically dehydrated. I wasn't going to let him turn me down again, though, so I tried to control my feelings.

I freaked out when I took Harvey's helmet off and realized we were in front of a bar. Harvey's bike wasn't the only one in the parking lot. Several other larger and more intimidating bikes were scattered throughout the area. Loud music flowed out of the old torn-down building and numerous scary biker dudes walked over to the entrance.

"I should have left you at the motel," I heard Harvey mutter over the music coming from inside. I knew he was talking to me, because it was me he looking at with those accusing eyes. As if it had been my idea to end up at a biker bar. I was about to say something until Lexi skipped over and hooked her arm through mine.

"Not a chance. You think me and Liv would have been cool with missing out on all the fun?" Those were her parting words before she dragged me away from the rest of the guys.

Even though they followed closely behind us, my heart skipped a beat when a super-intimidating biker walked in front of us and turned back to leer. He had a huge graying beard and a black leather vest that covered most of his large body. The snake tattoo he had on his face was practically staring back at me when he turned. He didn't say anything before turning back, and my heart got a chance to calm down.

Walking into the bar was even more terrifying than when we had walked into the mansion the night before. This place was filled with scary-looking adults and practically no one was our age. For a second I wondered how we were even allowed inside. Enforcing the law didn't seem like a priority.

No one stopped us. Everyone in the room was smoking heavily, so I had to resist the urge to scrunch my nose. Most of the men crowded around the bar or the various pool tables. I didn't expect other women in the place, but my eyes flitted over to a few of the bikers' companions. Some of the women were old, like my mom's age, and some were a bit younger. Most of them had tattoos and were hanging from someone's arm. The large wooden bar was to our left and a meaty-looking bartender handed out drinks.

I focused my attention on an older girl who was currently singing on top of the bar. She had on the shortest shorts imaginable even though it was pretty cold outside. Regardless, she shook everything she had on top of the bar. Some of the men were handing her money, but she wasn't a very good singer, so it was obviously for all the booty shaking she was trying to pull off.

A jukebox at the corner of the room was playing the karaoke track for her while she held an old microphone up to her lips. No one else paid any attention to her aside from me and the guys handing her money. It was like some weird bar/strip club establishment. Eventually, I tore my eyes away.

"Stay close to us, alright?" Harvey ordered Lexi and me. We both nodded in agreement, but I couldn't keep my eyes from wandering. Lexi's boyfriend reached out to hold her hand and I felt a little pang go through me. It was a sweet thing to do. I had no clue what we were doing at such a dangerous bar, but I realized what was happening once Harvey walked up to some of the guys playing pool and spoke to two bulky biker dudes. Rex walked up beside Harvey, while the rest of us stayed behind. I could hear a few words through the music but not much. One of the bikers put a huge wad of money on the edge of the pool table.

In the meantime Rowan brought out a few stools for us to sit on. Rex ordered a round of beers and everyone, aside from Lexi and me, started to drink. Something about the deal going on made me extremely anxious. What if Harvey and Rex lost? Would they have to pay the scary-looking men the money we didn't have? The air was heavy with apprehension.

The larger of the two biker guys, who had a mullet, started the game by breaking up the triangle of billiard balls. He hit the white ball so hard that the other ones went flying in almost every direction and several went into the pockets. I hadn't ever seen anyone play pool up close, but the look on Rowan's face gave me a clue as to whose favor the odds were in. The game had barely begun and it seemed like we were bound to lose. The bigger biker said something to Rex, who nodded and lined up his shot. Even with all of the concentration he was giving it, his pool stick still slid over the ball and made it flounder over to the side.

I watched Harvey give Rex a death glare before the other, much smaller biker did his own shot. One of the balls fell into a pocket, but Harvey made two of them go in when it was his turn. The intensity was stressing me out after several minutes.

I leaned over to Lexi, trying to get my worries out in the open. "Uh, are they winning?"

"No, and Harvey's good, but these guys..." Lexi let out a whistle to make her point.

"But if he knows he's losing—"

Lexi cut me off. "Harvey never turns down a bet. That's his thing. It's the reason we're in this mess."

I wanted to desperately for Lexi to explain, but Rowan threw his hands up in the air and growled when Rex missed another shot. My attention went back to the game and I forgot all about what Lexi was going to say.

There were very few balls left on the green surface of the table. I knew that the ones that belonged to the biker guys were even fewer.

I chose that moment to glance over at Harvey. His forehead was scrunched up severely and he was holding the pool stick tightly in his hand. He looked at me for the briefest moment and for the first time I actually saw that he wasn't in control anymore. Harvey was always in control. Even when we were stuck in the woods in front of Bob the Wolf, he had been in control. That was Harvey. He just made you feel like he had all the answers. I knew in that moment I was seeing something that no one ever got to see, him a little bit scared and a whole lot confused.

My eyes shot towards the bar, where the same girl was still shaking her butt. Her voice was pretty plain, but I wasn't sure if mine was any better. I certainly couldn't shake my stuff up there like her. God knew my dance moves would probably make every biker in the room cringe.

I did sing in the shower sometimes, and when Nick would come over and we would sing karaoke. Nick always told me that I had a good voice, but he was my best friend so I never believed him. I sure as heck couldn't dance seductively up on the bar, but Lexi could! I glanced back at the game, only to see things getting worse. I wondered what the biker guys would do to Harvey and Rex if they lost and didn't have the money.

With a big gulp, I stood up from my seat and grabbed Lexi's hand.

"We're gonna go get more drinks!" I yelled towards Lexi boyfriend, who never ripped his eyes away from the game and only nodded.

"We are?" Lexi wondered over the blasting music as I pulled her along. Up close, the amount of old men crowding the wooden bar seemed to multiply, which only made my fears do the same. I was either going to embarrass myself so bad I would have to leave the country, or I was going to fix things.

"I need you to dance on top of the bar!" I yelled suddenly at Lexi.

"Gladly, but I can't sing for shit! That's the only way they let you up!" Lexi claimed, pulling me a little back.

"You take care of the girl already on top of the bar and I'll do the rest."

Lexi looked at me doubtfully for a moment before a huge smile lit up her face.

"Let's do this! Show me what you got, Livvie-cakes!" Lexi said, before giving me a wink and walking up to the bar with confidence. She was officially on board with my crazy idea, even if I wasn't so much anymore. I followed behind and watched her whisper something into the meaty bartender's ear. He eyed her appreciatively before nodding his head.

I saw her try to hoist herself over the tall structure and scrambled over to push her up before the bartender got to cop a feel. I watched the girl already up on the bar look at Lexi warily and flip her off. The crowd of old biker men cheered at a new appearance, and then some more for the singing girl's hostility.

I couldn't believe when Lexi ripped the mic from the girl's hands and swayed her hips to the side. She ended up knocking the other girl down to the floor with a sway of her butt, until all you could see were a pair of scrambling legs, upside down, from the opposite side of the bar.

"Can I get a good song up in here?" Lexi yelled into the mic. Lots of people cheered and the song that had been playing was quickly shut off and replaced by a new instrumental. My heart sped up when I realized that I did in fact know the song.

How could I not? It was my dad's favorite. Not that my dad would have been very proud seeing me at a biker bar, ready to sing for tips in front of a bunch of drunk men.

Lexi turned and extended her hand out forward to grab me. I was about to let her when a sudden fear took hold of me. I couldn't go up there! I wasn't even sure if I could sing! The huge amount of people that were waiting for me to go up was also pretty daunting.

"Come on!" Lexi called, bringing her hand closer to my face. She was crouching down trying to get me. I could feel the crowd watching us getting impatient.

"I can't!" I finally stuttered out, scared out of my pants. I didn't want to disappoint Lexi now that she was already up in front of everyone and I didn't want Harvey to lose and end up dead, but I wasn't Mariah Carey either.

"Here!" Lexi said, bringing a small glass up to my face. "Do a shot and get up here already!" she ordered once I took it from her hands.

There was no looking back after I brought it up to my lips and let the burning liquid slide down my throat. Just like that, I grabbed Lexi's hand and let her pull me up in front of everyone. People began to cheer again and the song started over.

I looked over to the opposite half of the room to see that Harvey was still playing the game with concentration. He hadn't seen me yet. His head snapped up when I sang the first note, though.

The song was a country oldie with flirty lyrics and some strong notes that I had to hit. I started off sultry, which was pretty much something I thought I could never do. I knew that if I wanted the money that the bikers would offer, me and Lexi were going to have to give them a show to remember.

I guess the shot did its job, because I stopped caring about what people thought after a few seconds. I was there to sing my heart out. I was The Voice. Mariah had nothing on me. For a second I imagined I was in the shower with no one watching me, while I belted out a few more of the lyrics. I looked over to see

Lexi dancing in front of one of the younger biker guys and clapping her hands to get the crowd going.

I had to admit, we were a good team. I began to walk back and forth on top of the long wooden bar as if it were a runway. Suddenly, tons of hands were springing up into the air with dollar bills locked inside them. Lexi was doing a good job of grabbing them and sexily putting them into her bra for everyone to see. I started to smile, thinking that it really wasn't so bad being up there. I even began to grab a few bills and hand them to Lexi while I sang, pretending to be talking about whatever guy was in front of me. Meanwhile, Lexi was smiling and dancing around. She had grabbed a bottle of something from the bartender and was taking swigs of it, then threw it over the bikers' heads. Even the women in the crowd were clapping and singing along.

I knew I was an alright singer, but I was realizing that more hands than normal were popping up one by one thanks to Lexi's efforts. I was in the middle of the song when a random arm fell flat on the bar and next to my foot. The girl who had been on the stage before looked furious as she tried to lift herself up using the table in front of her.

I kept singing as I bent over and used the palm of my hand to push the girl's head back down towards the ground. I knew I looked kind of ridiculous just then, bending over and singing some of the words in a hurried voice, trying to get the girl to stop fighting it and give up. She looked ready to claw my face off but I didn't want her coming back up to steal our spotlight.

When I was sure that she was stuck under the bar, Lexi came over and grabbed my hand. I wasn't drunk enough to try dancing again, but I sure was after she handed me the bottle she had in her hand and I paused my singing to take a sip. Suddenly, Lexi and I were dancing side by side while the crowd went wild. Soon, people weren't just holding the money out, they were literally throwing it at us.

We were both scrambling to grab bills as fast as we could. It seemed like everyone in the bar had gravitated towards us. The song was about to end, when I hit the highest note. It felt so good, that for the final verse I pushed the old microphone towards Lexi's mouth.

Big mistake.

Lexi was pretty tipsy too and so hyped up from the moment that she took it and belted out the next line in the song, quite badly.

So bad that her voice cracked three times and she even got some of the lyrics wrong. Suddenly, like a splash of cold water, the crowd went silent. The instrumental kept playing but now we both stood like deer in the headlights, while everyone started to shift around.

I was about to walk off of the bar in defeat, when Lexi brought the mic back to her lips and yelled tipsily, "Who wants to see us take our tops off?!"

That got the entire crowd cheering once again and I started to sing as if nothing had happened when she handed the mic back to me. True to her word, Lexi slid her barely there tube top over her head and twirled it round in the air. I hadn't thought more money was possible, but I realized it was when hundred-dollar bills started to pop up.

I kept drinking from the glass bottle so I didn't really notice when Lexi came over and started to tug at my shirt. I was ready to help her take if off when something broke through the crowd. I felt like I hadn't seen Harvey in forever when he glared up at me. Rex had pushed through the crowd and made way for him to reach me.

"Let's not do that," he said, grabbing my legs and swinging me over his shoulder. Being swung backwards made me instantly dizzy and confused.

"Adios!" I heard Lexi say coyly and drunkenly into the microphone behind me, after what I think was her boyfriend ran up to the bar and grabbed hold of her as well.

My stomach was being pressed into Harvey's shoulder so I couldn't move. I finally got to see what was happening behind me when he turned towards the door. Most of the men were laughing now, unperturbed at us leaving now that they were seeing us carted off. Dreads and Rex were still far behind us, picking up bills from the top of the bar and on the floor. Dreads' head kept bobbing up and down from the effort.

Harvey and I were the first to get through the crowd and out the doors. With the high of such a fun experience and all of the unknown liquors I drank it was like my drunkenness was multiplied by a hundred.

This also meant that sexual Livvie was back.

I knew she was back when Harvey set me down and I started to lean over him, even though he had obviously set me down beside him.

"What was that?" he finally asked, grabbing hold of my clumsy arms that were all over him. I'm not sure if he really knew I was being frisky, since I was being so sloppy about it.

I don't know why I took that moment to ignore his comment and lean over the first and only car I saw near me. I knew it wasn't our car because the model was much newer and shinier.

"Why would you kiss me?" I said randomly. It had been the same thought on my mind since earlier that day, but only then did I have the guts to say it out loud. I was expecting a response, but Harvey only shook his shoulders and gave me a level stare. He hadn't bothered to think of an answer. I was instantly defensive.

"You throw yourself at every other girl, but when it's my turn, it doesn't mean anything!" I was leaning over the hood of the car now, getting comfortable. I shouldn't have been saying those things, but I couldn't bring myself to care.

"You should get off the car, Livvie," Harvey ordered. There was something about the way he was looking at me though that made me feel like there was lava running through my chest. I wondered for a brief second where the rest of the crew was, but didn't think of it for long.

"Am I not...sexy enough?" Oh my freaking God, even in my drunken state I couldn't believe I had said that out loud. I was too far gone to care for long. I wanted him to think of me as someone he wanted, someone he needed to have, and for some odd reason I thought that by draping myself on the hood of the car he would find me completely irresistible.

I got comfortable, while Harvey cracked an unsure smile. His expression fell off of his face when he heard the crack of my head against the windshield when my body got too heavy and my arms gave out. The force of gravity had made me fall slack towards the windshield and fall with a thud. My sexy moment was over when I felt the car's antenna break in half under my back, and the car's windshield made a horrible cracking sound.

"Holy shit, Livvie!" Harvey yelled in an alarmed tone before stalking over to me and picking me up off of the car. The rest of the group took that moment to walk out of the bar. I realized I had half of the antenna stuck to my back and ripped it off. I didn't know what to do with it, so I handed it to Harvey.

He didn't seem to know either and so he fumbled with it for a few moments before flinging it randomly in the air behind him. Too bad the car was parked there and the windshield chose that impact to be the reason why it would completely shatter.

Logically, an antenna breaking a windshield doesn't make sense. Except the thing lodged itself in between one of the cracks I had already made. All of us turned with our mouths open as the tiny shards of

* * *

glass all broke apart in midair and fell into the inside of the car. That's when the car started to beep wildly. We began to scramble, hoping that none of the scary guys from inside could hear it over the music. We needed to leave quickly, but even though Harvey was pulling me along with him, Lexi was proving to be much harder to move.

"I want a fucking slushie, Rowan!"

"Baby, I'll get you all the slushies you want, but we have to go now!"

"Promise?" Lexi was making puppy dog eyes at him and still wouldn't budge.

"I promise I'll buy you a slushie right now if you just hurry the fuck up!"

With a huff, Lexi finally complied.

"I'm gonna go get her that slushie. You know how she gets if I don't!" Rowan yelled towards Harvey as they parted ways.

"We'll be at the motel!" Harvey yelled back, already pulling me behind him. Hearing him say we'd be at the motel made me giggle like a middle-schooler.

"I know you're drunk but you have to hold on to me tight. Don't do anything you think is funny." I nodded at him as if I were a little girl and let him put the helmet over my head.

Once the helmet was over my hair my mind turned towards other more important things. Sexual Livvie wanted it bad. I made sure to wrap my arms around his torso tighter than usual while I started to daydream. It was a real-life miracle that I didn't fall off of the back of the bike.

I resolved to seduce Harvey when we hit our first red light and waited for it to turn green. Not serious, my butt.

Chapter Fifteen
I'm the Queen of Seduction

"What are you doing?" Harvey wondered once we had made it back to the motel parking lot. I knew it was just he and I until the rest of the group caught up with us. Sexual Livvie was trying to hold on to Harvey while she wobbled back and forth, trying to be alluring. Please make a note of the word *trying*.

"I'm trying to seduce you, duh," I said plainly.

I heard Harvey trying to stifle his laughter, but it eventually burst out of him.

"What's so funny?" I accused, slapping his arm and feeling hurt. We were standing face to face in the middle of the deserted parking lot. A lamppost loomed overhead, illuminating Harvey's amused features.

"Nothing!" Harvey tried to amend but he kept laughing at me. "How's it working for you so far?" he began to ask me. I knew he was just humoring me, but I was too drunk to care.

"Well, it's not going anywhere now!" I yelled, exasperated.

I watched as the humor died down from Harvey's eyes and he turned serious. I realized how close we were at the same time he did. I wanted to pull him back up to me when he took a step back and cleared his throat.

"We should get back to the room..." He trailed off uncertainly. I nodded my head dejectedly and let him lead me up the rusting metal stairs. We were slowly nearing our room number when the urge to say something hit me.

"Why did you kiss me?" There it was, the dreaded question. It just kept popping out of my lips and in my drunken state it was even harder to hold it back.

He shrugged again before speaking. "As if I knew." He mumbled it more to himself than for my benefit.

I felt him walk closer until our noses were almost touching. The warmth of his extended palm on my cheek made my heart race. I wanted him to lean down and kiss me. I wanted to mold my body against his and be able to stay there as long as I wanted.

"This doesn't mean anything." Again, more for his benefit than mine, it was sounding like.

"Mhm, okay," I mumbled until our foreheads touched. It was like time was suspended and we were stuck in endless space.

I stood on my tippy toes until my lips brushed against his. He didn't pull away, but he didn't push forward either. I was never going to get Harvey Lockwell to want me if I just threw myself at him, and in that moment it was clear. I smiled against his lips before pulling away.

The look of surprise on his face was worth the sacrifice of pulling away from him.

"You have commitment issues."

Harvey's lack of relationship initiative had just been thrown in his face and his response was nothing short of shocked.

"No," he insisted, but he was looking more uncomfortable than ever.

Harvey looked like he was about to fight the facts, but a sharp glow of headlights illuminated us both.

We watched Lexi stumble out of the car with a huge slushie cup in her hand. Rowan followed, or more like got dragged behind her, as she tried to find her way towards the stairs. Dreads came out of the car next. He had both his hands holding the huge cup, probably afraid to drop it, and his mouth sucked on the straw intently. Even Rex, who had been driving, had his own slushie. Rowan was cradling three other slushies in his arm while Lexi tugged him around. Her direction was off and she stumbled, never ripping her mouth from the straw unless it was to giggle at a missed step.

Harvey and I waited for them to reach the top of the stairs. All of us finally crowded into our small room with slushies in hand. Turns out Lexi had made sure that Harvey and I got some as well.

"I want more *Buffy*!" Lexi yelled excitedly. She'd gotten hooked on it earlier, while the guys were getting ready.

"Damn, this is good," Dreads said in response to his cold drink, finally coming up for air before bringing the straw back to his mouth. All of us agreed silently and Rowan started to play around with the DVD player until he got it going.

All of us crowded onto the mattress and sat against the headboard. We had a king-size bed this time, so although we were all touching arms we at least fit. Harvey's arm was warm and strong against mine, but I pretended not to notice.

My arm tingled where it touched his even if I was trying to be in denial. Lexi crawled towards the empty space between her boyfriend and me, before lodging herself between us. The room was in complete darkness, aside from the glow of the screen. Occasionally, you could hear someone sipping harder at their straw.

I let my head rest on Harvey's shoulder. It was automatic and for a minute I panicked, thinking maybe I was being too clingy. He hadn't professed his undying love or anything to me yet, which was the entire point of playing hard to get. My panic subsided when I felt the slight pressure of his head against mine. I could work with what I had for the time being.

We all watched Buffy kick demon butt, but no one else had a smile on their face like me. Every so often I would glance at the glowing numbers on the alarm clock and then back at the screen, until it was midnight. When the number struck twelve, I nestled a little bit deeper against Harvey.

I was pushing it a little with the midnight nuzzle, but I figured I could treat myself a little. It was my birthday after all.

The following morning was kind of a mess. Which was kind of an understatement.

Eventually all of us fell asleep sitting next to each other. When we woke up, there were old plastic cups rolling around on the bed and all of us had stiff necks from the night before.

Lexi and I brushed our teeth first and since we hadn't been the most sober the night before, we were both a little bit snappy. The guys had no chance in taking the bathroom away from us. I was in the middle of debating an outfit with Lexi when Dreads slammed the door coming back inside. The paper-thin door rattled from the force. All of us stood looking at him with confusion in our eyes. His own eyes were wide and alarmed as he flung his head from side to side, trying to find something.

Finally, when his eyes landed on Harvey, who was standing in the corner of the room, he spoke.

"I was outside having a smoke—" We all watched him take in a big huff before continuing. My heart started beating quickly just watching him. Dreads was the definition of calm, cool, and collected.

"—and I saw them! They're here! In the parking lot!"

No one had to say who he was talking about. We all pictured the black Escalade from a few days earlier. It was as if someone had set off a bomb in the room. We all scrambled around trying to pull ourselves together.

"We gotta go!" Rex yelled, jumping around and starting for the door. No one was more alarmed than he was.

"No!" we all said in unison.

Rowan decided to be the voice of reason. "We can't leave through the door. They'll fucking see us!"

He had a point. Their line of vision was directly on the door.

"Livvie and Lexi, grab the sheets and tie them up. We have to get our shit packed." That last order from Harvey was for the guys, who started to grab all of the bags and things we had brought with us.

I ran up to our king-sized bed and started to help Lexi rip the sheets from the mattress. I had no clue what we were doing, but followed Lexi's lead when she started to tie two ends together.

Eventually we had a long chain of cheap hotel sheets tied up.

Harvey grabbed hold of the fabric once we were done and Rowan wasted no time in walking towards the window and pulling it open. Fresh air hit the room with force while we watched Harvey swing the sheets out the window. Rex took that moment to grab a huge dresser in his hands and lift it over to where Harvey stood.

I watched the muscles on his arms bulge out from the effort. He set the dresser over the end of the rope and Harvey made sure that it couldn't be pulled out.

One by one we all started to make our way towards the rope. Rowan was first. I freaked out when I saw him take hold of the rope and use it to scale the side of the building. I heard him hiss, probably from the fabric burning his hands, and he let out a curse once he reached the bottom.

Lexi was next.

Surprisingly, she scaled the building with more ease than her boyfriend had. We knew we didn't have any time to waste, and so Harvey was next. Before he flipped his entire body over the edge of the window, he turned towards Dreads and Rex.

"Make sure she's next," he ordered. I didn't have to turn around to see the other guys nod. Harvey slid down the same way Rowan and Lexi did.

It was finally my turn. I wasn't ever afraid of heights but the fact that I had tied the sheets together freaked me out. What if I hadn't tied them together strongly enough? What if they ripped halfway?

I pushed my fears aside as I walked towards the window ledge. Now all I had to do was believe I had a smidge of upper-body strength and hopefully not kill myself.

Taking in a deep breath I tried to remember the day my dad had taken me rock climbing. It was before he had left, when he was still with my mom. I had been scared of the harness, thinking that it would fall apart. My dad had climbed up with me instead and with his body pressed into my back I hadn't been scared.

I tried to remember that feeling as I gripped the sheets with my sweaty palms and started my descent. I used the wall to push my legs off. I never opened my eyes and my heart almost came out of my throat when I felt someone's hands on my hips. The hands carried me the rest of the way down until my feet touched the cement.

I finally opened my eyes to find Harvey's body pressing against my back. The feeling was no longer part of my imagination. I was safe. Our things flew out the window next before the other two guys followed.

"Alright, we're going to circle them from behind. You said they were close to the main building, right, Dreads?" Harvey asked quietly.

Dreads nodded his head so that his dreads flew into the air.

We all made our way with our backs pressed against the building in a straight line. I was behind Harvey, who was first. As we turned the corner, the black SUV came into view. The truck looked even more intimidating than before, especially when I noticed movement coming from the passenger side. The windows were heavily tinted so I only saw the shifting of a dim outline.

Harvey started to run the minute he saw it and I followed suit. The car and motorcycle were behind the SUV and a good distance away, so all we had to do was make it to them before we were seen.

Harvey turned and motioned towards the car with his head. He wanted me to go with the rest of the guys and I nodded in response. I knew it would be easier that way. I was obviously the slowest runner because I found myself trailing behind everyone else.

It felt like the distance between me and Lexi, who was second to last, was growing wider by the second. I heard the rumbling of a car and wasn't sure if it was Harvey's bike or the black SUV.

I knew the sound of footsteps behind me, though.

Right when I was about to scream for help, a hand cupped my mouth. My eyes scanned the area and saw that no one was turned towards me. No one could see me being dragged away with the heels of my feet scraping against the asphalt. The large, strong hand at my mouth pressed harder when my muffled screams got slightly louder. I was losing my marbles right then and there, but no one could hear me.

I prayed for Lexi to turn, or anyone, but slowly realized that Harvey probably thought I'd reached the car and Lexi thought I was with Harvey. It was the only way they hadn't turned to see me start kicking the person holding me. I wondered when they would realize the truth.

I started hyperventilating when a blindfold went over my eyes. Someone struck me hard against the side of my head. All the while the same hand was still crushing my mouth. It never moved. The first hit hurt but didn't completely knock me out. I felt something cold hit me a second time, finally making me woozy.

I felt my body being flung onto a flat surface, probably the backseat, before growing woozier and finally giving up.

Chapter Sixteen
They See Me Rolling

"Jesus Christ," I hissed the minute I came to. My hand sprung up to grab at the side of my head, but I quickly realized that I couldn't move either of my arms. The fact that I had just been kidnapped kind of washed over me in a slow, painful drizzle. What a crappy birthday present, to be honest.

I knew I was awake but I couldn't see a freaking thing. Whatever had been tied over my face was blocking any light from passing through.

I also realized that there was a huge woolen rag stuck in my mouth. Whoever had tied it to the back of my head really knew how to gag a girl. What was the need for the gag, anyway? It wasn't like I was gonna discuss the weather when I woke up.

On that note, I started to think of several ways to get myself out of my predicament. I knew for sure that I was lying down in the backseat of the black SUV. It had been the last thing I knew before they knocked me out. My first goal was to get the gag out of my mouth.

I started to wiggle my chin all over the place, trying to loosen the hold that the fabric had on me. My lips started to move everywhere while I twisted my neck around like a crazy giraffe. Although I must have looked like a fool, I congratulated myself when the cloth started to undo and eventually fell down towards my neck. My mouth was free to complain. And I had a *lot* of complaining to do. If I was going out, it wouldn't be without a fight and a headache for them.

But first I needed to use my mouth for some smooth convincing.

I swung my tied legs over the leather seat slowly and prepared myself. I counted down before I sprang up and settled against the back of the passenger seat. My head felt like a hundred needles had punctured it the minute I sat up, but I ignored it.

"Lovely day we're having," I said pleasantly. My voice screeched in the ear of whoever was sitting in the passenger seat. My heart jumped in my chest when a guy yelled, leaving us both flabbergasted and neither with the upper hand.

"What the fuck!" the same guy yelled again. My body fell like a rag doll when the car swerved and the driver started yelling as well. This guy had a much deeper voice, leading me to believe he was older. In fact, the passenger's voice sounded really squeaky, as if he was currently going through puberty, because it tended to crack at some points. If he hadn't kidnapped me I might have found it endearing.

"Holy shit, boy! Why would you yell like a little girl at a moment like this?" the older man said. I was just trying to readjust my position when the younger boy started to speak.

"She's awake!" No duh.

"Really?" the older man asked, no doubt glancing back at me. "Just give her another bang on the head and she'll be quiet for the rest of the ride. Here." There was a pause where the driver shuffled around for something that I assumed was going to be used to assault me again. I stiffened, ready to plead my case.

"Aw," the boy whined before continuing, "Do I have to hit her again? She was hot. I doubt she'll give me a chance if I hit her again! You hit her."

I was momentarily flattered and insulted at the same time. The older man's voice was kind of familiar in a weird way. Couldn't place it, but it was a little grumpy and nasal at the same time.

"Well, I didn't get a good look at her, but I doubt she'll be worth the trouble when Big Daddy gets a hold of her."

My face contorted inside my face mask when I heard the name Big Daddy. Who the heck let people call them Big Daddy? It was so cheesy. Both of the men in front of me were talking as if I weren't perfectly conscious in the back seat.

"I can hear you guys, you know..." I trailed off in the same casual voice. I couldn't find it inside me to sound panicked, although I really was.

"Oh, right, here. Just thump her. You can be gentle, but get the job done. We gotta make this drive before sunset if we're to lead them to us." I had no doubt that the people he was referring to were my friends.

I wondered for a fleeting moment if they would come for me.

"Wait!" I yelled, hysteria finally rising up my throat. "I'll be totally quiet. I swear. I hardly ever talk. In fact, you could just let me off the side of the road here and you won't ever have to hear me again! Eh?" I was really pushing my luck with that last one.

The older man chuckled at my audacity.

"Good try, sweet, but I don't trust any of you. Especially not that hustling, good-for-nothing—"

"Dad." The younger guy spoke up after a few moments of being silent. "Do you always have to rant about Lockwell?" he continued after a lengthy sigh. My heart twisted in my chest at Harvey's name.

"The boy and his hooligan friends cheated me and your uncle out of a great deal of money! No one messes with us. He has to get what he's got coming!" The man really did sound offended. More than I thought possible for someone sketchy enough to kidnap me.

I decided to apologize for Harvey. It was only rational.

"I'm sure he didn't mean to," I said awkwardly after the man was done ranting.

The older man simply huffed. I wondered if he would try to explain, but I felt my body once again slam against another part of the SUV.

"Shit!" the older man screeched. I wanted nothing more at that moment than to have my eyesight back and to see what all the excitement was.

"What is that?" the younger guy asked in surprise. Then I really wanted to see. They could have held a piece of cake just out of reach and it would have frustrated me less. At least the guy answered his own question with another question.

"Is that a body?"

"Just what we needed at a moment like this." The man sounded preoccupied and I felt the vehicle start to move under my body once again. Jesus, was he just going to circle it and drive off? Was he gonna finish the job and just run the body over?

"It's a girl! A...hot girl," the younger guy eventually noted. I cringed for a moment, wondering if he had just called a dead girl hot. I was officially as hot as a dead girl too in that case.

"Boy, keep your head out of your pants for a second, would ya?"

"I agree," I piped up.

The boy was silent and I wondered if he was blushing. That didn't keep him from speaking up again after a few embarrassing moments.

"It's not my fault there's a hot girl in a miniskirt just sprawled on the ground," he grumbled sulkily.

"You're just going to leave her there?" I spoke up incredulously.

"Yeah, Dad! We should check it out!" The younger guy took my lead for an entirely different reason, but it worked.

The older man huffed before speaking. "Might as well, I can't get the truck around her anyway. Go move her."

"Really? You sure?" The younger guy didn't sound so excited anymore. He probably realized that he'd have to roll a dead body out of the way. No one wants to cop a feel from a corpse.

"Well, don't just sit on your ass, boy! Go do it!" the older man ordered. I heard one of the doors opening and the ticking of the car. The younger guy didn't bother to close it, which was how I heard his footsteps until they halted. I also heard his painful yell from the distance.

What was that?

"The hell?" It seemed like the older man had the same question.

My heart soared when I realized that both of them were out of the car and I was alone. My feet and hands were tied, but I prayed that the door was unlocked when I scooted over to it. I gave the door handle my back and let my hands do what they could with such limited conditions. When the door handle clicked and I was able to push the door open I couldn't have smiled wider. Whatever the distraction had been, I was forever thankful to it.

I couldn't see a thing, but I let my feet dangle out through the open space and took my first hop. I prayed that whatever the distraction had been that it was still working. Right when I was about to take another hop, I heard the sound of the opposite door being ripped open. I panicked and took another hop, except my feet lost their balance and I found myself falling straight down to the floor.

"Livvie!" I heard a voice holler from the opposite side.

"Harv—" My recognition was cut short when I fell down to the ground. Instead of simply falling I started to roll. I realized with dread that there wasn't any ground under me. I was an idiot! I had no clue if the ground that I was going to step on was smooth. My body felt like it was flying for several moments before it crashed painfully on actual rocks.

When I was little, my parents would take me to the huge park beside our old apartment complex. It was before my dad left and we moved into our current house. I loved that park and I especially loved the huge grass hill that it had. I would lie down horizontally at the very top, countdown, and then let my body roll all the way to the bottom. I would laugh the entire way down. And right when I reached the bottom, my mom would grab me in her arms and dust the dirt off my shorts. I would trudge back to the top and do it all over again just so that my dad could catch me instead the second time around.

This was not my grass hill. This was jagged rocks and thorns. I was quickly rolling down. I wondered how big the hill was when my body slammed again into the dirt and my head hit a rock.

For a second I was happy about the fabric covering my face. At least that was being minimally protected.

I realized that I was going to die. That was it. I was probably rolling off a cliff while Harvey watched my death from above. I wondered if he would miss me.

I would miss him.

Well, I would be dead, but I could still miss him, right?

I hit another rock with my cheek and cried out. I felt myself floating in the air, until suddenly, I stopped. Something hard and strong wrapped around my stomach and all of the air escaped me. I tried breathing, but for a second I couldn't.

Someone grunted and then my body rolled backwards over another spiky rock.

"Why would you roll off a fucking cliff?" Harvey's voice sounded strained and angry.

"It," I huffed, trying to regain my breath. I was still lying on a rock with what I assumed was Harvey's arm around me. "Looked like fun at the time."

I have no clue why I took that moment to be a smart butt.

"Remind me to laugh at that later," Harvey said in the same tight voice.

"Yep," I replied, closing my eyes and praying that he wouldn't let me go.

Slowly, I felt my body being lifted as if it were on a crane. I still couldn't see, but I was actually thankful because I would have been freaking out more if I could.

"What happened?" someone yelled from above us. It sounded like Rowan and my heart soared at hearing his voice. They had actually come to get me!

"Livvie rolled down the side and I had to go get her. Gimme a hand, yeah?" Harvey asked. I heard rocks rolling and the sound of hesitant footsteps coming closer. I realized the strain Harvey was under when someone grabbed hold of my legs and distributed my weight.

"We just have to get to the top now," Harvey said. His voice sounded less forced, but he still sounded winded.

"Rex and Lexi are pounding the shit out of those guys, but I think they'll be down soon," Rowan said, helping Harvey carry me. Everything hurt, but for a moment I wondered how hard Lexi was kicking butt. I was proud of her, even though I felt like I was ready to fall apart.

Eventually I knew when we reached stable ground because my world tilted to a certain angle, and even though everything spun, I could feel a flat surface under me. Several footsteps came towards us. Everyone was standing over me when Harvey finally pulled the fabric that had been covering my face.

My heart froze when I took in everyone's expressions of horror, concern, and pity.

"Ooooooh," all of them kind of said in unison, pulling away at the same time to get a better look at me.

"I wouldn't look half as good as you do if I'd fallen off a cliff," Lexi tried to lie through her teeth.

I wondered how messed up my face was, before turning towards the hill behind me. I finally found the exact place where I had rolled off to and my eyes bulged out when I realized I couldn't see the bottom. I dragged my body to the edge of the road and peered down, only to see several feet and a small, smooth step, then an endless pit of desert and darkness. There was a piece of purple fabric from my shirt stuck to some sort of branch thing right before the small step led towards the abyss. I realized I was crying when I found myself having trouble speaking.

"I almost died," I said in shock. There was no emotion in my voice, despite the tears.

Someone moaned from far away and before anyone could say anything to me, Lexi yelled, "Ready for round two, bitch?"

I turned to watch her stalk off towards where the moan came from and remembered my two abductors. Rex and Rowan followed her, probably for backup.

I was still crying and staring at some random space on the gravel when I saw Harvey's shoes come into view. He knelt right in front of me before his arms wrapped around my shoulders. I didn't expect anyone to get close to me, but I instantly melted into him and cried harder. I cried because my injuries hurt, but mostly because of how scared I was. It hit me that I had been kidnapped by probably crazy men and almost fallen off a cliff to my death. Talk about scary.

All of the fear and shock was making me cry into Harvey's flannel shirt.

"Shit," I heard him whisper from beside my ear. His head was resting on the crook of my neck and mine on his. I was so relieved to have his strong arms around me.

"Shit," he repeated.

"This is the worst birthday ever!" I wailed after coming up for air.

Harvey looked at me with pure astonishment.

"You're not supposed to almost die on your birthday. You're supposed to get older!"

I wailed some more, clinging to his shirt.

"Livvie." Harvey poked my shoulder, gently, but it still hurt a little.

"What?" I pouted with tears still streaking my face.

"Happy birthday." He gave me a small grin.

Chapter Seventeen
Twitch if You Like Me

Harvey insisted in carrying me back to the Corolla. It was gallant of him, but I think he was really just making sure I was getting in this time. My abductors were sprawled unconscious on the ground when I glanced over.

My eyes were kind of foggy from the tears, but I could still make out both of their bodies. No doubt, Lexi could be brutal when she wanted to be. I wondered if she could teach me a few things, since using cliffs as escape routes was my current defense mechanism. The black SUV had been turned off, but its doors were wide open. It looked smaller then, and lonely.

"Dude, should we...?" Rowan called for Harvey's attention with what I assumed were the SUV's keys in his hands.

Why yes, why didn't we steal the only vehicle belonging to the people who tried to kidnap and kill us?

"Fuck no, we owe them enough as it is. Now including those two." Harvey gestured at the two unconscious men on the ground.

I assumed Big Daddy would not be pleased. Just thinking of him as Big Daddy made me laugh. The image of the words "Big Daddy" printed on a driver's license next to a huge faceless man popped into my head. I couldn't help the giggle that escaped my lips. Oh no, something told me I was entering the hysterical stage from my trauma.

I reveled in the feel of Harvey's arms around me. He had noted my awkward giggling, but seemed too preoccupied with his thoughts. I wanted to be like "I'm okay! Look, I'm just going insane now. It's all good!" But I didn't think he needed to hear it right then.

After few minutes passed, I started to get over my initial shock. So I fell off a cliff, no big deal. I was sure plenty of people expected me to, or at least wouldn't be surprised that I toppled off.

Harvey eventually lowered me down onto the backseat of the car next to Lexi. I was ready to just sprawl on the seat and lie there for the next ten years.

I wondered what my face looked like. Everyone had already climbed into the car, and Harvey had left for his bike. I glanced over to see Lexi redoing her makeup. The girl kicked butt and then looked like a model right after.

Before the car started I stretched up to catch my reflection in the rearview mirror. My mouth dropped right when the car shot forward.

My face was messed up. Maybe I was exaggerating, but there were lots of scratches on my face and especially my neck. All of my features were red and blotchy and my hair resembled a bird's nest. I still had the bruise from when I ran into the pole. With everything combined, I looked like a mess. At least I fell asleep.

By the time I opened my eyes we had pulled onto a dirt path. I could see next to nothing except for the infrequent objects that the headlights would illuminate. There was a wooden sign we passed, but I couldn't read it fast enough. A tree stump came into view for a few seconds right before Rowan swerved around it.

"Where are we?" I wondered out loud.

"Campground," Rex answered from the passenger seat.

"Are we seriously going to sleep here?" Lexi whined from beside me.

"Babe, think of it as camping. The night sky, a freshly lit joint..." Rowan's voice turned smooth and rhythmic.

Lexi picked up where he left off in a mocking tone. "The cold hard ground under our backs, a shitload of bugs, and if we're lucky maybe some random animal crap we can step on."

"Buzzkill," Dreads said.

"More like bug kill, there's already a mosquito in here! Ew!" Lexi was practically having a panic attack. She started swatting violently into the open air. I reminded her that the car windows weren't even open, to which she snorted.

"You can beat up random men, but you can't handle camping?" I wondered incredulously.

"I've been beating off foster dads and brothers for years, but camping is my kryptonite. It's the root of all hell." No one commented on that first part, so I figured everyone knew already. I hadn't known that Lexi was a foster kid.

"Are you still living with people like that?"

"Only until I turn eighteen, which is in a few months. It's no big deal. It's almost over." Her response was dismissive, but she was trying really hard to make it sound that way.

"Do they know you're gone?" I'd never really given much thought to our disappearance in that way. Everyone had to have parents, but none of them had said anything.

"Probably not. As long as the checks keep coming, they don't really care." Again, she shrugged like it was no big deal, but I could tell that it kind of was.

"We're here!" Dreads screamed like a little boy. The car came to a halt and we all scrambled out, some more excited than others. I heard the roar of Harvey's motorcycle stopping directly behind us.

"So, what now?" Rowan asked no one in particular. I glanced around and saw that the little light that the lampposts provided showed a few camping tents and even some RVs.

We were the ones who were clearly unprepared.

"Well, I don't know, Rowan. Why don't you tell us? Huh, ranger?" Lexi's tone was sarcastic to the max.

Before Rowan provided a response, my voice broke through the couple's tension.

"Harvey was a Boy Scou—"

"Livvie, no!" Harvey practically shouted.

"Harv was a Boy Scout? Holy shit!" Rowan exclaimed. Dreads couldn't believe it either.

Rex approached just in time to hear the little tidbit I provided before breaking down in a fit of laughter. Rowan and Dreads quickly followed. If I wasn't mistaken, I would have said that Harvey was turning red under the lamppost above him. It was nighttime though, so what did I know?

"Fuck you guys," Harvey said before walking away. He was smiling a bit when I made eye contact with him so I took it as a good sign.

At one point Harvey took the reins and started telling the guys what to do. Our area was pretty big but it was getting incredibly cold out. Lexi didn't stop complaining and even thought it was hilarious how much she was harassing Rowan. I eventually wanted to start complaining with her. There was something about hearing Harvey take control and tell everyone what to do that was insanely attractive, though.

I had it bad. All I needed was to start writing him haikus on public bathroom stalls.

After what felt like an eternity, the guys got a fire going. I'd napped for most of the ride, so I wasn't exactly tired. An old musky blanket was brought out from the depths of the car. It kind of smelled bad, but we laid it out on the dirt ground anyway. The ends were frayed and it scratched my skin. I was more worried about the blanket and wherever it had been than our surroundings. We all lay down unceremoniously. It had been a long day for all of us, but especially me. I could feel my body pulsing from everything it had been through, even though I still had some leftover adrenaline. Several minutes passed and I wondered who'd fallen asleep. I knew it obviously wasn't Lexi because her voice slit through the silence.

"Fuck this, I'm sleeping in the car."

I propped my head up to watch her stand and wring her hair out.

"Uh, might as well follow her. You all know how she gets." Even though Rowan had a point it honestly sounded like he was looking for an excuse to get his butt back into the car, too.

"There's a thorn in my ass," Rex complained before rising as well and following them.

Someone coughed, which sounded a lot like Dreads. It wasn't long before Rowan came through with that joint he had talked about and Dreads followed them into the car several feet away.

• • •

And then there were two. I wondered if it was planned. I mean, what were the odds of Harvey and me being the last ones?

Was he waiting for me to say something?

I focused my attention on the night sky that was hovering right above us. The stars were vibrant but tiny against the dark blue. I knew Harvey was looking at them too.

"Stars are cool. I want a t-shirt made out of stars," I declared.

"You sound higher than Dreads right now." Harvey let out one of those quiet laughs that consisted of a short gust of air. He had so many different laughs. The kind where he sounded like a little kid who just found something so funny, the sexy chuckle he did when he thought something was ridiculous but cute, and then the subtle quiet laugh he did when things got serious but there was something funny anyway.

I wanted Harvey Lockwell so bad, but I wasn't sure he wanted me.

"Sorry I overreacted about the cliff thing." It hadn't felt like overreaction, but maybe it was.

"You didn't overreact, Livvie. I didn't even ask you if you were alright. I should be sorry." His voice sounded gruff then.

"It's no big deal."

"Yeah, it is, but you're just too nice," Harvey said.

"I am not! I'm just...just..." I had no idea how to describe myself without saying the obvious, that I was kind of vanilla. Boring and basically flavorless.

"Good? Innocent?" I caught Harvey shaking his head, like he couldn't believe that I didn't want to accept it. I thought of all the things I had done since embarking on such a crazy trip with him. He was wrong. I had done things that I probably never would have done in a million years.

"I. Am. Not!" I tried to argue.

Harvey sat up at the same time I did and brought his body closer to mine. I tried not to feel affected by how close he was but I loved it. I loved when he got into a conversation and forgot all about personal space. Heck, I loved when he forgot about personal space in general.

"Did you know that every time you cuss or say something dirty your eye twitches?"

Say something dirty? I tried to remember ever telling him something racy when I was drunk, but I honestly couldn't remember. Maybe sexual Livvie got way more excited than I gave her credit for.

"That's not true. How would you even notice that?" I fired the words at him in the hopes of getting my point across by muddling the conversation.

"Say *shit*, then," he challenged.

"Shit," I said without hesitating, but was shocked when I felt my right eyelid closing without me wanting it to. I said the word again when I realized this, and then again when I recognized with dread that he was right. Plus, my voice sounded so weird. The word didn't come out smoothly at all, unlike Lexi or the rest of the guys, who cussed like they owned it.

"Livvie, you're practically a saint!" Harvey exclaimed, jumping up and down.

"That one was a fluke! I have to blink sometime and it just happens when I speak. I'm not a saint!"

"Prove it, then." His entire tone changed from amused to defiant. I could see the outline of his lips in a smirk. I wasn't about to let him think I was the same girl from before, because that girl didn't get Harvey Lockwell's attention.

"Is there a lake here?" I tried to make my tone casual.

"Yeah, I saw one up north when we were gathering wood. Why?"

"Up north? Harvey, you're such a Boy Scout," I claimed, ignoring his question and gripping the bottom of my shirt.

"Fuck no!" Harvey replied to my taunt. He was completely silent when I pulled my shirt off. "What are you doing?" His tone was intentionally bland.

"Less clothes and more lake, come on!" I ordered, already working on the zipper of my jeans.

I heard Harvey calling for me but I started to where I hoped was north. I nearly had a heart attack when his lips brushed the side of my face.

"North's this way, dummy," He said before grabbing my hand and pulling me in the opposite direction. A full round of chills came over me from the lack of clothing and the way his breath graced my skin.

The muscles on his back moved up and down, I noticed as he led the way. The same tattoo I had noticed the first time he was shirtless around me caught my attention.

What was it with boys and tattoos? They were great. I supported them one hundred percent.

We reached a small lake after half running a small distance. The water was almost black, but you could see the moon reflected on top of it prettily. I was freezing my butt off, but I slipped out of my pants anyway before I stood in my underwear. I watched Harvey start on the zipper of his pants before calling out to him.

"Need some help?" I asked sweetly. It was my birthday. Playing hard to get would have to wait another day, when I wasn't trying to prove a point.

Harvey laughed before taunting me. "You couldn't handle it."

I really couldn't, though, but I wanted to.

I didn't wait for him. I ran straight into the water. My bones felt like they were freezing but the relief the water gave me was worth it. For the first few minutes I was alive. I swam around the water and tried not to think about whatever was happening underneath my feet.

The water suddenly quivered as Harvey dived in. I shook some of it off of my face and waited for him to rise up. After a long moment, I looked back towards the ground to see if I had imagined him dive, right before feeling his hands run up my thighs and eventually grab onto my hips. My entire body was dunked underwater and for a moment I didn't see anything. Eventually, when we rose back up I splashed him in the face for pulling me under.

I started to swim backwards, away from him, with a laugh. He stayed put and watched me swim several feet away before turning upright. My hands rose up to my bra and trying not to think about it too hard, I unhooked the clips before grabbing the wet fabric and flinging it towards the ground.

Harvey's mouth dropped open with the slightest bit of confusion. His hair was slicking to his face. I didn't bother to look very long before diving back underwater and swimming towards him. When I was sure he was right in front of me, I took in a long breath before sliding my body right against his. My hands ended up around his shoulders by the time my head made it out of the water.

He wasted no time in bringing his lips to mine, which was exactly what I wanted. I relished the feel of him under my fingers, strong and smooth. Everywhere I touched was new, like an exploration, even the places I had touched before. I wrapped my legs around his unconsciously. His lips on mine were soft as always, but they moved with purpose. I felt the tip of his tongue right along my bottom lip and gasped. My gasp shook both our bodies and we rocked back and forth in the water for a bit. The water didn't even feel cold anymore. The contact of both our chests pressed together sent a tingle right towards the pit of my stomach.

I wasn't really sure what we were supposed to mean to each other right then. I knew that it was likely he would push me away soon, but I wanted to feel loved right then, even if it was the temporary kind.

"Saint, my ass," I said in between kisses.

I felt his smile on my lips before his breath tickled my face.

"Whatever, you still twitched."

He was right.

Chapter Eighteen
I Do. I Really Do.

We didn't stay too long in the lake. Eventually the water turned super cold. We were both laughing and shivering when we crawled out. Harvey grabbed hold of my hand to pull me out. I tried not to think about how perfectly his hand held mine and the shocks it sent up my arm.

We picked up several discarded pieces of clothing as we made our way back and it wasn't until we were in front of the Corolla that I realized that I had no idea where my bra was. Thankfully, it was still dark and I found my shirt before we got back under the lights. My confidence only went so far and I still couldn't believe what I had done. Even though we were dressed, our bodies were still dripping from our dip into the lake.

We ended up sprawled over the ratty old blanket from earlier with the sky above us. Harvey held my hand and played with my fingers without speaking. For a moment I closed my eyes and wondered if that was what being with someone was like. Just two people reveling in being able to feel each other's existence.

I, Livvie, was lying side by side with Harvey Lockwell in complete contentment.

"Who left you?"

Harvey's voice broke through my happy thoughts and for a moment I didn't know how to answer.

"What do you mean?" I asked in a hushed voice similar to his.

"You said earlier that you were used to being left behind," he prompted me, while his fingers wove in between and around mine.

I wasn't going to tell him. I just didn't want to ruin things with a retelling of my crappy life story, but before I knew it the words were tumbling out. I told him about my dad, how he left me when I little, and how much I missed him. I even told him about Brian and how I wished he was more like my little brother than my own kid. I spilled everything about Nick and how he was utterly amazing as a best friend. As I was touching the topic of Nick, I realized how guilty I actually felt about leaving him to take care of Brian and for being such a lame friend. I had essentially ditched my best friend back home, granted for an amazing adventure, but still.

Harvey stayed moderately silent during the whole thing, the only contact between us still being our hands. Occasionally he made some noise of disapproval or a quiet chuckle depending on whatever I was telling him.

I felt him stiffen beside me when the topic of Jim the Creep came up. I hadn't wanted to discuss him since it was embarrassing and awkward, but once I started I couldn't help myself.

As my retelling of Jim's proposal carried on, Harvey's hand started squeezing mine tightly. At first I thought it was for moral support, but as the story went on the grip got tighter and tighter.

"Uh, Harvey?" I paused midstory.

"Huh?" he asked with a voice equally tight.

"You're kind of killing my hand," I let him know in an apologetic tone even though he was the one squeezing the life out of my fingers.

I felt him fumble, releasing me, before he mumbled an apology and urged me on. I felt transparent after telling him everything.

I secretly loved that he didn't comment or criticize any of the things I told him, but only listened. Only at the end of it all did he say something.

"It used to piss me off that you tried to be so perfect." We had ended up facing each other on our sides. His nose lightly brushed mine as he spoke and it took me a moment to think about what he had said.

"But," he continued, "I didn't know you then."

I stayed silent, half-amazed that Harvey had given me a second thought before we ended up running away. Sure, I pissed him off, but that meant that he knew I existed at least. Suddenly, a real wolf's howl echoed through the air, rattling us both. I knew we were both thinking of Bob and my wolf whisperer skills.

I followed him into the car after a few minutes. The smell of weed wafted out of the windows and tickled my nose. I was realizing that I didn't like the smell much.

Harvey and I crawled into the back seat, where Lexi and her boyfriend cuddled together. There was just enough room for one person, so Harvey surprised me when he pulled me up on his lap and shut the door. The rest of the guys were fast asleep. I didn't think about what Harvey and I were supposed to be at the moment and simply focused on snuggling close. I breathed in Harvey's scent from the water and hid my head in the crook of his neck. It was the last thing I did before I fell asleep instantly.

Everyone stretched their limbs out the following morning. Sleeping in a car was hardly the most comfortable thing on the planet, but at least it made for some funny chemistry between Lexi and Rowan. Lexi's grudge against the outdoors was as strong as ever. The guys gave each other amused looks, except for Rowan, who was taking all her bickering with a frown.

Eventually we picked up our clothes from the trunk of the car. Even my underwear smelled like weed, I realized when the smell wafted up to my nose. Lexi and I separated from the rest of the group when we turned into the women's showers. I tried not to think about how dirty showers that belonged to a campsite could be.

They were clean enough, although the yellow hue of the tiles kind of freaked me out. I showered quickly before donning a pair of skinny jeans and a lacy peplum top that Lexi had picked out for me. She was already doing her makeup in front of one of the mirrors when I walked out.

I was in the middle of making my hair into a messy bun when I noticed the huge smirk on Lexi's face as she eyed me.

"What?" I wondered out loud, trying not to flinch under her catlike examination.

"If I wasn't already going to lend you my foundation for the bruises on your face, I would have for *that*."

I followed Lexi's line of vision all the way to the base of my throat before letting my face heat up.

"That's not—"

Lexi's snickering made me pause. "Girl, own it! Well, I mean, cover it up, but own up to it," Lexi said with another smirk as she eyed the enormous hickey on my throat.

"I guess?" I tried to speak, my eyes rounding at the sight of it.

"Ha! I knew you'd be all over each other."

"Wait, did you guys plan last night?" I asked, my horror rising. Was this a campaign? A unified effort? A part of me was gracious, but mostly mortified if that was indeed the case.

"Maaaaaaaybe," Lexi singsonged, still working on her makeup.

"That's...that's..." I had no words.

* * *

"Livvie, seriously, don't look so freaked out. That's what friends are for."

Even my friends were trying to get me a boyfriend.

"Please, we're doing Harv a favor. It's about time he stopped being such a slut," she finished with a slight smile. I smiled back and continued to work on my hair.

"I was gonna wait until after, but I guess now will work." Lexi spoke, taking out a cupcake wrapped in plastic. The kind you get from a vending machine.

"Harvey mentioned it was your birthday yesterday. So—" Lexi unwrapped the chocolate pastry before taking out a lighter from her makeup bag and stabbing it into the cake.

"Happy birthday." She smiled, flicking the lighter on and holding it up to my face.

I wanted to cry. The gesture was so nice and unexpected. I was going to put the lighter off with my tears if she didn't stop soon. With a wobbly smile I blew out the fire and watched her take the lighter out. She was about to hand me the cupcake, but I ended up crushing her in a quick awkward hug.

"Thank you," I said, finally taking the chocolate cupcake from her.

"No problem, Livvie-cakes." Lexi smiled.

Lexi finished her makeup and decided to apply her skills to my face next. I tried not to flinch as she did all sorts of things to my face. Some of it hurt, since my bruises were still fresh, but anything in exchange for having them disappear a bit. Lexi was in the middle of putting some powder on my face, which was bringing on a sneeze from me, when she paused and looked directly at me.

"Livvie?"

"Huh?" I asked, wiggling my nose under the brush. My attention was mostly caught up on not shooting a snot rocket on her.

"Thank you," she said, still brushing over my face.

"For what?" I asked, breathing in deeply and trying to keep everything in.

"For being a friend. Most people at school usually think I'm a slut or a whore, even though I've been going out with Rowan since like seventh grade. Everybody's judgmental as hell."

"Seventh grade?" I asked, my eyebrows shooting up to my hairline.

Lexi laughed and moved a bit further away to grab something else from her makeup bag.

"Yeah, he used to be short and a little chunky, but he was the nicest guy back then. Still is." The way Lexi said it made my heart squeeze tight. I couldn't picture tall, lean, and tattooed Rowan as what Lexi said, but it had to be true.

"That's amazing," I said in wonder. I really couldn't picture Lexi or Rowan with anyone else but each other.

"Yeah, Lexi agreed before smiling down at me and finishing up.

I stole a quick glance at my face before we walked out of the bathroom and was relieved to see it half-presentable. The guys were huddled in a group when we approached them, except for Rowan, who still hadn't showed up.

We were just about to reach them when a car pulled up with the word *Sheriff* painted on the sides. Lexi pulled me back behind a tree trunk, while a tall man in sheriff's attire walked out. The top of his head was bald, kind of like Jim the Creep's, while his left hand rested neatly on the gun hoisted by his side. He scrutinized the guys.

"Morning, boys," he greeted, sizing everyone up. My breaths started to come out in quick, uneven spurts, while Lexi gripped my arm tightly.

I heard Harvey murmur a hello. The sheriff wasted no time in asking for identification.

"Maybe he's looking for me? I'm the only one still underage," Lexi whispered from somewhere behind me. It was true—I was officially considered an adult as of the day before. Regardless, my heart froze and for a second I wondered if the sheriff was looking for me. Maybe my mom had cared enough to send someone looking for me, even though I desperately wished she hadn't.

The sheriff looked over the plastic cards with a tight-lipped expression. As he was handing the cards back he spoke.

"We received a few complaints about a certain smell coming from you all. Do you have anything that you would like to tell me about?"

I nearly stopped breathing. I listened just long enough to hear Rex make a crack about the showering facilities. I wanted to listen to Harvey's response, but someone had pulled me backwards. When I turned I caught sight of both Lexi and Rowan. Their expressions of horror probably mirrored my own. Before I knew what was happening, Rowan was bringing his finger up to his lips and dodging ahead of me towards the car.

"I'm going to need to search your vehicle—" I heard the sheriff when I turned back. My eyes darted towards the trunk of the car and I couldn't believe what I was seeing for the first few moments.

Rowan was in the middle of crouching beside the trunk of the car and pulling out all of the drugs that the sheriff was obviously on the prowl for. Lexi and I couldn't do anything, just watch as the sheriff began to circle the car.

It could have been three seconds between the time that Rowan got the last plastic baggie and the sheriff finally made it to the back.

Suddenly, I found my hands full of the stuff I hated to smell so much and lugging it behind Lexi. All three of us were carrying the packages in our hands and scrambling in different directions.

"What do we do?" I hissed though my teeth in a low tone. I felt like I was about to have a heart attack. Only a few trees concealed us from the rest of the action.

"Just...just..." I could see Lexi trying to think of something to say.

"Bury it!" Rowan whispered with excitement. I stood there with my mouth half-open, watching him fall to his knees and start digging a hole with his fingers. I turned to watch Lexi doing the same, before following suit. The slimy dirt slid under my fingernails as I pulled at it frantically. At least Rowan had a decent-sized hole in the works when I took a glance at him. Time felt like it was slipping away. We all tried to be quiet as we covered the plastic baggies with dirt and rocks. We weren't even bothering with concealing everything too well, since most of our hands were shaking.

I started to relax just a fraction when I managed to get the bags I had been handed partially concealed. I stood up a little higher, because my legs were cramping up, which turned out to be the worst mistake ever. We all heard the car door bang shut, before the sheriff's voice shot right at me.

"Hey! What are you kids doing back there?" The sheriff's tone made me want to start crying the minute I felt it coming in my direction.

All three of us slowly stood up from behind the trees with equally terrified looks on our faces. Rowan was first to walk out from behind the trees, with Lexi second and me last. My head was ducked down, because I didn't trust myself to meet the tall man's eyes.

"Care to explain what the three of you were doing, hiding behind those trees?" The sheriff's tone was stern. Everything was quiet, except for the sound of my heavy breathing. I could feel Harvey's eyes on me, telling me to relax. It was weird, but I even knew the feel of his eyes on me.

"Yeah, I was giving my girlfriend her ring."

What? My head sprang up in confusion, mirroring the sheriff's. I watched Rowan run a hand through his hair and look at Lexi. I didn't realize my mouth had dropped open until some sort of insect started buzzing dangerously close and Harvey came over to bring my chin up. Lexi had her back to me, so I couldn't gauge her expression. It couldn't possibly have been what I was thinking, but it was.

Rowan cleared his throat. "I was gonna give this to you after...all this shit happened. I know we aren't getting married, yet, but I want you to know that there's no one else I want. You've always been the girl for me."

Everyone was quiet, captured by the moment.

Time froze as Rowan fumbled to grab something from out of his jeans pocket. It was the most adorable thing, how he was nervous and just a little clumsy. We all realized it was a ring box when he propped it open and took out the small silver ring. Lexi let out some sort of gasp before bringing her shaky hand out to him. I didn't even notice the hot tears that had pooled in my eyes until it was too late and I was crying.

"Holy shit, Rowan!" Lexi squealed and after letting him slide the ring onto her finger she jumped into his arms. It was the craziest, most unexpected thing that could have happened. Even the grumpy sheriff was trying not to smile when I looked over.

I could hardly contain my happiness for her, so when she turned around to look at me we both started yelling and jumping up and down like crazy. The sheriff must have taken that as his cue to leave, because after his short goodbye the car's motor started rumbling away. My head was spinning from the anxiety and then the excitement when Harvey started to lead me away with a smile and Lexi and the rest of the guys made their way to the car.

"Why are you crying?" Harvey asked, half smiling and half looking concerned.

"I don't know, it was just so..." I had no words for it so I burst out with a laugh. I was still smiling when I wrapped my arms around Harvey's waist and rested my head on his back.

"Where are we going next?" I asked, before the whirr of the motorcycle drowned me out.

"Jesse's," Harvey said.

I wondered what that meant, but figured when we got there I would know.

Chapter Nineteen
I Could Really Use an Eye Exam

Everything was great until it hit me that I needed a bathroom break. My mind raced back to the time when Harvey commented on my pad boobs. We were definitely past the point where he thought I stuffed my bra.

We had been on the road for the last six hours and the sun was just hiding away, when I took the opportunity after stopping at a red light to poke the back of Harvey's shoulder.

"Can we stop somewhere?" I yelled above the loud purr of the engines around us. Harvey turned towards me at the same moment that a car drove up to the right side of us. It was filled with overly muscled frat boys. Their obnoxiously loud music was blaring out of the open car windows, while their bucket hats bobbed up and down to the beat. Any other moment I would have freaked out at having so many guys staring at me, but my arms were wrapped around Harvey, so it didn't really matter.

I was in the middle of ignoring them and yelling at Harvey that I had really had to pee, when the main driver yelled something towards me.

"Can I get your number?"

It just so happened that I yelled the word pee at the same time that he finished saying number. My entire face froze in an embarrassed expression, before my neck mechanically turned towards the car in horror. The rest of the guys were hooting and laughing.

"Fuck off," Harvey yelled towards them before shooting them his middle finger. I was equal parts embarrassed and actually kind of flattered. By that time the light had turned green we shot forward. I wondered when we would be stopping, because I wasn't sure if it had to do with the day's excitement, but I felt right on the verge of having to explain another very embarrassing moment in my life to my future grandchildren.

Thank God that Harvey took the next right turn into a gas station. I jumped right off the bike, even before he stopped it completely. I didn't wait for anyone, before I nearly sprinted over to the main entrance. Somewhere behind me I heard the wheels of the Corolla coming to a halt.

I saw the majestic glow of the women's bathroom sign up ahead, before my euphoria was shattered by a thick Russian accent.

"Bathroom for customers only," the voice said from behind me. I wondered if he was kidding me, but the stern expression on the little man's face told me otherwise. His head poked up just a few inches from the checkout counter. I could see the top of his balding head softly glowing under the lighting. My eyes bulged out while I walked around in circles trying to find something to buy. I could see myself peeing all over the floor, as I scrambled around the place. Finally, I grabbed the first thing I could and speed walked to the cashier. I didn't make eye contact with him. I was too busy trying not to think about flowing rivers and waterfalls.

"Four ninety-five," he spat out.

"Five dollars? For that little thing?" I wasn't really sure what I was buying, but from the tiny size of it when I'd held it, I doubted it was worth five dollars. I couldn't even see it anymore, since the little man had pushed it deep into a plastic bag and was watching me with narrowed eyes.

"Fine! Sorry," I mumbled, reaching deep into my jeans pockets and hoping I had enough. I thanked the gods when I managed to bring up four one-dollar bills and enough quarters to complete the amount. The man took his time ripping the receipt from the machine and handing me my plastic bag. He even had the gall to sarcastically wish me a nice day as I ran towards the bathroom.

Once inside I nearly threw the plastic bag inside a stall. I whipped my entire body to scan the walls of the bathroom. I realized that there was another woman in there with me, but she was busy applying some sort of makeup, so she didn't bother to look at me.

I thanked the lord profusely once I was inside the cubicle. Peeing was a regular function for some people, but to me, it was a holy experience just then.

I walked out from the stall with the plastic bag hanging from my wrist and quickly washed my hands. I finished doing what I was doing at the same moment the woman beside me finished applying her makeup.

"Cute shirt," she acknowledged with a smile.

We both walked out of the bathroom, before the lady started making small talk. She asked if I was from around there, to which I answered no. Eventually, as we passed the little man, the woman beside me winked at him and waved. I watched her acrylic fingers dance in the air before I walked outside with her. The lady was probably twice his size, but the expression on the little man's face was completely ecstatic. I bet he hadn't made her buy anything for using the bathroom.

I had to say my goodbye to the woman when I spotted Lexi and the rest of the guys standing off towards the back of the lot. I was surprised when she leaned over to hug me. I hugged her back a little bit dazedly.

"You take care now," the woman said sternly before walking off towards the corner of the building. I nodded my head at her retreating back before walking over to Harvey and the rest of the gang.

Everyone was dead silent when I finally got there, which made me feel instantly apprehensive.

"What?" I said at Lexi's confused expression and Rex's taunting one.

"Did you just hug a hooker?" Harvey asked incredulously.

"You did realize she was a tranny, right?" Rowan added. My mouth popped open right before I quickly turned back towards the gas station in time to hear the lady ask a truck driver if he was looking for a good time. It finally dawned on me that the woman had spoken in a very deep voice. Like, insanely deep.

"But, she was very nice," I said slowly. I don't know why I was so surprised that a tranny hooker had been so pleasant.

"Hookers are very nice," Rex replied, bringing a corner of his lips up into a smirk and nodding his head, as if he were imparting incredibly useful knowledge.

"Ew!" Lexi said, before slapping Rex in the stomach with the back of her hand. Rex acted mortally wounded, but quickly recovered.

Harvey shook his head at me and grinned. Everyone dispersed towards the car, but I followed closely behind Harvey, still trying to wrap my head around the fact that I had hugged a hooker like it was no biggie.

We were back on the road when I realized that I still had the plastic bag wrapped around my wrist. I had no place to put it now that we were moving, so I

focused on setting it more securely on my lap instead
of floating in the air.

For some reason, I expected the ride to take a
lot longer, but we started to wind our way around the
streets of a neighborhood. The houses weren't very
big, but at least the place was decent. We all came to a
stop in front of a small one-story brick house. A
Mustang was sitting outside in the driveway.

"Is this it?" I asked once Harvey and I stood on
the grassy spot before the sidewalk. Harvey turned
towards me and nodded. He looked kind of troubled,
like whatever we would find inside the house was
something he didn't want to face. The rest of the guys,
including Lexi, walked over to us and waited for
Harvey to lead the way.

I was behind Harvey when he rang the
doorbell. The light beside the front door turned on
and the lock clicked. I don't know why I felt like
holding my breath, but I did.

Someone pulled the door open. I blinked a few
times in the awkward silence that ensued. It didn't
matter that the guy looked half-pissed, he was still the
single most attractive guy I had ever seen in my life. I
wondered in shock if I was on the verge of literally
drooling when he angled his stare towards me for a
fraction of a second. It hit me that he looked like
someone I knew, and then I realized that he looked
like a, frankly, better version of Harvey. He had the
same brown eyes as Harvey, but a darker five-o'clock
shadow. Some of his tattoos peeked out the sleeves of
his t-shirt. I was in awe.

"Harvey." He sounded kind of pissed. Not the best greeting in the world.

"Jesse," Harvey replied in the same tone, albeit a bit less hostile.

Jesse didn't say anything else before bringing the door open just an inch more and walking inside. Harvey started to follow, which was our cue to do the same. I walked slowly enough to step alongside Lexi.

"I know I'm practically engaged and all, but Jesse Lockwell can get it," she whispered to me with a sigh. I sighed in response as we both watched the back of Jesse's head.

We walked into a dimly lit living room and stopped there. There was a couch, a lamp, a small TV, and nothing else. I could see the entrance to a small kitchen to my right and a hallway to my left.

A very pregnant girl walked out of the kitchen with a jar of peanut butter in one hand and a spoon in the other. She looked pissed, as well as very tired. I wondered how late at night it was.

For a second I was disappointed because Harvey's brother was having a baby. It wasn't like *I* wanted to have his baby or anything. But it was always kind of sad when a really attractive guy ended up being taken.

For all of his good looks, Jesse didn't really give off good vibes. In fact, he looked like a person who rarely smiled.

The girl didn't spare us another glance before rolling her eyes and walking down the hall. Jesse stared at his girlfriend without a clear expression, but it definitely wasn't a look of someone in love.

Jesse's phone rang just then. We all watched him pick up the call.

"Yeah, I got them right here," he said after listening to the other side for a few minutes. "I'll make sure they go tomorrow. You have my word," he said before hanging up the call.

We all watched him sigh and run a hand through his hair before looking over at us.

"Do you realize how much shit you're in?" he addressed Harvey, completely ignoring us.

"Yeah, I know. Things just got out of hand."

Jesse didn't look very impressed with Harvey's response. "I've been getting calls from Big Daddy all week and all you can say is that things got out of hand? No shit, they got out of hand!"

We all just kind of stood behind Harvey, trying not to flinch. He wasn't even mad at us, but I was sure we were all feeling the heat. I wanted to apologize even if I wasn't really sure what for.

"We have some of the money. It's not all of it, but..." The more Harvey spoke, the more disappointed his brother looked.

Eventually, Jesse turned cold and stoic enough to listen to Harvey's retelling of the last few days. It was a little weird to hear everything we had done coming from him, but we all stayed silent.

Eventually both of the brothers agreed that we would meet with Big Daddy's *people*, whatever that meant, and try to work something out. To keep us out of trouble, Jesse would be coming too.

Jesse started to talk about two spare rooms he had. Lexi and Rowan ended up crashing in what was being remodeled to be the baby's room, Rex and Dreads got the living room, and I ended up sharing the last room with Harvey. No one said anything about Harvey being paired with me. They were acting as if we were a couple, which was kind of awkward. Were we a couple? I honestly didn't know.

Eventually, I changed into some sweats. I went into the bathroom to brush my teeth and was just about to walk back into my room, when out of nowhere someone turned the corner. I realized it was Jesse when he leveled his stare towards me.

"Excuse me," I mumbled, since I was flustered. I tried walking around him, but he took up most of the narrow hallway.

"You're new," he said. I tried not to flinch from the tone of his voice.

"I am?" I stuttered.

"You're not one of his usual friends."

"Yeah. I kind of ended up here by accident," I tried to explain with a shaky shrug of my shoulders.

He looked at me intensely for a few moments before making some sort of grunt and walking away. I could have been running from a burning building with how fast I scurried away. I was still on an adrenaline rush when I ran into Harvey. His hands grabbed both my arms as I nearly crashed into him.

"You okay?" he asked, half smiling.

"Peachy!" I replied with an awkward lopsided smile before walking away from him, towards the bed.

I was in the middle of getting comfortable under the covers, when I heard Harvey say the most unexpected thing.

"Glow-in-the-dark condoms?" he said, kind of dazed.

"What?" I shot straight up from the bed to look at him. I hadn't remembered setting the plastic bag on the table on the other side of the room, but now it lay limply beside Harvey, while he held a small black-and-green box.

"You bought glow-in-the-dark condoms?" His expression was a mixture of amusement and confusion. I brought the covers over my head and started to laugh crazily instead of replying to him.

I wanted to give him an explanation but I was laughing too hard. It wasn't even cute laughter. It was the hysterical kind with varying degrees of insanity.

"I didn't mean to buy those, I swear!" I eventually got out.

"Livvie, if you wanted to take advantage of me, you should have just said so," Harvey said, which only made me laugh harder.

"The guy at the gasoline station said I couldn't use the bathroom unless I bought something and I...I don't even know." I was stuck trying to explain and control the laughter that kept bubbling up.

"So you bought condoms?" Now Harvey was laughing just as hard.

"That make your—" I paused, trying to regain my breath and not being able to finish my thought anyway.

"—look like a glow stick!" I finished with an immature snort.

By that point Harvey had taken a seat at the edge of the bed with his head in his hands. His shoulders were shaking from the spurts of laughter that kept bubbling up.

"Quit laughing at me!" I eventually said, hitting him on the arm but not being able to control my laughter either. At one point Harvey took a long enough breath to scoot over towards me and plant a kiss on my lips.

I kissed him again, while wrapping my arms around his neck and bringing him closer. He flipped us over so that I was straddling him before trailing kisses down my neck. I was in the middle of a moan, when the door was pushed open. I jumped from the surprise, before making eye contact with a mildly surprised Jesse.

"Came in to discuss some stuff, but we'll see to them in the morning." With that he walked out, closing the door behind him.

"You have the funniest expression on your face, like you just sucked on a lemon," Harvey said beside me.

More like the embarrassment lemon. Harvey's brother had looked so uncomfortable. It was all I could think about while Harvey spoke.

"So, those condoms…" Harvey said quietly. He was staring at the same spot where his brother had stood just seconds ago.

My heart started to race inside my chest. I wanted to, except not really. I knew it was part of my list, but it was something I wrote on there without even thinking. Being presented with the actual possibility of losing my V card was ten times scarier and more serious. I was terrified of giving it up now. Harvey made me feel good, better than good, but he wasn't my boyfriend. He wasn't in love with me either and although I could fall in love with him in an instant, I still hadn't.

Harvey was probably thinking that I subconsciously bought the condoms, but that wasn't the case. Maybe it kind of was, but now I was pretty sure I wasn't really.

"Can't," I choked out. "Aunt Flow is visiting."

Liar. I was a filthy rotten liar. I prayed he didn't realize I was crap at making things up. I didn't even know why I said what I did. I didn't have to lie. I could have just said I wasn't ready. He would have understood.

"Your aunt's visiting?" Harvey had a Dreads moment when he started to look around the room, looking for my great aunt or something to pop out from behind the closet doors.

"No! Like Aunt Flow…"

"Oh!" Harvey said, realization washing over him.

Boys would be boys. He took a second to look over at my face.

"Livvie, you could just tell me the truth." Hiss look was understanding at least, which helped tone down the shade of red on my face a bit.

"I'm not ripe," I said with an awkward shrug of my shoulder. Harvey looked confused.

"You know, like green bananas? Not exactly...ready," I finished lamely. The look he gave me told me he was trying to figure out exactly where I was trying to go with my explanation.

"You're full of metaphors today." He smiled.

Chuckling beside me, he stood up to shut off the lights. He held my hand while I stared into darkness. We weren't in love, but we didn't exactly amount to nothing. Not knowing where you stood with someone was torture, especially when they kept giving you signs that they cared.

I felt him nuzzle into the back of my neck, right into my hair, before he sighed. I was in the middle of drifting off to sleep when I started to think.

"How did you know I was lying?" I asked, referring to my Aunt Flow excuse. The room was silent for a while, but I felt his smile against my skin.

"You're transparent, Livvie."

I wished he was transparent too.

Chapter Twenty
No Introduction, Please.

When I woke up, Harvey was already out of bed. I could hear murmuring coming from somewhere in the house. I figured everyone was having an early morning meeting without me. At least no one hogged the shower, which meant that I quickly jumped in and out.

My hair was still dripping when I hesitantly tiptoed into the kitchen. Harvey, Jesse, Lexi and Rowan were all sitting around a round kitchen table. Every head turned towards me when I walked into the room. For a second I panicked, thinking I forgot to put my clothes on. My eyes landed on Lexi, who was already patting a chair beside her with a smile.

I tried to make myself appear small as I made my way next to her. It seemed to work, because the guys jumped back into their discussion. I wondered briefly where Rex and Rowan were. I realized that the pregnant chick was also missing. I had absolutely no clue what the guys were talking about, but it sounded like they were strategizing about the meeting.

Eventually, we all heard a screen door bang shut, followed by the sound of footsteps. Rex and Dreads both walked into the already crowded kitchen. I had to look twice when I realized that they were both wearing shades and black hoodies.

"We got it." Rex spoke in a really deep voice. He sounded like he was regurgitating something from deep inside.

"What the hell are you guys doing?" Lexi was quick to ask. She was looking at Rex like he was an idiot.

I turned just in time to see Jesse pinch the bridge of his nose and turn his head away. He couldn't even stare at us for more than five seconds before getting pissed off.

"More like what the hell are you guys wearing?" Rowan asked, giving them the same look filled with confusion.

My head spun towards Harvey, only to see him settle on a resigned expression. Like he'd tried his best.

"What you guys asked for! We got you all a pair of some sick shades and some black hoodies to blend in. We're ready to keep shit on the down low." Rex was looking a little too proud about his purchases. We all watched him with varying degrees of bewilderment while he ruffled inside a few Walmart bags that Dreads held out to him. Dreads' head kept bobbing up and down with excitement as Rex droned on.

"Black hoodies to blend in? We're seeing them in an hour in the middle of the day," Rowan reminded the two other guys. By this point I knew I had the weirdest look on my face, but I was desperately trying not to laugh.

"It's not going down tonight?" Dreads asked this time, looking over at Rex like a wounded puppy.

"You thought it was at night, then why the hell would you buy sunglasses?" This time Jesse spoke up.

"Who doesn't look rad in shades?" Dreads was quick to make a point.

Lexi had stayed silent up to then. She stared at the guys with an amused expression that mirrored my own. Both of them shook their shoulders in an 'I dunno' fashion, before going back to investigating their purchases.

"I can't deal with this shit so early in the morning," Jesse murmured before standing up and pushing his way out of the room.

I didn't even have to look at Harvey to see him shaking his head. Finally, Lexi and I let out our laughter and joined the two boys who were still rummaging through the bags to see if we could find something to put on.

"I think it's really nice that you guys wanted to prepare," I said, watching a grinning Dreads light up. The rest of us left Harvey and Rowan in the kitchen while we all huddled in the small living room and started playing dress-up. The hoodies were three sizes too big for Lexi and me, so we ended up flinging the ends of the too-long sleeves at each other's faces.

Then we tried on different pairs of glasses. We finally decided which pairs looked best before sitting beside the guys and watching TV. Jesse didn't emerge, and I figured he was probably with his baby momma in the other room. I could hear Harvey and Rowan faintly discussing things.

We were going to meet up with the same people who had shot at us and even kidnapped me. For some odd reason, knowing that Jesse was on our side kind of made me relax a little. He seemed to be in charge of everything, and for once, Harvey wasn't the only one in command. It was probably a sibling thing.

Jesse emerged from the hallway into the living room when it was time to head out. That was it. It was showtime. I wondered what would happen once we got everything straightened out. We'd all go home and then what?

I felt as if we were walking towards a battleground when in reality we were crawling into our cars. I hitched my leg over Harvey's bike and hugged him tight. I felt him lean on me for a fraction of a minute and smiled.

We hadn't spoken that morning, but it felt good to be next to him. I had no clue where we were going but tried to take inventory of our surroundings. We rode on a freeway for a good portion of the time, but eventually the terrain became more desolate. Then we drove onto a road set against a mountain. I could feel the wind whipping my hair all over the place the higher we wound around the mountainside. My ears started to pop too, but I tried to ignore it. Where the hell were we going?

Jesse was in the lead. He drove the black Mustang and I could see it up ahead. I was pretty stressed out about what we were about to do, but I wasn't gonna lie and say I wasn't feeling an adrenaline rush too. Harvey and Jesse ended up wearing the shades too.

My heart nearly dropped to my knees when we stopped. I waited for Harvey to make sure that the bike was set firmly on the ground before checking out the location. We'd parked in a small clearing right by the side of the road. The wind blew my hair even worse when Harvey removed my helmet.

Jesse efficiently stepped out of his car with a phone stuck to his ear. Probably calling Big Daddy's people about our arrival. I knew we had money from the impromptu concert, but I really didn't think that we had enough to please the people who were coming to meet us. When Jesse took a huge duffel bag from inside his car and launched it towards Harvey, I nearly stumbled off the bike.

"Is that full of money?" I asked. If my eyes had opened any wider just then the eyeballs would have fallen out.

I was secretly glad for the shades we were all wearing.

"Yup," he said. He seemed disconnected, but I ignored it and wove my fingers through his. It was enough just then.

"When we win, we win big," Rex gloated.

"You also lose big, dumbass," Lexi cut in, reminding all of us where our real problem had started at.

I ruffled through my memories to understand what he was talking about. I couldn't believe that the rest of the money in the duffel was from the pool game Harvey had bet on at the shady bar. But the more I looked towards the bag the more it sunk in. Harvey and Rex hadn't just won that pool game, they had to have won multiple times.

"I don't understand. Rex, you were really bad," I said, eyeing him suspiciously.

"Only when I need to be." He flashed me a devious smile.

Just then two huge black Escalades rolled up beside us. I resolved to be tough, until one of the doors started to open and I stepped behind Harvey for protection. I freaked when a super young guy walked out from one of the trucks and waved Jesse over.

He hadn't spared a glance at Harvey, but he walked up with his brother anyway. My hands grasped thin air as Harvey walked away from me. I briefly saw him hand the duffel to Rowan. The rest of the guys formed a protective line in front of Lexi and me.

At first, it looked like they were all having a casual conversation. As casual as you could have in a remote location with a duffel full of money. Until the young guy took out a gun and aimed it right at Jesse. The rest of us let out an awkward chorus of screams, which momentarily took the young guy's attention off of the two brothers.

That's when he waved the rest of us over to him.

We seriously had no choice but to all walk over in terror. I could feel my knees going weak, as if my cartilage had suddenly turned to jelly.

"This is how we die," I whispered. I imagined my death in ten different ways, all in the span of a few seconds. The mental movies ranged from being shot to falling from the side of a cliff again.

"We're not gonna die, Liv," Lexi said, although a bit shakily.

"That's her! That's the girl who knocked me out!" I heard from inside the truck that was parked in front of us. It sounded a lot like the voice of the younger guy who had kidnapped me.

"What did we talk about, eh?" My ears caught the sound of another voice. I remembered it as the voice that belonged to the older man who'd also kidnapped me.

"I mean," the younger guy corrected, "the girl who almost knocked me out!"

"Oh, please! You were out like a baby!" Lexi suddenly yelled towards the idling car.

"Babe!" Rowan chided, turning towards his girlfriend with a crazy look.

"Now look here!" An offended tone shot back before a man sauntered out of the vehicle. Everything about him was thin. His torso, the finger he stuck in the air to make his point, even his mustache was thin. He wore a casual button-down shirt, dress pants, and steel-toed dress shoes, which were a nice extravagant touch if you asked me later.

Also, he looked like someone I knew but couldn't place.

"Why didn't you tell me you dumbasses ran into them already?" Jesse whispered heatedly towards Harvey. I didn't hear Harvey's response because I was too paralyzed from the confusion.

I'd gotten the mystery-flavored lollipop. Like when you have to find out what the real flavor is from a flavor that you've tasted before. That was me, trying to figure out why the man in front of us looked so familiar.

"My son did not get knocked out by a girl!" But we all knew he had.

An even scrawnier and much younger guy walked out from the truck next, red-faced with what I could only guess to be embarrassment or anger.

"I would have knocked *you* out if I wasn't against hitting girls!" the guy yelled in Lexi's direction. And they said chivalry was dead.

I found it funny that he suddenly had respect for the female gender when he'd knocked me out with a pipe before. He obviously couldn't handle Lexi's right hook.

"Enough!" a new voice broke out. A voice that I didn't have to place, because I knew exactly who it belonged to.

It came from the person who was now getting out of the other SUV. He'd been quiet and unassuming till that moment, probably preferring to observe everything from inside the car.

"I let you kids think you could hustle me for too long. It's time you pay up before I—" That's when he noticed me.

I could see the recognition in his stare. He hadn't noticed me until then, but now his gaze didn't falter. I wanted to hug him, but the idea that he wasn't real kept bursting into my head.

"Dad?" I let the word slip through my lips.

"No, Livvie." Dreads leaned down towards me and elbowed me gently. "It's Big Daddy." He said it like I'd just committed a faux pas.

I knew he was trying to correct me, but he was the one who was wrong.

"Livvie Sweet?" My dad said my nickname in the same tone I remembered.

"What the hell happened? I didn't even recognize you with that hair and those clothes and these kids..." My dad kept scooting closer. It was then that I realized that everyone had started to give me space.

They didn't want to get infected with whatever I apparently had.

"What are you doing here?" I asked, suddenly more overwhelmed than I had been just minutes before.

"What are you doing with these duds and where is your mother?" My dad was sounding more and more alarmed. I could see him searching the deserted space we were in. Hoping my mom would pop out from behind the Corolla and yell *surprise.*

"Duds? What about you!" I yelled, suddenly feeling frustrated. Not that my dad was a dud, but I was still defensive about my friends.

"Your dad's Big Daddy?" Dreads wondered aloud before Rowan punched him in the stomach to shut him up.

"Yeah," I said with a hitch in my voice, right before I ran up to my dad and hugged him. It was what I'd wanted to do from the minute I saw him. Forgetting that he was a criminal, I ran up to him with all the speed that a girl who had run away from home and from the cops could. It couldn't be. My dad was Big Daddy! My dad was...not that big. I'd have to figure out why they called him that later. It was all so crazy, like a dream.

My arms wrapped around him in a fierce hug and I hid my face in the crook of his neck. It couldn't be real, but it was. I didn't really care what my dad did for a living—really, the fact that I had him holding me and calling me every single nickname he had given me since I was little was everything that mattered. That was my fault; I forgave the people who did bad things around me because I loved them.

I was filled with happiness and excitement, and I could feel it showing on my face when we finally let go.

"Well, if it isn't my favorite niece!" the taller man said. Suddenly, as his face neared and I got a better look, memories started to flash in my mind. For a moment, I felt like I was floating through the air, falling and laughing, and then I felt the ghost touch of a strong pair of thin hands holding my forearms before I hit the ground.

"Uncle Bobby!" I said, gradually remembering him from my childhood memories.

"I hardly recognized you, Marshmallow!" he said with awe before coming in for a hug. It was all quickly turning into a family reunion. Only when his thin arms released me did I look back towards my friends. Except, I didn't really like everything that I saw. Jesse looked uneasy, Lexi and the rest of the guys all had mixed emotions, but Harvey was the last one I saw.

Harvey looked absolutely sick, and the fact that he wasn't even looking me in the eye momentarily took all of my happiness away. I pushed through it. I wasn't going to let the important people in my life be at odds with each other. I could fix things. Nothing a little rational duct tape couldn't fix. I'd start with some proper introductions.

"Dad, this is my boyfriend, Harvey."

Oh shit.

I said it. I put a label on it without even thinking it through. Harvey looked at me, then to my dad, then back to me with a wide-eyed stare, before going back to me and slightly nodding his head. He was quietly telling me no, that I was wrong. He distanced himself from me a little to drive the point home.

* * *

Everything was wrong. I'd just gotten silently rejected in front of my dad. He denied it in front of our friends too. Lexi was looking at me with wide eyes too, trying to make me feel better with a look of understanding, but she was fumbling. The rest of the looks showed pity or disbelief and that summarized my first taste of heartbreak.

I couldn't even look Harvey in the face, because I would end up crying and that was the last thing I needed. My dad looked like he was working himself up for a fight. I didn't know where else to look except at my uncle. Uncle Bobby looked much more understanding about the entire thing.

Before I knew it, my uncle was pulling me inside one of the Escalades, and no one was doing anything about it.

"Keep the money," my dad said before following closely behind me.

I could hear him talking about us catching up and him getting me back home. My dad was doing everything to distract me, but it wasn't working.

I wanted to tell my dad to wait, tell him that they were my friends, but to everyone's discomfort, I started to cry. I couldn't get any of the words past the lump in my throat. I felt shitty and used. I guessed Harvey couldn't amend it and say we'd actually been acquaintances with benefits in front of my dad.

"Sweet, sit still and focus," I heard my dad's crisp voice order me. "We'll talk about the boy another time, but you have a lot of explaining to do about everything else."

I sniffled some more, but eventually managed to stop crying enough to speak. I wanted to roll my eyes at my dad's prime opportunity to actually act like a dad, but no matter how hard I wanted to act like a snooty teenager, I just couldn't. My dad was my safe harbor from the complete humiliation I'd just endured.

"Dad, I really don't think you should be saying anything. With you in the mafia and all." Ah, there. I was able to manage some of that teenage sass.

"Mafia?" My dad started to chuckle, a deep throaty thing that warmed my insides with familiarity, but not enough to make me less sad. "Is that what you think I belong to?" he asked, with his eyes twinkling in amusement. His stare reminded me too much of Harvey's, which was a horrible and unflattering comparison.

"Yeah, I mean why else would Harvey owe you so much money?" I asked.

"I'm not in the mafia. I'm a businessman." He shrugged like he didn't really want to elaborate.

"What kind of business?" I narrowed my eyes at him. I deserved to know the truth. He sighed for a moment before answering me.

"It's a gambling business. Very low-key. No big deal." He smiled at me, showing all his teeth. The two men sitting in the front seat looked at each other uncertainly.

"Like an illegal gambling ring? Is that where all of your money comes from? Do you even pay your taxes?" My voice was rising in volume towards a more frantic tone. My dad flinched but he didn't deny that he was laundering money or anything else.

"Why don't you take this time to explain why you ran away from home? Your mother didn't even call to tell me." He sounded kind of pissed during that last part, but he was trying to calm me down. He wanted to turn the tables. I could let him get away with that. I really didn't want to make him feel bad about what he did, even though it was wrong. It just seemed like I would be attacking the core of who he was if I showed him my disappointment.

So I told him what happened. I mentioned how his SUV rolled up to my school and he explained that he'd meant to surprise me by picking me up, but instead found Harvey and his friends. He'd been looking for them for weeks, trying to claim some money that they owed him. I asked him why he shot at us if he knew he was chasing me too, but he said he hadn't recognized me. He'd thought I was just another one of Harvey's friends. He looked super guilty about that last part and kept apologizing until I told him to stop.

Obviously I wasn't going to delve into the details of my nonexistent relationship with Harvey, but I did highlight the rest of the gang's good points. I tried to ignore the gruff noises my dad would make whenever I mentioned Harvey because I figured we were both anti-Harvey at the moment and I didn't think it would be a good idea if we were both negative. I was already transparent enough that even my own dad figured out I'd been used, then cast aside.

Ignorance was bliss, and I was going to forget the last twenty-four hours even if it killed me.

"And now you should agree that I deserve more answers." I ended my conversation with a huff, a la Big Daddy.

I let him take a deep breath. It genuinely pained him to have to explain everything.

"I didn't think I would ever have this conversation with you," he finally said.

"Go on," I urged, having already spilled most of the beans myself.

"Your mother was never happy with what I did for a living when we were together. It's always been one scheme after another with me, and even I knew it wasn't good for a family. Worst thing is, when I married her, it was your uncle that helped me start up the business." My dad chuckled at the irony.

"So you run a casino-type thing?" I tried to guess by putting the pieces of my childhood and the present together.

"You could say that. I own a few other reputable businesses, but that's just to keep the main one under wraps," my dad said before taking a piece of my hair and twirling it in his fingers. I'd always loved the undivided attention my dad was able to give me.

"Aren't you scared of getting caught?" I said, trying to reason with him.

"Old habits die hard, as they say. Plus, it's worked pretty well for your old man, don't you think?" He gestured at everything surrounding us. It *was* a nice SUV, with the beige leather seats and the backseat TVs.

"What about Harvey?" I couldn't help myself.

My dad gave me a stern look before finally deciding that there was no harm in telling me.

"I knew Harvey's father from many years before. He was a sick son of a—" My dad caught himself, probably remembering that I was his daughter and not one of his shady friends.

"Needless to say, the man was addicted to the game. Never knew when to call it a day. A few months ago the Lockwell kid walked into one of our warehouses with his friends and I instantly knew whose kid he was." He stared off somewhere, thick into his story.

"Looks just like him, by the way," he mentioned as a side comment. Leaning in closer, he continued.

"Anyway, the kid was playing hard that night. We ended up playing a few rounds of poker together. The kid was good, but not good enough. I was waiting for him to give up, but he kept digging himself his own grave with one bad hand after the other. I saw the moment he decided to cheat. Rookies like him are transparent as hell." My dad's eyes widened for a fraction of a second.

"Pardon my French, baby doll."

"It's okay, Dad," I urged him to continue.

"Right. Well, I let him believe that he cheated me, but before I knew it the kid and his friends had hightailed it outta the warehouse like bandits. With my money, mind you! I wasn't going to let some punk hustle me, so I planned to give him a little visit, but the kid was impossible to find!"

"But you found him with me." I finished his story with a flourish.

My dad nodded at my conclusion.

And so we drove on, back home. I wondered if my friends were heading in the same direction. What if they didn't? What if I was back to being the same lame person as before?

At least I was with my dad.

We stopped at a very luxurious hotel when nightfall came around. I let my dad lead me inside and check us in. My dad's name wasn't Richard to the concierge, but Carlos instead.

I found out that he expected me to have dinner with my uncle and cousin after I was already in the hotel room. I wasn't feeling too friendly towards my new cousin, but I agreed.

Uncle Bobby and my dad were already waiting at a table in the hotel restaurant. It was a bit on the late side, so there weren't that many other people in the room, aside from a middle-aged couple sitting in the far corner.

"Look at how big you are." My Uncle Bobby, beamed up at me. I couldn't believe that I didn't remember him until my own memories bashed me in the head. I hadn't seen much of my uncle while growing up, but he had been one of my favorite people when I did. I knew he was my mom's older brother and only sibling, so it was kind of weird to see him with my dad, who wasn't even his brother-in-law anymore. Well, he was, but not for long if Jim the Creep got what he wanted.

It wasn't long before my dad and my uncle's bickering made me forget about my surreal surroundings. They argued over what kind of wine to order, my dad arguing something about the fermentation process, and my uncle saying that the wine my dad wanted was going to ruin our entire dining experience.

It was like watching a TV show in real life. My cousin, Calvin, finally appeared. He was freshly showered and I internally smiled at the yellowing eye he had.

"Well, hello, beautiful," my cousin said before plopping his skinny body down on the chair in front of him. Beautiful? I was still wearing the clothes from that morning, including the underwear. Stunning.

I listened while Uncle Bobby told him to shut it.

"Tone it down, boy. That's your cousin you're talking to." My Uncle's gruff voice made me laugh and Calvin wrinkle his nose. Once he stopped trying to flirt with me, he quickly became your typical annoying cousin.

My dad let me get my own room next to his. I had to sleep in the same clothes, but he promised to buy me new ones the next day.

The following morning we rode out towards home. My dad did make good on the promise to buy me clothes. I tried on things I hoped Lexi would approve of and as a result my dad wouldn't. He didn't stop me from buying them, but he acted like it physically pained him to pay for the stuff.

The following days I got to ride with my uncle and surprisingly enough, teasing Calvin proved to be the most interesting thing on the trip. He was incredibly cocky for a guy who probably didn't weigh more than 130 pounds.

The ride back home was shorter. It made sense since we didn't stop as many times and drove straight back, not in the twisted curved way we'd taken while we ran. It was in the late hours of the night that we finally rolled up in front of my house.

I expected it to look different, like maybe the roof had caved in during my absence, but the porch light was on and my mom's car was parked in the driveway. So much for being missed.

I'd just stepped out of the SUV when a pair of new headlights illuminated the street. My heart sped up when I realized it was a familiar Corolla. Someone rode up in front of it on a motorcycle, and for a moment I feared they would keep driving away.

They'd followed me home! Harvey and my friends had been right behind us. I could feel a hopeful smile start to grow on my face, only to extinguish itself when I watched Harvey whiz right by me without a second glance.

My dad and uncle watched Harvey with avid curiosity, but neither of them made a move to stop him. All of us quickly followed Harvey's lead once we had broken out of our stupor. I ran up just to see Jim the Creep's skinny arm push open the front door.

That's all I saw of my good friend Jim, because the next moment Harvey pulled his fist back and slammed it into his face. Hard. I heard a distinct crack before hysterical screaming erupted from somewhere inside the house, probably from my mom, who had come down to investigate.

I seriously could not believe my eyes. Jim had shot back into the house with a weird moan and Harvey simply stood there looking down at him for a moment.

"Leave some for the rest of us, kid," my dad said. He came up in front of me and eventually past Harvey. My dad and uncle were both in the middle of rolling up their sleeves when they went in. I wanted to focus on the commotion happening inside, but Harvey walked right by me in the opposite direction. I couldn't believe that he would leave right after punching Jim in the face and I turned to tell him so.

Except he wasn't anywhere near me. He was already climbing back onto his bike. I started to yell for him to come back, my body finally kicking into gear. The Corolla had already left.

I was equal parts surprised and hurt when Harvey ignored me and started to drive away. There were so many things I needed to tell him and the guy had just left. Kaput, drove off into the night as if I wasn't yelling his name behind him.

"You suck!" I finally yelled at the empty road in front of me. Just like that, the boy I was almost sure I was in love with had sped out of my life.

What sucked the most was even though he'd hurt me, I was starting to think that I was a little bit in love with Harvey Lockwell.

Chapter Twenty-One
Hiding the Evidence

When I walked back inside, my dad was in the middle of roundhouse kicking Jim in the face while my uncle held him up. Needless to say, it scared the crap out of me, but when I turned around to look at my mom, she wasn't screaming anymore. Her expression was no longer terrified, but looking kind of amused.

"Are you enjoying this?" I asked incredulously. What was going on with the world?

My mom snapped out of it at the sound of my voice and shook her head to clear out the romantic fog she was apparently in.

"Alright, enough!" she finally said in my dad's direction. She didn't sound very convincing, though. I watched my dad step back for a moment to inspect his handiwork. He shook his hands out, causing the blood on his knuckles to fly around. It was kind of cool to see your dad beat the crap out of someone like a badass and for a moment I understood the look on my mom's face.

"You need to leave," my mom said. I thought she was talking to my dad and uncle, until I realized that she was talking to Jim. Jim looked incredulous, or so I assumed, since both his eyes were shut.

"I hate to beat it to you, but she's right, my Uncle Bobby said. He chuckled to himself at his pun. My uncle's attempt at a joke made me hurt more than Jim. It was getting weirder and weirder to be home.

"Poor guy," I said, feeling Calvin's presence behind me. Not that Jim hadn't gotten what he deserved, but no one had been very gentle about giving it to him.

"Him? My dad just made a pun after beating the shit out of someone. You don't know how many times he does that on a regular basis. If anyone needs to be felt sorry for it's me." Calvin said. He was clearly embarrassed on his dad's behalf. He did have a point, so I shrugged in agreement.

Jim caught my attention again, stumbling up our staircase with my mom and dad trailing by his side.

"It was about time we got things settled," Uncle Bobby said, flexing his skinny arm. I wanted to laugh, since my dad had been the one throwing the punches, but Uncle Bobby was giving off some serious Rocky vibes.

"Calm down, old man," Calvin murmured to his dad with an eye roll.

It took a few minutes, but eventually Jim slid down the stairs with his bags. I hadn't even been here to watch him move in, but at least I got to see him out. Jim started to slur about my mom being a liar and not telling him about her marriage, but it was as if my parents didn't hear him.

Where was my little brother? Before I knew it I was jumping up the stairs, taking two at a time, before running into Brian's room. I saw the lump of his body popping out from under the covers. Then I started to sob because I had missed my little brother so much and I was so happy Jim the Creep was gone. I was feeling a tad emotionally unstable at the sight of my brother.

Brian squirmed when I leaned over to hug his shoulders, but he didn't wake up. Brian slept like the dead. He hadn't even heard Jim getting the crap beat out of him. I wiped a few of my tears and gave him a kiss on the cheek before walking back downstairs. Everything felt like it was as it should be, at least in my house, and for the moment that was enough.

Until I walked into the battlefield.

Everyone was arguing with everyone, except for Calvin, who was scrunched in the middle of the adults. My mom was shaking her head up and down like an out-of-control bobblehead. Clearly, she was trying to yell the loudest. My dad and uncle were trying to get their points across with angry voices, while poor Calvin stood looking like a deer in the headlights. When I walked into the room Calvin's reverent glance made me feel like a god, until everyone else noticed me and started yelling in my direction.

"Who gave you the right to bring your dad back?" God did a miracle that night. There was no other possible way my mom's head didn't completely topple off her shoulders that night without his help.

"—can't believe I had to find you where I did—" my dad yelled. Finally deciding to be the pissed-off, concerned parent.

"—that's just not you—" my uncle, still believing that I was five, also yelled in my direction.

"I gotta take a piss so bad—" Calvin tried to interject, grabbing the center of his crotch and doing a little dance. He looked pained and terrified.

The easiest thing to do was pull Calvin out of the throng and direct him to the bathroom. Then I faced my parents, squaring my shoulders. It was time to take things into my own hands.

"I left because I got caught up in something, but mostly I left because, frankly, Mom, you weren't being very good at being a mom. I was tired of having to deal with all the responsibility, Jim being a total creep and you too blind to see it, and having Dad away was seriously hurting me. I didn't bring him back, it just happened that way. So why don't the both of you have a nice long chat about your bad parenting, sketchy lifestyle, and your relationship. Do something for me and Brian, just this once." I ended my speech with a flourish of my hands and a gasp for breath.

The room was dead silent, right as Calvin came back in. The only thing you could hear was the sound

of his zipper being pulled back in place and then
silence again. Everyone was still staring at me while
my parents tried to recover from my outburst.

"Nice try," my dad finally said.

"Yeah, you better believe you're grounded," my
mom added, finally on the same page. But for some
reason, the idea of being grounded didn't put a dent
on my happiness. My parents were finally agreeing on
something. It was weird, but enlightening.

I thought they would say more, until I saw my
parents look at each other and then leave the room.

I was left with my cousin and uncle.

"You did good, Livvie," my uncle said with a
twinkle in his eye. I turned my head in his direction to
smile at him. The more I thought of it, the more I
realized he was right. It had gone better than
expected. No one had chopped my head off, which was
a win in itself.

The following day I woke up to the sight of my
mom actually making breakfast, after taking the day
off work. My dad and uncle argued about salt versus
pepper and whether you should put either or both on
eggs. They argued about a lot of things, but food was
usually the main topic.

Calvin was in the middle of stuffing his face
with food. It felt good to sleep in my own bed again. I
was in a relatively cheerful mood until both my
parents sent me withering glances. I smiled a goofy
smile anyway, trying to lighten them up.

As it turned out, I wasn't to leave the house
unless it was to go to school. Which sounded like my

regular schedule before the trip. My uncle and cousin decided to stay at our house for a few weeks until they found their own. It was surprising, because although I hadn't given it much thought, I'd automatically assumed that the male members of my family would soon be disappearing.

I was in the middle of swallowing a forkful of eggs when I caught my dad smacking my mom's butt. I don't know what made me cringe more, the sound of the assault or my mom's responding giggle. Then I was kind of happy that my dad had smacked my mom's butt, which was on a whole other level of weird.

I heard Brian's footsteps before I saw him. I was almost scared to turn around. What if he was mad at me? What if he felt like I'd abandoned him and now had a massive grudge against me?

I swallowed all my guilt and fear before turning around to see him. I watched him catch sight of me. There was absolutely no reaction. Did I have egg on my chin? I tried smiling at him, a big, forced effort.

"Livvie." His face broke out into his regular sweet smile after a few tense moments. I was expecting a slow-motion reunion where Brian would run into my arms and the sun would shine through the windows right over our heads in a spiritual glow, but the kid only smiled at me before climbing on a chair and asking for breakfast. Definitely not as monumental as I had hoped, but good enough. His mouth dropped onto the table when he realized he was sitting right in front of our dad. Now *that* was a reunion. I wasn't the only one who held my dad on a pedestal. Tears were shed, mostly mine for some reason, while Brian hugged and tried to catch our dad up on every comic book plot he'd read since he'd left.

I was surprised when my parents told me to get ready for school. They were going to make me go back as soon as possible. It was then that I noticed that even Calvin was dressed for the day, and only Brian and I were left in our pajamas. I wasn't about to face anyone's wrath by arguing, so I headed upstairs after breakfast to take a shower and put on some fresh clothes. My dad took one look at me when I walked downstairs and promptly told me to go change. It was a little too late for that, since he'd been the one to buy me the clothes in the first place. My mom, at least, didn't bat an eyelash at my new wardrobe.

School seemed completely different when I first walked through the doors. Were the walls always so cramped? Everything seemed smaller.

The office ladies looked happy to see me all for five seconds before they took one look at me, remembered my TV debut that happened to air on the seven o'clock news, and gave me the death glare. The office ladies no longer saw me in such a good light, apparently. They snickered and gave me the stink eye for the duration of my presence, and they weren't very helpful when it came to excusing my absences. My mom made up some bullshit story about me getting pneumonia, but we all knew everyone had seen me in the news footage.

* * *

Luckily, Calvin was only a junior, and not in any of my classes. I'd missed a week and a half of school, which was kind of stressful. I was also lumped into the 'bad kid' pile, which would have been amusing if the results weren't so annoying.

Thanks to my dad's smooth talking, I was excused for half of my absences, but they weren't sure if I would have to appear in court for missing so many days regardless. My mom looked like she was ready to kill me on the spot the minute she heard the news, but at least my dad's presence seemed to calm her a bit. I still hadn't heard from Nick, but I had left him a voice mail the minute I was allowed a phone.

I was sitting in a miniskirt and combat boots when the office lady, the one who had first approached me with the idea of tutoring Harvey, offered to walk me to class. They made up some cover story about helping Calvin find his way around, but really they were making sure I wouldn't ditch again. At first she seemed shocked when she saw me, before turning her nose up and looking sorry. I wanted to tell her that it wasn't like I was cooking meth in my spare time, but that would have caused even more of a stir. I was half in shock when our parents left Calvin and me at school, right smack in the middle of the day.

It was all too fast, but a part of me had hope that maybe I'd see my friends. The office lady led us to the cafeteria right in the middle of lunch. Everything looked the same as it should have been, until I caught someone's attention, and then someone else's, and finally everyone's. The room erupted in whispers. I should have known that in a small town like ours things would be said. Some not very nice things, I realized when I heard a few of the louder ones.

"Do you think they're all whispering about me?" Calvin asked. He looked kind of flattered by the attention, so I didn't say anything to convince him otherwise. I was grateful to have my cousin next to me, because for once I didn't have to do the walk of shame alone.

The room fell back into silence as I made my way towards the table where Nick and I used to sit. I crossed my fingers, hoping to see his head of messy brown hair. My best friend turned just in time to catch sight of my cousin and me being stared down by the entire school.

I don't know what I was expecting once I saw Nick again. Maybe a hug? A screaming match? Anything, really. It was a little bit like seeing Brian again, a total toss-up.

"Dude," Nick said, finally breaking the silence now that I was standing right in front of him.

"Nick," I responded with a hesitant smile on my face.

"Where the hell—" he started to ask in a serious, almost angry tone.

Have you been, I finished his sentence in my head.

"—did you get those boots?" he asked, excited, with a pointed look at the fashion article in question. I let out an abnormal amount of air out through my nose.

"I missed you, Butt!" he said before finally giving me the hug that I wanted. I was so glad that my best friend had taken me back. I didn't waste time introducing him to my cousin. I was about to sit down, until I noticed there was another person sitting at our table. Brian's babysitter was in my usual seat, glancing at me uncertainly.

Nick quickly gave me the lowdown on everything that had happened, particularly focusing on the news of his new relationship. My best friend had a boyfriend.

"No fucking way!" I exclaimed, giving Arnold a huge grin.

"No fucking way that you said no fucking way!" Nick countered, looking completely shocked.

I told them everything that had happened on the trip, including the Harvey bits, which were really the best and worst part. Half the school was trying to listen in, though, so I kept some stuff brief.

I won't lie, though, knowing that some of the girls were listening to the Harvey parts made me feel pretty special. Calvin heard most of it and by the end started sputtering something about avenging my honor, to which Nick said, "Calm down, Tybalt."

It was enough to distract Calvin, since he was too busy trying to figure out a response.

In the middle of my story, I glanced around the cafeteria trying to find any sign of the rest of the gang, even Harvey. I hadn't expected them to hang out in the cafeteria anyway, but it was still depressing.

"He's not here. None of them are," Nick said, catching on. I tried not to let the disappointment show in my face while I carried on with more stories of my recent adventures.

The rest of the day consisted of catching up on endless amount of homework and taking tons of quizzes. No one commented on anything, but I could feel people staring at me. I officially knew was notoriety felt like, and it wasn't very comfortable. Even the teachers treated me differently now, like a ticking bomb they didn't want to deal with. It was weird, since I was still the same lame person. Everyone else just thought differently.

The next few days, I kept looking for signs of them, even going as far as visiting The Cave. I finally realized that maybe they hadn't wanted to come back. There was no way for me to find them.

I was back to being invisible. Although I was better dressed and had my best friend back. Nick spent less time with me and more with Arnold, but he deserved to bask in the glow of young love, so I didn't let it bother me too much. Calvin quickly gained the nickname Starvin' Calvin and started to hang out with every female in his grade and beyond, quickly ditching Nick and me when we were at school.

Along with the downward slope of my mood came my house arrest. I wasn't allowed to go anywhere. The guys tried to distract me, but I could have really used a girlfriend to complain to.

At least they made sure to fill me in on the details of the gossip surrounding me. People were speculating that I had been abducted like in that action movie, *Taken,* with Liam Neeson, which was kind of funny because my dad had brought me back.

School was a blur of work and trying to get back in my teachers' good graces. Mrs. Lasowski's inexplicable distaste for me was finally founded on something, at least.

Most days seemed overly dull, though. Although it felt kind of comfortable to fall back into normal, a part of me was sad that some things would never change.

At night, I'd replay everything that had happened, especially between Harvey and me. I tried to read into every look he gave me, every touch, anything really. All of it amounted to nothing in the end because he'd rejected me before and kept rejecting me then.

I tried to self-medicate with romantic movie marathons. I even used my twelve-year-old brother as a shoulder to cry on.

But a girl can only be sad until she's angry. After a week, I was more than angry. I was furious. Who did Harvey think he was? If he thought I would be pining for him like some heartbroken girl, then he had another thing coming. So what if he had punched Jim in the face for me? That didn't mean crap when he kept avoiding me.

Harvey Lockwell could kiss my ass.

Chapter Twenty-Two
Keep Your Guard Up

The second week of school was less depressing. I wasn't being dragged down by heartache, but instead fueled by anger, so that was a plus. Monday was uneventful, unless you counted Mrs. Lasowski calling on me for everything and asking me questions that no one in the class had a chance of answering on a good day as an event. I preferred to wipe it from my memory so that's what I did. By Wednesday I was still pissed off, but I'd stopped trying to see Harvey everywhere I went. Which was why on Thursday, when I caught sight of broad shoulders under a gray t-shirt and a stance just like Harvey's standing in the lunch line, I had to blink twice and scan the room for hidden cameras.

I couldn't see his face, but people around him were doing their best to stay away. All clear signs that Harvey was trying to get his own lunch tray with spaghetti and meatballs.

The more I saw his casual stance, the angrier I got. Who did he think he was, eating lunch like a regular human being? He hadn't gotten lunch in the cafeteria in all of the four years we'd been in school. I took it as a personal attack.

I didn't even realize the moment I walked up behind him. He still hadn't noticed me, so I grabbed at his shirt leave before pulling him. He stumbled a little before turning around.

He wore a smug look on his face when he saw me. Mine was confused and then embarrassed when I saw that I hadn't almost attacked Harvey. I'd almost gone crazy on Garrard.

"What are you doing here?" I asked. I was floored. The last time I'd seen him I was trying to grind on his leg. Not the best lasting memory.

"Not the person I was looking for, but you'll do." He smiled mischievously, but completely ignored my question. I watched him grab hold of my upper arm in a stupor. His grip was hard, but not enough to actually leave a bruise. I immediately tried to loosen his grip, but it was impossible. Several people were staring at us in confusion, and we were holding up the lunch line, but no one made a move. The lunch ladies were oblivious, as always.

My eyes scanned the room, trying to catch sight of Nick or even Calvin, but my cousin was nowhere in sight and my best friend was really busy flirting with his boyfriend.

"Let go," I ordered, snapping back at Garrard. He got really close to my ear just then, before whispering harshly.

"Tell me where Harvey is and I'll let you go." At that point, he'd dragged me out of the lunch line and towards a nearby corner. Some of the students still staring at us started to whisper heatedly. I realized with horror that most of them probably thought I was in some romantic embrace. I looked down to see how close Garrard and I were, before feeling the brush of his other hand around my waist. I resolved to write a very strongly worded letter to the head of the school district about student safety. Who'd let Garrard in? He wasn't even a student.

"I don't know!" I hissed between my teeth.

"You're his girlfriend. Don't fucking lie," he said, still locking me into his threatening hug.

I laughed at the irony. Even Garrard thought we were together. It came off as taunting, though, so I had to endure him tightening up his hold on me.

"I don't know anything about Harvey because he's not my boyfriend!" How long was it going to take to get the point through? Was this how Harvey felt, because I'd gotten his point loud and clear the second time.

"Fine. You're going to find out where he is for me," he said. I let him pull me along towards the exit doors only because it was near Nick and Arnold. It was the perfect chance to get some backup. No one else was going to come to my aid.

"Help me!" I yelled in Nick's direction when Garrard dragged me right in front of him.

"No, you're cuter," Nick giggled at Arnold.

"No, you are, lovebug." I almost gagged at Arnold's pet name for Nick. It was unbelievable. My best friend was literally ignoring my cry for help. I was getting kidnapped in front of him, but he didn't notice because he was too busy being cute with his boyfriend. It was all too much.

Garrard pinched my arm.

"No talking. You don't want to piss me off." He was right. I didn't. He led me out of the cafeteria and towards the front office. The fact that he knew the layout of the school was kind of freaky.

"You're gonna go in there and find out his address." His chin pointed towards the double doors.

"How am I supposed to do that?" I asked, incredulous. Any other time before my runaway act, getting student information from the office would have been easy, not anymore.

"Figure it out. Or I will and it won't be nice." He grabbed my chin and turned it in the direction of his pants before pulling his shirt up a tad. He had a gun. Holy mother of God, the boy had a freakin' gun.

I started sweating. It was all fun and games until the drug dealer showed you his gun.

"'Kay!" I finally squeaked out in a much-too-cheerful tone.

My entire body was shaking when I finally walked into the front office. I wondered if I could tell the lady in front of me about the potential killer waiting outside, but I doubted she would have believed me. My credibility was at an all-time low and if I messed things up people could get shot at.

The office lady stared up at me. I couldn't get an excuse out fast enough so she had to stare at me for the longest time until she grew peeved.

"Yes, Ms. Jefferson?"

"I need to...speak to Principal River." My voice was surprisingly steady.

The woman looked uncertain, but eventually she nodded.

"He's out for lunch, but shouldn't be long. You can wait in his office," she replied.

I followed her into a small hallway and into the principal's office. I'd never seen his office until then, so it took me a moment to take inventory. I was surprised when the office lady left me there alone. At least she didn't completely distrust me. My eyes zeroed in on the computer sitting on the large desk in front of me.

When the monitor lit up I realized that I'd have to log in. Did I become a hacker in the span of that time? No. I could hardly remember my own passwords. I glanced around the room, searching for a clue, but I was so stressed out that nothing made sense.

I was so screwed. Principal River was bound to walk in any minute and find me hyperventilating at his desk, but I couldn't do anything about it. In a last-minute effort I typed *1, 2, 3, 4* into the login screen and pressed enter.

There was no way in hell the numbers were supposed to work, but the screen loaded up anyway. Principal River's screen saver was a picture of a cat in a basket with a huge bow on its head. I didn't have the nerve to laugh, but some hysterical giggling was bubbling under the surface.

I quickly searched for Harvey's name in the school database. As I scribbled Harvey's address onto a sticky note, I heard Principal River's greeting coming from the front of the office. I was so frazzled I misspelled the street name twice. I could hear his footsteps nearing and in my panic I shut down all of the windows and even the computer itself.

I was in the middle of jogging back towards the other side of the desk when my pinky toe banged into the corner of the desk. I flinched and cussed under my breath before falling into one of the chairs in front of me. Served me right for doing what I was doing, but damn if it didn't hurt like a mother.

My breathing was hard and I could feel one of my eyes twitching involuntarily.

"Good afternoon, Ms. Jefferson. Heard you needed to speak with me?" Principal River's voice was pleasant. I watched him drape his suit coat over the back of his chair before he smiled at me.

I racked my brain for something to say. I made a note to require twenty-four hours' notice the next time I had to hack into someone's computer and steal information.

"I wanted to thank you!" I nearly shouted.

Thank you for having such a dumb password.

• • •

He quirked a brow, and I wondered if he was concerned about my mental stability.

"Thank you for everything you do!" I nearly crawled over his desk to grip his hand. I shook it forcefully before finally letting go. My palms were sweaty and I was kind of embarrassed when he discreetly wiped his hands on his pants.

"Is that all?" He sounded sorry for me. Before my eyes started to tear up, I smiled and nodded my head at him. I left in a hurry, past the office lady, and out the door in record time. I was bent over with my hands on my thighs when Garrard pulled me up by gripping my arm again.

"Did you get it?" I nodded my head.

"Wait!" I yelled when he started to tug me away again.

"What?"

"Give me your gun," I managed to whisper.

"Are you retarded?"

"Or empty it out. I won't give you the address unless you get rid of the bullets."

I praised myself for thinking on my feet. I'd stuffed the sticky note in my shirt back in the office, so unless he decided to pat my down thoroughly, he wasn't going to find it. I thought he would be harder to convince, but he nodded his head. I let him pull me all the way to the school parking lot.

He finally let go of my arm when we reached a black Mercedes. I watched him pull the bullets out of the gun. The process reminded me of pulling out the little candies from the Pez dispenser. He dropped the bullets into my cupped hands and then stared at me with a mocking smile when he saw that I didn't know what to do with them.

They were cold and felt deadly in the palms of my hands. The last thing I wanted was to keep holding them. I looked over at a nearby dumpster and then back at him. He extended his hand in the dumpster's direction, which I took as him allowing me to throw them away. I threw them into the dumpster by the handful and cringed when the metal echoed.

I walked back towards Garrard and his extended hand, only to walk past him and towards the passenger seat.

"What the hell are you doing now?" he asked.

"You didn't think you would go without me?" My smile was mocking just like the one he'd given me.

Chapter Twenty-Three
Ready for Round Two

Garrard drove the car like a total tool. He had one hand over the top of the steering wheel and his seat cranked all the way back. Now that he didn't have a loaded gun I was feeling a little braver. I imagined him hitting something and popping himself in the face with his stupid arm from the impact, which helped a little.

"Turn left here." I was acting as his GPS. The more we drove the more my voice dipped into a monotone. By the time I directed him onto Harvey's street I was in complete character. I wondered if doing the voice for GPS systems was a valid career option.

"You have the most annoying voice." Guess not.

We pulled up to a two-story house in a rougher neighborhood than I was used to. I caught the gleam of Harvey's bike in the driveway, which reassured me that we were in the right location.

"What did he do to you, anyway?" It seemed like everyone always had a reason to hunt Harvey down. Garrard cut the ignition before answering.

"When you buy a burger, do you take two for the price of one?" he asked. Staring at Harvey's house.

"Only if I have a coupon," I answered.

"I don't give out coupons."

Or burgers, I wanted to add, but that was pretty obvious.

He didn't say more. I quickly followed him out of the car. My head snapped up to the sound of the front door opening. Harvey emerged from inside the house with his eyes trained on Garrard. He looked like he was expecting Garrard to find him. What he wasn't expecting was me.

I watched his eyes widen before he practically ran towards us.

"Fuck you! Let her go!" Harvey yelled.

Garrard threw his hands in the air mockingly. "I didn't drag her here." It was true. He hadn't.

"Don't lie!" Taking a page from Garrard's book, Harvey wrapped his hand around my arm and pulled me behind him.

"Look, I don't give a fuck about whatever's going on between you and your girl. I came to get my money." Garrard's patience was in the negative numbers. You could tell by the vein pulsing in his neck. I was angry at Harvey just then, but I was angry at myself too for liking the sound of being Harvey's girl. I pictured myself getting the word 'desperate' tattooed on my forehead as punishment.

* * *

"Relax. Rex told me what he did. We'll pay for your shit in full. Just let me go and get it from inside."

Before I knew it, Harvey had led me into his house. Garrard didn't get the same treatment, so he had to wait outside. I followed Harvey up a narrow flight of stairs. He hadn't said a word to me and he continued his silence while he rifled in his room, looking for something. I glanced around the room, noting his bed and the dresser beside it. The bed was made and it was surprisingly clean for a boy's room, aside from the loose change and receipts scattered on top of the dresser. I watched him pull the duffel from our trip out of his closet before hearing his footsteps slamming down the stairs.

He'd left me alone in his room.

I hadn't thought my plan out as far as ending up in his personal space, and I didn't understand how I'd ended up there. I turned around and saw that there was a desk against the wall with some picture frames and his laptop. Harvey Lockwell's room was...basic. I knew I shouldn't, but I started snooping a little. I'd never been in a guy's room, aside from Nick's, but his interior décor was ten times better than anyone's I'd ever been to. Harvey's room was plain.

I found myself creeping closer to his closet. I gently slid one of the two doors so that it was open just a crack. I could see his t-shirts and some jeans hung up. Towards the bottom there were some shoes, but mostly sports equipment. In the far corner I could see the faint outline belonging to a strip of something. I squinted my eyes to make sure what it was. I could see some of the patches that had been sewn onto the sash.

I was almost positive I was staring at Harvey's Boy Scout sash. I tried to run the door so that I'd have enough room to pick the sash out, but the door wouldn't budge. I tried reaching for it but it was too far, so the next thing I did was try to squeeze in through the opening.

Bad idea. I was skinny, but not that skinny. I got halfway through until the door locked in place leaving me without a hint of leeway. One of my boobs was inside the closet, while the other was still in Harvey's room. The edge of the door was flat against my forehead. I tried to push myself out, back into his room, but I was lodged in there good. I tried to sandwich the door between my hands and push it open, but it was locked in place.

My struggle was beyond real. I started to squirm when I realized the pressure from the door was making it hard to breathe. Harvey found me lodged halfway in his closet when he walked back in.

"Surprise!" I did some jazz hands, an uncomfortable result of my embarrassment. Too bad he could only watch one of my hands dance in the air, since the other one was hidden inside the closet.

"Tell me you're not stuck there." Harvey was looking amused.

"I am. I'd tell you more but I can't really breathe."

I made a last-minute effort to dislodge myself, but it was no use. Harvey had the problem of trying to grab the edge of the door to push it off. My body wouldn't let him get his fingers in. He tried to stick them in between my chest and the door, until we both realized my boobs wouldn't really give him a margin of space to work with.

Luckily he tried the space between my stomach and the door. He didn't exactly manage to pull the door open and free me. I did it on my own when his fingers made me ticklish and I laughed so hard I spasmed until the door gave out. It smacked into the wall opposite of me and was about to come back and hit me in the face if Harvey hadn't caught it midway.

I stumbled back into his room once I was free, until I tripped on a rug and fell face-first into his bed. Not the way I imagined my first time in a boy's bed, but what else could I do?

Eventually I managed to sit up on his bed and blow the hair out of my face. Harvey had watched me the entire time, still by his closet. He looked like he was having a surreal experience.

"Is he gone?" I asked.

"Who?" Harvey tried to shake his head, but he still looked confused when he was finished.

"Garrard?"

"Oh, yeah."

I'd come to give Harvey a piece of my mind but when I found myself sitting in his room all I could think about was how much I missed him. I missed our adventures together. I missed our friends. But mostly, I missed having him kiss me.

"He's a dick," I whispered. I was trying to remind myself that Harvey didn't deserve me after what he'd put me through. He hadn't even tried to get me back. I was the one who showed up at his doorstep.

"Yeah, he is." Harvey replied.

"No, you. You're a dick." I felt my eye twitch.

"I did what I was supposed to do." His eyes hardened. I could tell that he believed what he was saying. I shook my head at him because I still thought he was wrong.

"Push me away and then make me feel like crap?" I could feel my eyes start to water. It wasn't how I wanted our meeting to go. In my head I had envisioned myself as a ruthless warrior, maybe the kind that punched boys who broke hearts in the face. I wasn't any of those things.

I watched Harvey look up and then back down at me. He finally sighed before sitting beside me on the bed. I should have moved away but my heart was beating too fast at having him close.

"Shit. Don't cry," Harvey said. I sniffled anyway.

"If you let me explain, I promise you'll agree with me."

I didn't say anything back. I wasn't sure I really wanted him to explain, but he started talking anyway.

"My dad." He paused and I watched his expression turn momentarily bitter, like the mention of his father was sour in his mouth.

"My dad liked to drink and gamble, a lot."

I suddenly knew how fragile our moment was. I took the risk of intertwining our fingers together. Sometimes you had to hold the people who were opening up to you.

"His addiction got so bad that we went weeks without food or clothes or all the things that are supposed to be important. He kept saying how he just needed one big hit and we would be set. Every day he left us was the day he was supposed to win, but it never fucking was." Harvey's voice was somber, but he still didn't look at me. His fingers were warm in my hand.

I urged him to continue. My dad had mentioned some stuff about Harvey's dad, but some of it was still new to me.

"One day he lost everything. He bet more than he had to the wrong people. When he told them he didn't have money to pay they threatened to kill him. The bastard promised them something else instead."

He took a long pause that felt like an eternity. All the while my heart was in my throat and the urge to ask him what his dad had promised was bouncing around my chest, threatening to come out.

"A bunch of guys burst into our house. I went fucking crazy trying to stop them and so did my older brother, but they just beat the shit out of both of us and took her. My dad was nowhere in sight. When I woke up again my mom was back, but it was really late and everything about her was messed up. The most twisted thing about it all is that I'm just like him."

I felt his fingers twitch in my hand so I held on tighter.

"No, you're not," I said automatically.

His laugh was cynical. Finally, his eyes landed on mine.

"Yeah, I am. Every bet, every game, every move, I can't say no."

"Is that why I'm not yours?"

His smile was sad.

"If you were mine, I'd bet you too."

I wasn't sure if it was true. I hoped it wasn't. I thought back to our time together. Harvey had tried to protect my feelings when we first hooked up. He'd even tried to protect me from what we thought was a wolf. He'd stood in front of Garrard just to shield me. Some things just didn't add up.

"I bet you you're not like your dad," I said, sticking my chin up with determination. He finally cracked a small genuine smile.

"Nice try, Liv."

"It's true!" I said, my voice rising after such a long silence. He didn't say anything and so I braced myself and went for it. There was only one way to prove it to him.

I pulled his face towards me and crushed my lips to his.

His lips moved slowly against mine at first. I had never been the one to start kissing him, so for the few moments I was in control, I had no clue where to take things. Eventually, Harvey took over and started to lead instead. His lips were soft and demanding and when he brought a hand up to cup my cheek in a typical Harvey fashion my entire body sighed in contentment.

We were a frenzy of eager lips and hands that searched for anything they could grab. Eventually he deepened the kiss, his tongue sliding into my mouth. I tried to meet him there, our kissing reaching a faster pace. My heart froze in my chest when we finally pulled away.

"I wouldn't trust you if you were like him."

"You have the shittiest judgment," he responded.

I laughed before shaking my head. He was wrong, he just didn't want to admit it.

I kissed him one more time before pulling away. We were lying on his bed by then. Like always, I didn't really know what we were to each other but I knew that at any moment we could have taken things further.

"Can you take me home?" I whispered.

So he took me home.

Chapter Twenty-Four
All Things Go

The following Monday I woke up with one thing on my mind: Harvey and the rest of the gang would be back.

Harvey had clued me in on their disappearance by explaining that the school had put them in suspension after the police video ended up on the news. They said something about putting the other students in danger and all that jazz. They hadn't suspended me because of my previous record as a good student, but Monday was the day I'd hopefully get to see them again.

I spent the entire morning jittery with mixed emotions. I'd given Harvey my new phone number so that he could give it to Lexi. I'd been texting her every day leading up to Monday. I was sitting in my last class before lunch, texting Lexi under the table, when the lunch bell dismissed us.

I was so busy writing out my message that I didn't notice that everyone else had already left, even Mrs. Lasowski.

I was almost out the door when the smell of coffee caught my attention. Sitting on Mrs. Lasowski's desk was a steaming cup of joe beckoning me. The woman drank coffee by the bucket.

I wondered when she would be coming back for a moment, but figured it wasn't important.

"Alright, Livvie, this is your time to shine," I whispered to myself, rubbing my hands together like a maniacal fly.

I focused on the cup under my nose, and with the uttermost concentration, coughed up the biggest loogie I was capable of.

The loogie was midair when I felt a presence in the room with me. I didn't shift my body, but my eyes flew to the doorway, fearing the worst. It wasn't Mrs. Lasowski, thank God. It was Harvey.

I couldn't stop thinking of how gross I looked, so I finally just let the spitball drop towards the waiting coffee cup. Harvey was trying to fight off a smile. It almost looked like it pained him to find me amusing, which was a good sign, right?

Harvey finally broke the silence in a complimentary tone. "That was one hell of a loogie." I laughed at his compliment.

The kiss he gave me after was better than his compliment.

I wrapped my arms around his neck while his lips landed on mine—not for long, though, because he trailed kisses on my neck and shoulders before setting me upright.

"You just kissed me after complimenting my loogie," I said, a bit amazed.

"Number one," he said before kissing me again.

Number one: Date a guy who drives a motorcycle. Duh.

"Does that mean you're asking me out?" I wondered aloud when his lips gave me one last chaste kiss before pulling away.

"Will you say yes?" he asked, smirking at me.

"Probably not," I said just to mess with him. That spurred him to kiss me again.

"Okay. I'd say yes," I admitted, grabbing him and pulling him in for another kiss that was quickly becoming a makeout session.

I thought back to all of the things in my list that had come true, from getting drunk with Harvey for the first time, to stealing my first and probably last credit card.

As for the last thing on my list... I had my new boyfriend and Mrs. Lasowski's desk right in front of me. Just because I was back home didn't mean I was done doing some pretty bad things.

"Do you still have those glow-in-the-dark condoms?" I asked in between kisses.

"In my wallet, why?"

Several minutes later I was propped over Mrs. Lasowski's wooden desk with Harvey on top of me. I had a hard time convincing Harvey about doing it on the desk, but eventually I was persuasive enough.

"Livvie, stop squirming," Harvey said, trying to position himself better on top of me. I don't really know why I thought losing my virginity on a school desk had been a good idea, because clearly it wasn't. Harvey was doing everything right, obviously, but I was a colossal mess.

I didn't know where to put my hands and it wasn't like I had enough room to spread them out anywhere. Harvey was in the middle of trying to rip open a condom packet, while I pulled a stack of graded papers out from under my butt.

"Huh, you got a ninety-five on this," I commented, eyeing the first paper on the stack.

"Really?" Harvey asked, half-interested.

I didn't have time to answer because he was kissing me again and making me forget about everything. I felt his hand go up my rib cage right to where I wanted it. I was in the middle of actually moaning again, when a creak sounded off to my right.

"What the hell do you think you're doing?" Mrs. Lasowski's voice shocked us both long enough for our bodies to fall off the table.

I was on the ground on top of a half-naked Harvey after tumbling off the side. Nothing I could possibly do had the power of hiding me from the humiliation.

"You signed up for this, you know," I said through tight lips.

Harvey didn't say anything, but I knew he was already shaking off the embarrassment and growing increasingly amused.

PRETTY BAD THINGS

Oh yeah, we were definitely going to get ourselves into some trouble together.

Embarrassing trouble.

THE
END

About the Author

Yoly Marquez is an avid writer, reader, and all around book lover. She wrote her first book when she was sixteen years old and is currently a book cover designer for other authors. You can find her with her nose buried in a book, buying yet another pair of shoes she doesn't need, or working her next novel. She is currently a college student trying to figure out new ways to deal with the Arizona heat. *Pretty Bad Things* is her first published work.

You can visit Yoly on her website at:
yolymarquez.com

CPSIA information can be obtained at www.ICGtesting.com
Printed in the USA
BVOW03s1059230416

445350BV00001B/19/P

9 781508 867265